KU-469-872

Having the most beautiful sapphire and diamond ring slipped with loving care on one's finger does tend to dominate one's mind.

Consequently, it wasn't until after she and Joss had enjoyed the intimate little dinner for two, and had returned to the comfort of the front parlour, that Gwen's thoughts returned to recent events, both happy and sad, and the promise she had made to Annie the previous day.

'Have you someone in mind to replace Mrs Brice?'

Only for an instant did Joss's gaze stray from the chessboard, set on the table between them, to cast his worthy opponent a quizzical look. 'Hardly my province any longer, my sweet. Domestic arrangements are your concern.'

'Oh, heavens!' Gwen hadn't for a moment considered this. 'Yes, I suppose they are. Or very soon will be, at any rate.'

Dear Reader

Although I cannot claim to have written books throughout the majority of its hundred-year publishing history, it's a privilege to have this, my sixteenth story, published to celebrate Mills & Boon's centenary year.

As one might expect, tastes in literature have certainly undergone some changes during the last one hundred years, as have the aspirations of most women. The lives we live now bear little resemblance to those endured by the greater number of our sex a century ago. Although it hardly seems credible now, women still had to wait quite some years after the first Mills & Boon novels were published before they won the right to vote.

One thing we clearly continue to have in common with our predecessors, however, is our love for romantic fiction, which still remains popular with women not only in this country but all over the world.

And long may it continue to do so!

Anne

MT DISCARDED

0130905528

LADY GWENDOLEN INVESTIGATES

Anne Ashley

WARWICKSHIRE
COUNTY LIBRARY

CONTROL No.

MILLS & BOON®

Pure reading pleasure™

All the characters in this book have no existence outside the imagination of the author, and have no relation whatsoever to anyone bearing the same name or names. They are not even distantly inspired by any individual known or unknown to the author, and all the incidents are pure invention.

All Rights Reserved including the right of reproduction in whole or in part in any form. This edition is published by arrangement with Harlequin Enterprises II BV/S.à.r.l. The text of this publication or any part thereof may not be reproduced or transmitted in any form or by any means, electronic or mechanical, including photocopying, recording, storage in an information retrieval system, or otherwise, without the written permission of the publisher.

® and TM are trademarks owned and used by the trademark owner and/or its licensee. Trademarks marked with ® are registered with the United Kingdom Patent Office and/or the Office for Harmonisation in the Internal Market and in other countries.

First published in Great Britain 2008
Large Print edition 2008
Harlequin Mills & Boon Limited,
Eton House, 18-24 Paradise Road, Richmond, Surrey TW9 1SR

© Anne Ashley 2008

ISBN: 978 0 263 20163 5

Set in Times Roman 16¼ on 17¾ pt.
42-0808-76086

Printed and bound in Great Britain
by Antony Rowe Ltd, Chippenham, Wiltshire

Anne Ashley was born and educated in Leicester. She lived for a time in Scotland, but now makes her home in the West Country, with two cats, her two sons, and a husband who has a wonderful and very necessary sense of humour. When not pounding away at the keys of her word processor, she likes to relax in her garden, which she has opened to the public on more than one occasion in aid of the village church funds.

Recent novels by the same author:

A NOBLE MAN*
LORD EXMOUTH'S INTENTIONS*
THE RELUCTANT MARCHIONESS
TAVERN WENCH
BELOVED VIRAGO
LORD HAWKRIDGE'S SECRET
BETRAYED AND BETROTHED
A LADY OF RARE QUALITY

*part of the Regency mini-series
 The Steepwood Scandal

Author Note

Although it is acknowledged
that the heroine of this story, being the
widow of a knight, should not be addressed
as Lady Gwendolen, for the novel's title
only this rule has been waived.

Chapter One

Were the inns in England always this busy nowadays? Gwendolen wondered, while neatly avoiding a harassed-looking ostler leading a pair of steaming horses across the crowded forecourt.

It was only to be expected, she supposed, that five years spent abroad might result in her forgetting certain aspects of life back here in the land of her birth. Not that she had ever had much experience of travel, of course…of life, even, before her marriage to Sir Percival Warrender.

Pausing in her musings, she stepped to one side, thereby allowing the stagecoach passengers to traipse unhindered from the inn and return to their conveyance. None of them seemed to notice the bitterly cold gusts of wind sweeping across the forecourt at frequent intervals. Gwen, on the other hand, had been very much aware of the unpleasantly low temperature from the moment she had alighted from her hired carriage, and drew her fur-lined cloak more tightly about her. Having lived in a much warmer climate for very many months, she had forgotten, too, just how chilly it could be in England even in March, when travel became more widespread.

The frequently inclement weather was something else she would need to accustom herself to again, she mused, as she took the added precaution of raising her hood against further cold blasts, the result of which severely restricted her field of vision. One moment she was enjoying the protection the busy posting-house's pleasantly warm interior offered the instant she had stepped over the threshold; the next, she felt as if she had just walked into a stone-hard wall.

Almost at once a strong-fingered hand fastened itself about her left arm, just above the elbow, instantly steadying her. Some few moments later a deeply attractive and clearly refined voice eventually enquired into her well-being, but not before she had detected the muttered oath, only partially smothered, preceding the belated query. Hence, she wasn't unduly surprised to discover, upon finally raising her head, that the face peering down at her betrayed a deal more impatience than concern.

She took a step away, the better to focus on a pair of dark eyes set in a ruggedly masculine countenance that wasn't even remotely handsome. 'I do beg your pardon, sir. Entirely my own fault,' she declared, generously accepting all blame.

As she removed her cowl with a casual flick of one hand, there was, just for an instant, a marked softening about the set of thin lips, while brown eyes considered the burnished-copper highlights streaking through chestnut locks.

'Very true, ma'am, it was,' he agreed in the very next breath, the softer expression having disappeared so completely that Gwen wasn't at all sure she hadn't imagined it in the first place. 'May I suggest, therefore, you attempt to take more care in future. Journeying about the country, even at this time of year, can prove a hazardous undertaking, without having to contend with acts of downright stupidity perpetrated by fellow travellers.'

'Well, really!' Gwen muttered, after he had doffed his hat in what she considered a most condescending manner and had begun to stride away in the direction of the main entrance.

Having to deal with abrasive fellows such as that was possibly something else she would need to grow accustomed to, she supposed, as she continued to watch her tormentor's progress across the room until he had disappeared from view.

Undeniably she had had little experience of such unpleasant fellows. Her formative years, spent in a quiet country parsonage, and her marriage to a very considerate and protective husband, had certainly proved to be a shield against the more unpleasant aspects of life. All the same, she wasn't completely unworldly. Furthermore, she had no intention of withering, like some delicate bloom touched by an icy wind, merely as a result of a little unpleasantness.

Besides which, she was not entirely alone and defenceless, she reminded herself. Even though she had no immediate family now living, and had been widowed for several months, she could always rely on dear Gillie's loving protection and unfailing support.

Her blue eyes scanned the coffee room, seeking and quickly locating the plump figure of her lifelong companion-cum-maid. At that moment, the devoted servant just happened to be locked in conversation with a harassed- looking individual, whom Gwen could only assume must surely be the landlord. From the slight look of disappointment so easily discernible when the maid turned in her direction, Gwen guessed there was no private parlour available. Which, considering the number of patrons bustling about the inn, was in no way surprising, she decided, gesturing towards a row of settles set at frequent intervals along one of the walls.

Because the seat nearest the substantial fire was already occupied by a fashionably attired gentleman, Gwen was obliged to slip into a settle sited a little further away from the source of heat. As the seats were placed back to back, she had little difficulty hearing the gentleman talking softly to the inn's cat, which she had noticed had been curled up beside him and, typically feline, closest to the fire.

She had absolutely no difficulty either, just a few moments later, in recognising the cultured voice that announced authoritatively, 'My groom will have the carriage round at the door in five minutes.'

'It's dashed good of you, Pont, to put yourself out this way,' the well-dressed gentleman responded, while Gwen herself took the added precaution of slipping further down the high-backed settle so as to avoid detection by the new arrival. 'It's a deal more comfortable travelling in a private carriage than going on the mail-coach.'

'I've already told you, Merry, I'm not putting

myself out,' his companion responded, proving instantly that he wasn't always downright rude and could evidently be quite obliging when so inclined. 'I've managed to conduct my business here in Bristol speedily, as you know. And I did intend to pay a brief visit to the capital within the next couple of weeks. As well go now as later. So long as you don't object to making that slight detour to Bath first?'

'Not at all, old chap,' the abrasive gentleman was speedily assured. 'Haven't set foot in the place since great-aunt Beatrice passed away, ten years or more ago.' There followed a significant pause, then, 'How have the girls settled in at the seminary?'

'It's still early days. Nonetheless, according to the headmistress's letter, very well indeed…considering.' The deep and prolonged sigh was clearly audible to Gwen who continued, unashamedly, to eavesdrop. 'All the same, I'll not be completely easy in my mind until I've seen for myself, and spoken to my wards.'

'It was a bad business…a very bad business, Pont, especially as both girls had grown so fond of that poor governess. She was quite alone in the world, I seem to remember you saying, no immediate family.'

'Not as far as I'm aware. I recall her mentioning she'd lost both parents when she was quite young. I do happen to know for a fact she corresponded with someone residing in the capital— a friend, I can only suppose. Naturally, I should have taken the trouble to apprise this person of what had occurred. Unfortunately no letters were found among her belongings offering a clue to the person's identity. Which was most odd, because I know for a fact she both wrote and received a number of missives during those many months she was in my employ.'

There was no mistaking the thread of sadness in the abrupt gentleman's voice, proving yet again that he wasn't wholly devoid of compassion. Although a moment later Gwen wondered if she had credited him with more feelings than he possessed when he added, 'Oddly enough, I had come to look upon her as one of those rare members of her sex—a refreshingly sensible young woman. Then she ups and does something utterly birdwitted. Takes herself into Marsden Wood, a place she well knew had earned itself something of an unsavoury reputation in recent years. Furthermore, she does so in January, for heaven's sake! Now, I ask you, Merry, what in the world can have possessed any level-headed creature to go exploring a wood on a dismally damp winter's afternoon? And what's more… alone!'

Although, in part, to pass the time while awaiting her servant's arrival, she had, still without suffering the least pang of conscience, continued to listen to the conversation, Gwen had no very clear idea of precisely what was being discussed. That some misfortune had befallen a woman while out exploring some wood or other was evident. What became obvious too in the next moment was that the gentleman known as Merry was as much at a loss to understand the unfortunate female's actions as was her abrasive employer.

'It would take a greater brain than I possess to attempt to explain what motivates many females to act as they do. But that particular woman's actions on that day were sheer folly, especially after you'd made it clear from the first that to venture alone near the wood might prove unwise.'

The unexpected rumble of laughter that followed the pronouncement suggested that Master Merry had perhaps been well named. 'And a die-hard misogynist like yourself, Pont, could never hope to unravel the mysteries of the female mind.'

A further pause, then,

'Why, my dear friend, you above anyone should suppose I dislike all women, I cannot imagine. On the contrary, over the years I have thought well of several. Like yourself, I've never been tempted into parson's mousetrap. But that, let me assure you, is simply a matter of choice. I've yet to meet a female with whom I could happily share my life.'

'Nor are you ever likely to do so while you continue to remain so fastidious, Pont, for ever searching for the slightest flaw in either looks or character.'

'My dear Merry, you delude yourself,' was the immediate, drawled response. 'I should never waste time or energy attempting to seek the perfect woman, simply because such a creature does not exist. Nor do I actively seek imperfections in the opposite sex, either. There's absolutely no need for me to do so, of course, when they surface within minutes of my making any female's acquaintance.'

A bark of decidedly mocking laughter quickly followed. 'Now, you take that idiotic creature I encountered a mere few minutes ago,' Gwen's ridiculer continued, evidently having warmed to the subject. 'No need for me even to attempt to strike up a conversation to know she was utterly birdwitted. Walks into a crowded posting-house with a cowl pulled low over her face. Couldn't possibly have seen where she was going, and looks startled when she cannons into me...I ask you!'

'Ahh, but was she pretty?' the other enquired, after an appreciative chuckle at the derision that had simply oozed from his friend's every word. 'I bet you didn't even notice, Pont.'

'Truth to tell...no, can't say as I did,' he admitted. 'Noticed her hair, though. Dashed pretty colour! Streaked with copper, it was, and curled quite prettily. Never seen anything quite like it before, though whether the hue was Mother Nature's gift, I couldn't say. So many of 'em, as you well know, resort to artifice in order to attract.'

'What a nerve!' Gwen exclaimed before she could stop herself. Fortunately, though, neither gentleman seemed to have heard, as the rude individual at precisely the same moment had expressed a desire not to leave his horses standing too long in the cold wind.

Gwen waited a second or two before peering round the end of the settle in time to catch a last glimpse of the close friends as they strode side by side across the coffee room. Aggrieved, justifiably so in her opinion, she was experiencing far too much resentment towards the taller man to appreciate that for a large gentleman he carried himself with a dignified air, his gait both smoothly effortless and remarkably graceful. Instead she favoured his retreating form with a basilisk-glance.

'Odious, odious creature!' she muttered, turning back in her seat.

It wasn't his low opinion of her sex that annoyed her. Innate honesty prompted her silently to acknowledge that she herself had come into contact with numerous woolly-minded females during the quarter of a century she had been on God's good earth. It wasn't even his condemnation of her actions a short time earlier, either, that rankled. Indeed, it hadn't been the most sensible thing to walk into a crowded inn with one's vision severely restricted. No, what she found unpardonable was his suggestion that her hair was possibly not wholly natural. Evidently he was accustomed to associating with females who would resort to any means in order to attain their ends. She was not so naïve as to suppose such women did not exist here in England. Her eyes suddenly twinkled with a very satisfied glint. But at least no female, virtuous or quite otherwise, had been foolish enough to tie herself irrevocably to such a self-opinionated bore as that person appeared to be!

'Why, Miss Gwennie! I've never seen such a mutinous look on your face, not since that time your sainted mother—God rest her soul!—refused to allow you to play in the garden with Miss Jane until you'd finished your lessons.'

Memories of her long-suffering mother's attempts to instil in her, her only child, at least a basic education swiftly erased the lines of annoyance from Gwen's brow. 'Ah, yes, dear Jane was so much cleverer than I. Just as well I didn't attempt to follow her example by earning a living. I was always slower to learn.'

'Only because you wouldn't apply yourself. Leastways, that's what I recall your mama always said. When something interested you, it was always you took the lead.'

The maid slipped into the settle opposite, apologising as she did so for being away for so long. 'But you really oughtn't to walk into inns by yourself,' she went on, adopting the scolding tone she had used throughout Gwen's childhood. 'You ought to have remained in the carriage as arranged. You never know what nasty folk you might bump into.'

'True! How very true!' Gwen agreed, tongue-in-cheek, before deciding finally to thrust the un-fortunate encounter with the abrasive gentleman from her mind completely. 'I assume you were not successful in securing a private parlour?'

'No, Miss Gwen. Seemingly there's only two, and both in use at the present time, though the landlord did offer to put himself out and serve us in one of the unoccupied bedchambers, if we were—er—willing to pay the price.'

'Needless to say you declined,' Gwen responded, smiling to herself. One could always rely on dear old Martha Gillingham to know how to deal with any presumptuous fellow. She might have been in service throughout most of her life, and her education limited, but she was quite a remarkable judge of character, and was never slow to recognise when someone was attempting to take advantage.

'I said as how my mistress didn't intend to break the journey for long, and that we'd be comfortable enough eating our broth in the coffee room.'

'Which is no less than the truth,' Gwen quickly avowed. 'According to the post-boys, we should reach our journey's end, barring any mishap, before evening.'

'And as long as the old master's housekeeper has received your letter, everything should be in readiness for our arrival.' The maid beamed across the table, her small, round eyes positively aglow with excitement. 'You must be longing to see your new home, Miss Gwennie. I know I am.'

'I'm longing to see Jane again far more.' Gwen released her breath in a sigh. 'She must have changed a good deal in the years since I've seen her. I know I have.'

Martha's smile faded. Her plump features clearly betrayed a moment or two's thoughtful contemplation before being replaced by a look of gentle affection. 'Not that much, miss, you haven't,' she eventually countered. 'You still get that same wicked glint in your eye you had as a child when you're amused by something, or annoyed. And you're still not afraid to speak your mind on occasions neither, though thankfully you're a deal less headstrong than of yore.'

Gwen didn't waste her breath in fruitless argument, simply because there was a deal of truth in her loyal maid's utterances, and merely said, 'Well, let us hope dear Jane hasn't retained that stubbornly independent streak of hers. She may have been overjoyed to obtain that position as governess to those two orphaned girls, granting her the God-given opportunity to remove to the West Country. And so conveniently close to dear Percival's house, too! But it doesn't automatically follow that she'll be any more willing to come and live with me now that I'm taking up permanent residence in my late husband's home.'

A shadow of mingled resentment and regret flickered across Gwen's delicately featured face. 'I haven't forgotten she refused to oblige me six years ago.'

A completely trouble-free last stage of the long journey resulted in the post-boys' prediction of a late afternoon arrival proving accurate. Consequently, Gwen was privileged to enjoy the first glimpse of her new home bathed in flattering pale-golden sunlight glinting welcomingly on mullioned windows. An untidy and overgrown garden detracted somewhat from what might otherwise have been a very pleasing setting for the Restoration building, as did the profusion of choking ivy clinging to the front wall.

If the truth were known, though, Gwen wasn't so much concerned about the architectural merit of the house that was shortly to become her permanent place of residence, at least for the foreseeable future, as she was about the atmosphere prevailing within. Much, she strongly suspected, would depend on the character of the female her late husband had employed almost twenty years before to maintain the smooth running of his household.

Gwen knew next to nothing about Mrs Travis, save that she was a female now well into middle age, and that Sir Percival had considered her to be a first-rate cook-housekeeper, completely trustworthy and conscientious. So unless she discovered the woman to be quite otherwise, Gwen was prepared to allow things to remain as they were. More importantly, her own dear Gillie had promised not to interfere in the running of the house, and to continue with her duties as personal maid-cum-companion. So one might be inclined to take an optimistic view, expecting everything to run smoothly, and everyone to rub along together remarkably well. Except that Gwen, now, was nothing if not a realist, and was well aware that things frequently didn't work out as one might have wished. Furthermore, love her though she did, she wasn't blind to her dear Gillie's faults.

Martha Gillingham had assisted in bringing Gwen into the world, and had always been treated as a member of the family, rather than a servant. Consequently Martha had never had too many restrictions imposed upon her.

The maid had never been afraid to speak her

mind, airing her views whether called upon to do so or not. So, should it be discovered that the house wasn't being maintained to the high standards to which she herself had always adhered, when she had held the position of cook-housekeeper in the late Reverend and Mrs Playfair's home for all those years, she wouldn't be reticent to point out any deficiencies on Mrs Travis's part.

Gwen quickly discovered there was thankfully no possibility of an early confrontation between the two women, when she was admitted by a housemaid who wasn't slow to impart the unfortunate tidings that Mrs Travis had taken to her bed.

'Terrible poorly she be, ma'am. Took bad a few days back, but would drag herself about, as she knew you'd be arriving some time this week, and now the chill's settled on her chest, so it 'as.'

'Has a doctor been summoned?'

The housemaid appeared astonished, as though it were unheard of for a practitioner to administer to a servant. 'No, ma'am...I mean, Lady Warrender.'

'I should prefer you address me as Mrs Warrender,' Gwen said, never having grown accustomed to the courtesy title bestowed upon her, simply because her late husband had received a knighthood in recognition of his unblemished record and acts of heroism whilst serving in His Majesty's Army during the previous century. 'And your name is?'

'Annie, ma'am…Annie Small.'

Gwen was unable to suppress a slight smile as the name was somewhat incongruous. The rosy-cheeked Annie was definitely on the buxom side. 'A doctor must be summoned at once,' she ordered, her mind swiftly returning to the matter in hand. 'I understand from Sir Percival's man of business in London that a male servant is also employed here?'

Annie rolled her eyes, a clear indication that she didn't wholly approve of the male employee. 'Yes, ma'am, Manders. He be outside some-where. Don't come into the 'ouse much, on account of 'im being a lazy good-for-nothing and not seeing eye to eye with Mrs Travis, as you might say. Made 'imself a snug little place above the stable, so 'ee 'as. You can usually find 'im skulking up there.'

Although she was aware that prejudice often clouded judgement, Gwen strongly suspected that much of what Annie had related had not been too far removed from the truth.

From what she had seen thus far, the garden, although adequate in size, was by no means totally unmanageable for an employee willing to pull his weight. Anyone working outside, even in the remotest corner, would have little difficulty hearing the sounds of an arrival. Yet no one had appeared when the carriage had pulled up at the door in order to assist the post-boys and Gillie in bringing the baggage into the hall.

'In that case, Annie, it shouldn't be too difficult a task for you to locate his whereabouts, and dispatch him for the local doctor. But first I'd like you to take me to see Mrs Travis.'

The cook-housekeeper occupied a small apartment, consisting of two rooms, directly off the kitchen. Gwen's first and very favourable impression was one of combined cleanliness and order. This was quickly overshadowed by a rush of concern, as she set foot inside the bedchamber, to find a thin, angular woman doing her level best to rise from the bed.

Mrs Travis's assurances that she was now feeling a good deal better after her day's inactivity, and was more than capable of creating a wholesome evening meal for her new mistress fell on deaf ears, as both Gwen and the loyal Martha headed across the room with purposeful strides. Severely weakened by the infection, Mrs Travis was no match for one, let alone them both, and returned to the warm comfort of her bed without attempting an undignified struggle, though clearly betraying signs of distress at being denied at least an attempt to fulfil her duties.

'No one, I'm certain, supposes you contracted the malady on purpose,' Gwen declared, after listening to the tearful apology. 'Martha, here, is more than capable of catering for my needs, until such time as you are able to resume your duties. Which I sincerely trust will not be long delayed.'

At this assurance that her position as housekeeper was in no way in jeopardy, Mrs Travis began to appear a good deal easier, with the lines of concern that had been steadily increasing beginning to fade from above the lacklustre eyes. The further assurance that she was considered worthy enough to receive a visit from the local practitioner seemed to deprive her of the power of speech, and it wasn't until Gwen alluded to the maidservant, Annie, that she was able to regain command of her voice.

'But Annie hasn't a permanent position here, madam,' she revealed. 'When the master's man of business, Mr Claypole, wrote and told me a few weeks ago of your arrival back in England, he said as how I might employ extra staff in order to prepare the house for your arrival. He knew well enough there was only me and Manders here, on account of his visiting once a year to check for himself how things stood in the poor old master's absence. He took his duties seriously. Never once forgot to pay our wages come quarter-day, and insisted I write to him, no matter how trivial the matter, if I was concerned about anything.'

As she too had been favourably impressed by Mr Claypole's conscientious attitude, Gwen experienced no qualms whatsoever over retaining his services when she had called to see him shortly after her arrival in the capital at the beginning of the year. Her concerns now, however, were not about her business affairs, which she felt sure were in trustworthy hands. Her late husband had not left her a pauper. In fact, the opposite was true. He had ensured that she could live in comfort, and although she had no intention of wasting money on frivolous luxuries, she fully intended to concentrate her efforts on turning her late husband's house into a home in which she might happily dwell.

Consequently, early in the evening, after the doctor's prompt visit, and a swift exploration of each and every room in her new home, Gwen made a start on her objective. Taking herself up to the best bedchamber, which boasted a commanding view of the sadly neglected front garden, she began to unpack her belongings, some of which had been acquired during her recent sojourn in London.

In the process of hanging yet another new gown in the wardrobe, Gwen paused for a moment to cast a thoughtful glance across at the young maidservant who was proving to be both an obliging and cheerful soul, only too happy to remain later than usual in order to lend a helping hand.

'I understand, Annie, that you're not a permanent member of the household here?'

'No, ma'am. Mrs Travis 'eard I were back at the cottage, taking care of me ma and the young 'uns, and so sent a message over asking if, mayhap, I'd like work for a week or two. Weren't going to turn it down, not with 'ow things are at present. But I'll need to find m'self something more settled again afore too long, now Ma's on the mend.'

After unravelling the salient points of this response, and asking a few more pertinent questions, Gwen discovered that Annie was currently seeking new employment owing to the fact that her last mistress had chosen to leave the area and reside permanently in Bath. Although having become extremely attached to the elderly lady for whom she had worked from an early age, Annie retained strong family ties, and had chosen not to accompany her mistress, but to return temporarily to the family home in order to care for her younger siblings, while her mother recovered from a severe bout of influenza.

'Mortal bad she's been, ma'am. Surprised she weren't took, after the 'ard life she's 'ad,' Annie went on to reveal so matter-of-factly that Gwen was hard pressed not to laugh.

It wasn't that she didn't feel a deal of sympathy. It was merely that, having been the daughter of a clergyman, she had frequently come into contact with those much less fortunate than herself, and knew from experience that Mrs Small's circumstances were sadly the norm for those less privileged members of the human race. Worn out by years of childbearing, hard work and a meagre diet, Annie's mother was yet another victim of her class, growing old before her time. The wonder of it was that the poor woman had managed to reach middle age, something which her spouse, seemingly, had failed to achieve, having lost his life in an accident involving an unruly piece of horseflesh belonging to his employer, the Earl of Cranborne.

'And was it because his employer felt in some

way responsible for your father's demise that he permitted your mother to remain in one of the estate cottages?'

'Don't expect so, ma'am. Much more likely it's on account of our Jem working up at the stables as well. Our Betsy's employed by his lordship too. She's a chambermaid up at the Hall. But she stays up at the big 'ouse now. Just as well, 'cause it's been mortal crowded in the cottage—what with Ma and the three young 'uns, not to mention Jem 'imself.' Annie raised one plump shoulder. 'I've got used to better, I suppose—a room to m'self. So the sooner I finds another situation, the better.'

'And couldn't you find work at Cranborne Hall? It would offer you the opportunity to remain close to your family.'

'Not 'eard there's anything going there.' Annie shrugged again. 'Wouldn't make no neverminds even if there were. I don't want to work up there.'

Gwen was intrigued to discover this. 'Why is that? Is the Earl not well liked in these parts, Annie?'

'Oh, it ain't that, ma'am. I don't want to stay a parlourmaid all me life. Wants to better m'self, become housekeeper or some such. Not much chance of that 'appening if I went to the Hall.'

'And are there no other large households here-abouts, or well-to-do families that might offer employment?' Gwen wasn't in the least reticent to make use of this golden opportunity to discover more about her friend Jane's employer who, she was very well aware, was rumoured to be one of the wealthiest landowners in Somerset. Although she had never heard a word to his dis-credit, her late husband having enjoyed more than just a casual acquaintance with the gentleman in question, and his father before him, she thought it would be no bad thing to, perhaps, attain an unbiased view from another source before she paid a visit herself.

'I recall my husband mentioning a Mr Northbridge, a close neighbour of his, I believe.' She chose not to reveal at this juncture that she had a very dear friend employed as governess in the household. It wasn't that she was ashamed of Jane's status. Nothing could have been further from the truth. No, it was merely that she thought she would receive a more candid opinion of the aforementioned gentleman if she kept certain facts to herself.

'Lord bless you, ma'am! I'd never get a job there!' Annie exclaimed, much to Gwen's intense surprise.

She then began to experience slight feelings of unease. 'Why is that, Annie? Is he not— perhaps—a well-liked person?'

'Oh, no, ma'am, it ain't that. It's t'other way, if anything. I'm not saying he's liked by everyone, but he is by most. And that's a fact! He can be sharp, mind,' she went on to divulge, after a moment's thought. 'Ain't afraid to say what he thinks, Mr Northbridge ain't. But 'ee's fair. My big brother, Ben, him that toils down at the smithy in the village 'ere, would work for 'im tomorrow, iffen there were a situation going. Trouble is, nobody ever leaves Mr Northbridge. Not unless they're taken away from the place in a box, that is!'

Gwen stared across at the parlourmaid for a moment in stunned disbelief. 'What in the world do you mean by that, Annie?'

'Well, 'tis this way, ma'am. Like anyone else, Mr Northbridge's got 'is faults. All the same, there's no denying folk lucky enough to get taken on at Bridge House stay there, and only leave when the Almighty decides it's time for 'em to move on. Mr Northbridge knows fine our Ben would be 'appy to run the stables for 'im, and he's promised Ben he'll be given a job soon as there be one. But m'brother's not daft, ma'am. He knows 'ee might be working at the smithy a good while yet.'

Gwen listened to these disclosures with decidedly mixed feelings. On the one hand, it was comforting to know that her dearest Jane had found herself a position where the head of the family was held in such esteem; on the other hand, though, it might prove no easy task to achieve her objective—namely to prise her dearest friend, the female whom she had always looked upon as a sister, away from this pillar of the community and persuade her to come and live with her now.

There was no denying that Jane had grown into a fiercely independent young woman. The only child of well-respected, if not affluent, parents, she had been both proud and determined to make her own way in the world. Gwen was equally aware that there would have been a greater chance of attaining her dearest wish if this unknown Mr Northbridge had proved not to be such a paragon. Undoubtedly she would discover precisely what manner of man he was for herself in due course.

In the meantime, though, there were other matters requiring her attention, she decided, quickly returning to the unpacking of the various trunks cluttering the bedchamber. Her first visit to Bridge House would need to be postponed for a while, at least until her own home had been restored to full working order.

In point of fact, it was over a week later before Gwen began to think seriously about making that short two-mile journey to Bridge House to see Jane Robbins. She had had much to occupy her since her arrival, not least of which had been engaging the services of Annie on a permanent basis, and hiring one of Annie's young brothers, Joe, to help bring some much-needed order to the neglected garden.

Although the steadily recovering Mrs Travis had been very well pleased by Annie's appointment, declaring that she was an excellent maid, one who could be relied upon to work without supervision, and not cut corners, Manders had betrayed no similar delight when informed that there would shortly be an extra pair of hands not only to help about the garden, but also to assist with all the other outside tasks.

His decided lack of enthusiasm hadn't altogether surprised Gwen, for as the days had passed she had become increasingly convinced that Annie's low opinion of Manders was fully justified. The resentment she had easily perceived in his expression, when she had informed him of the changes she intended to make, she strongly suspected, didn't stem from the fact that he believed she thought him no longer capable of doing his work. Oh, no, it was much more likely to have been because, having someone else working alongside him every single day, he would no longer be able to idle so much time away in some out-of-the-way corner, feet up, pulling on his pipe. Already there had been noticeable improvements in several areas of the garden, and it was no longer a rare sight to see Manders himself pushing a wheelbarrow along one of the overgrown paths.

Her housemaid's sudden appearance in the cosy back parlour, which Gwen had quickly selected for her private domain, drew her attention away from the activity taking place in the garden. For a short while she absently watched as Annie made up the fire, before enquiring into how her two newest employees were settling in.

If Annie felt surprised by this show of interest in her welfare, and that of her much younger brother, she certainly betrayed no sign of it. 'Champion, ma'am,' she declared, rosy face beaming. 'My room in the attic's nice and cosy.

And I knew right enough I'd be happy working under Mrs Travis.'

'And what about your brother? How's he settling in?'

'Well enough, Mrs Warrender. He's finding no trouble with the work, young though he is. But 'aving a room all to 'imself is summat strange for 'im. Used to sharing with Ma and the little 'uns, you see?'

It said much about the conditions endured by the majority of those less fortunate members of the human race that sleeping alone in a room measuring little more than six feet by eight was considered the height of luxury.

'Yes, I'm sure Joe must find it odd. But I'd rather he stay where he is for the present, where you can continue to keep an eye on him.' Gwen turned once again to stare out at where the thirteen-year-old Joe was hard at work doing battle with a bramble patch. 'The day might dawn when he'd prefer to share those quarters above the outhouses, and I shan't object if he chooses so to do. As I saw for myself, only the other day, there's ample room up there for three people. But for the time being I think it best he remains close enough for you to keep an eye on him. He's still a child, after all.'

Gwen knew she didn't need to say anything further. Annie was no fool, and although the maid herself was more than capable of holding her own against a taciturn individual like Manders, it didn't automatically follow that her sibling might quickly learn to do the same. So, for the time being at least, it was worth keeping a watchful eye on proceedings, if only to be certain that young Joe wasn't being put upon by his co-worker.

Gwen's thoughts then turned to other events that had occupied her during her first week in her new home. She certainly hadn't found time hanging heavily on her hands, even though she hadn't received a single visit from a neighbour. In view of the fact that both Annie and the local practitioner, Dr Bartlet, had mentioned that what had seemed half the county, at some time or other, had fallen victim to the particular malady that had struck down poor Mrs Travis, the lack of callers in no way surprised her. All the same, she did think it rather strange that she had received no word from Jane, not even the briefest of notes awaiting her, especially as she herself had made a point, the instant she had arrived back in the country, of apprising her dearest friend of precisely when she expected to be taking up residence in her late husband's home.

As was her wont, Gwen wasn't slow to act once she had come to a decision, and asked Annie to send Martha Gillingham to her immediately and then instruct Manders to have the one and only horse-drawn vehicle the late Sir Percival Warrender had ever possessed brought round to the door.

The journey to Bridge House was blessedly of short duration. None the less, it was with a feeling of intense relief that Gwen alighted from the antiquated conveyance that afforded no more comfort than a farm cart, vowing as she did so to decrease her bank balance in order to acquire a new carriage at the earliest opportunity.

She then turned her full attention on the early Georgian dwelling before her. Set in a garden that was both extensive and well maintained, Bridge House was, as Jane had once described in one of her letters, a very handsome building indeed. Clearly it was a residence belonging to a gentleman of substantial means. Furthermore, if the property was a reflection of his character, he was a person of elegance and good taste.

Apart from one or two details she had discovered from both her late husband and Jane, and those few interesting snippets she had gleaned from Annie in recent days, Gwen knew next to nothing about the owner of the delightful property, save that he was closely connected to several aristocratic families, he could also boast a fine residence in the capital, and he remained a bachelor.

'Which in one way is a great pity, Gillie,' she declared, after mulling over the few facts she did know about him. 'Had he been married, it would have spared you suffering this atrocious journey. I could then have asked to see Mrs Northbridge. As things stand, I have no choice but to drag you along. I might be a respectable widow, but I still cannot go calling on single gentlemen without giving rise to a deal of gossip.'

'That you can't, Miss Gwennie,' Martha agreed. 'Might be different if you had a few more years in your dish and a face like a horse's rear. But the fact is you haven't.'

'No, and I suppose I should consider myself most fortunate for that, too,' Gwen responded a little unsteadily, as she reached the impressive colonnaded front entrance. 'Let's hope Lady Luck continues to favour me and we should discover Mr Northbridge away from home. I can then ask to see Jane without fear of causing offence.'

'You could have written again during the past

days, telling Miss Jane of your safe arrival down here,' Martha pointed out, reaching for the highly polished door-knocker before her young mistress could do so.

'Yes, I know I could have done,' Gwen agreed. 'But until I know for certain that Jane's willing to share my home, I don't want to make things awkward for her. I know her too well. At the very least she'll insist on working her notice, or remaining until Mr Northbridge has managed to engage another governess. Furthermore, letters have a habit of going astray or falling into the wrong hands. I had no intention of advertising my close association with Jane, at least not until I've discussed things with her first.' Gwen lowered her eyes, thereby concealing the look of bitter regret. 'I was once guilty of assuming too much where she is concerned. I have no intention of repeating that gross error of judgement.'

The summons was answered promptly by an elderly male servant who, on discovering her identity, betrayed no reluctance whatsoever in admitting Gwen, or revealing that his master was in residence.

'If you'd care to wait in here, madam,' he said, leading the way into a most charmingly decorated and comfortable front parlour, 'I shall enquire if the master is able to see you.'

Given that her late husband had always maintained he had remained upon the best of terms with this particular neighbour, Gwen didn't suppose for a moment that Mr Northbridge would refuse to see her, unless of course other matters required his urgent attention. What she didn't expect, a moment after she had detected the click of the door, was the clearly astonished voice declaring,

'Good gad! I'd heard Warrender, the old rogue, had married someone years his junior, but I never supposed for a moment she'd turn out to be a chit not long out of the schoolroom!'

Chapter Two

It was more the oddly familiar rich tone than the blunt exclamation of surprise that induced Gwen to abandon her contemplation of the neat flower-bed just beyond the window and to swing round to face the new arrival squarely. Then it was as much as she could do not to reciprocate with an expression of shocked dismay of her own.

If nothing else, a quarter of a century of life had taught her never to be complacent, or take things for granted. Although considering herself more favourably circumstanced than most, she had not hitherto lived a completely cocooned existence, protected from every cruel knock. She knew well enough that life was littered with pitfalls, ready to entrap the unwary. But never until that moment had she supposed that fickle Fate could be quite so mischievously vindictive.

Briefly she raised her eyes heavenwards, as though hoping to prompt some divine intervention, or at the very least discover the answer to that one burning question torturing her mind— why, oh, why must Jocelyn Northbridge, a gentleman whom she couldn't possibly hope to avoid in the future, if she wished to resume her former very close friendship with Jane Robbins without delay, turn out to be none other than the thoroughly obnoxious individual she had encountered, albeit briefly, in that Bristol posting-house a mere ten days or so ago?

Gwen suppressed the shout of hysterical laughter rising in her throat as effectively as she controlled the sudden desire to flee from his presence like an overwhelmed child. She then quickly took heart from the fact his expression betrayed no sign of recognition whatsoever, and in those moments that followed, while he continued to study her with a look that could best be described as amused disbelief, a germ of steely determination that never again would she allow him to dismiss her as yet another light-minded female, not worthy of at least token civility, seeded itself deep within.

A close association over a period of very many months with certain members of a noble Italian family proved invaluable. Gwen raised her pointed little chin in faint hauteur, in much the same way as she had witnessed her good friend the Contessa di Canolini doing on numerous occasions when dealing with any bumptious fellow.

'You appear somewhat stunned, sir,' she said, aping, too, the darling Contessa's bored tone to a nicety. 'If your failure to observe the social niceties in asking me to sit down stems from the fact that I've called at an inconvenient time, I can only apologise and assure you that you'll not be importuned for longer than necessary. If, however, you doubt my authenticity, I'm in a position to prove I am indeed the widow of Sir Percival Warrender.'

Had it ever been Gwen's overriding ambition to set him at a disadvantage, her satisfaction would have been short-lived indeed. Only for the briefest of moments did he betray a flicker of something that could well have been attributed to mild discomfiture at being reminded of basic civilities. Then he merely strolled forward in that infuriatingly relaxed way of his that she well remembered, and stared down at her, unblinking, from his superior height, while gesturing towards one of the chairs placed before the welcoming hearth.

'I require no proof of your identity, Lady Warrender. I shall unmask you soon enough, should you prove to be an impostor,' he told her, sounding infuriatingly confident. 'And as for my reaction—I'm sure you must be well used to it by now. If the truth be known, I expect you were taken, more often than not, for old Warrender's daughter, not his wife.'

Gwen didn't attempt to deny it. 'There was a vast disparity in our ages, it is true,' she agreed, before a certain twinkle, which Martha Gillingham would have recognised in a trice, began to flicker in her eyes a moment before she added, 'And I suppose I must be generous and make allowances. Anyone having attained middle age might consider someone in her mid-twenties a mere child.'

The unkind and altogether inaccurate barb undoubtedly hit its mark. Consequently she experienced a degree of satisfaction to see those dark eyes narrowing perceptively a second before he swung round, and headed across the room in the direction of the decanters. All the same, she had no intention of engaging in open hostilities or attempting to attain the upper hand on the few occasions she was likely to find herself in his company. She was neither vindictive by nature, nor was she one to harbour a grudge. She was quite prepared, henceforward, to award him the same civility as she would any other casual acquaintance, providing he, in turn, reciprocated, and didn't attempt to treat her as though she were a mere featherbrain.

'No, I thank you, sir,' she said, belatedly taking a seat by the hearth, while declining the offer of refreshment. 'I never imbibe in the forenoon as a rule, but do not demur if others choose to do so.'

She didn't suppose for a moment he'd care a whit if she objected or not, for already she had gained the distinct impression he was a gentleman of strong character who, more often than not, would follow his own inclinations, no matter the opposition. Yet she knew it would be grossly unfair of her to assume on so short an acquaintance that he went out of his way to be hostile or even contentious. She was inclined to believe that what she had gleaned from her housemaid was not far removed from the truth. She gained the distinct impression too that, being a blunt, no-nonsense kind of fellow, he would possibly appreciate plain speaking in others, and so decided to adopt just such a policy in any dealings they might have in the future.

Only before she could commence to explain

the reason for her visit, Mr Northbridge, who had been staring at her rather intently since settling himself in the chair opposite, confirmed the conclusions she had thus far drawn by declaring, 'Ma'am, I cannot help thinking we've met somewhere before. Yet for the life of me I cannot imagine why I should suspect as much, since I'm positive we've never been formally introduced, owing to the fact that your husband never returned to his home after your marriage.'

For a moment or two Gwen remained in two minds, not knowing whether to admit to the brief and unfortunate first encounter, or allow him to remain in ignorance. Then a sudden well of pride decided the matter. She had no intention of alluding to an insignificant incident that would set her at a distinct disadvantage. After all, hadn't he little enough respect for her sex, without her fuelling his biased inclinations?

'It is absolutely true, sir, I never visited this county before I recently took up residence in my late husband's house.' Evasiveness on a grand scale it might have been, but at least she had refrained from telling an outright lie. 'I was born and bred in the north of Hampshire, and never once stirred from the county until after my marriage. Perhaps you were a frequent visitor to that part of the country and our paths crossed there.'

For a second or two his regard remained uncomfortably penetrating, then he shrugged, evidently having decided to dismiss it from his mind, and merely offered a token apology for not having called upon her. 'The truth of the matter is, ma'am, I've been away from home, and only arrived back here late yesterday evening.'

'I never made the least attempt to discover whether or not you were in residence,' Gwen wasn't slow to confess, having experienced no second thoughts about maintaining a policy of plain speaking where the gentleman seated opposite was concerned. 'The truth of the matter is, sir, it is the female you employ as governess that I particularly wish to see.'

Study him though she did, Gwen found it impossible to assess what was passing through his mind during those following moments. He certainly didn't appear taken aback, or even offended by the admission, for that matter. No, if anything, she thought she detected what might well have been a guarded expression, before dark brows rose in exaggerated surprise, and he regarded her much as he had done when he had first entered the room.

'You must allow me to felicitate you, ma'am. I

had no notion Sir Percival retained such—er—reserves of stamina in his latter years.' He paused for a moment to observe the bewilderment, which his visitor did absolutely nothing to disguise, widening vivid blue eyes. 'All the same, in this particular instance I fear I cannot oblige you. Besides which, you should find it no difficult matter to engage a suitable female yourself to educate your offspring.'

A full half-minute passed before Gwen had comprehended fully. 'But—but I bore Sir Percival no children,' she eventually managed to reveal, her voice betraying such mortification that it was clear she was experiencing the utmost difficulty understanding why he should have harboured such an absurd notion in the first place. 'There was never any question of children,' she added, not realising precisely what she was revealing to her interested listener, who turned away briefly, thereby concealing a flickering, enigmatic smile.

'Forgive the assumption, ma'am,' he responded, with just a trace of unsteadiness in his voice. 'However, in my defence I must say it was an understandable mistake to make. Furthermore, if you have no children in your care, I fail to understand why you should require the services of a governess.'

'I do not wish to employ a governess, sir…any governess,' Gwen swiftly assured him, after having silently acknowledged there was some justification for his jumping to the totally wrong conclusion, ludicrous though it had undoubtedly been. 'I merely wish to attain your permission to exchange a brief word with your governess, Miss Jane Robbins.'

All lingering traces of amusement vanished in an instant from Jocelyn Northbridge's ruggedly masculine features. 'I regret to say I am unable to acquiesce to your request, Lady Warrender. Miss Robbins, sadly, is no longer in my employ.'

Gwen made not the least attempt to hide her astonishment, though after a moment's reflection she began to appreciate that it was perhaps understandable why, given her employer's caustic temperament, Jane had eventually sought another post. What wasn't so clear was why Jane had failed to furnish her with a forwarding address. After all, she had been well aware that her childhood friend would shortly move into the locale. Why on earth hadn't she left a note in Mrs Travis's care, or sent one to London for Mr Claypole to pass on at Gwen's arrival in the capital?

She began to experience a definite feeling of

unease. 'Do you happen to know where Miss Robbins presently resides, sir? Could you possibly furnish me with her direction?'

For a moment Gwen feared he might, for reasons best known to himself, withhold the information, but then he informed her, without betraying the least emotion, 'Yes, I am in a position to do that, ma'am. She has taken up permanent residency beneath the shading branches of a large yew tree in St Matthew's churchyard.'

Jocelyn Northbridge could never have been accused of harbouring much sympathy towards females who suffered the vapours. In fact, his tolerance hovered only just above zero. Yet in those moments that followed his blunt disclosure, when he watched what he had already decided was a very sweet countenance lose every vestige of healthy bloom, the chivalrous streak in his nature welled as never before, and an unexpected desire to protect almost overwhelmed him.

Within seconds he had poured out a generous measure of brandy and was forcing the glass into a finely boned hand. 'Drink!' he ordered at his most dictatorial, a command seemingly that she could not or did not choose to disobey. Then he was able to observe, with a degree of satisfaction, the subsequent shudder and coughing fit restore a semblance of colour to delicate cheeks.

For a few moments he continued to watch her closely, all the time cursing himself under his breath for a boorish, unfeeling fool. Even a simpleton might have guessed that Warrender's widow and Miss Robbins were likely to have enjoyed more than just a casual acquaintance, he told himself. Yet his voice when he offered an apology for breaking the news in such a callously abrupt manner remained quite impersonal, betraying none of the annoyance at himself or regret he was experiencing.

'Evidently you and Miss Robbins were well acquainted, ma'am?'

'As she was sadly orphaned at an early age, we grew up together, sir.' Her voice, though soft, was blessedly level and free from any threat of tears. 'She was my mother's goddaughter. I looked upon her as a sister.'

As Joss turned at that moment and headed towards the bell-pull sited on the far wall, Gwen failed to see the self-deprecating expression flickering across his features. 'You must allow me to summon your maid, ma'am. You have suffered a grievous shock.'

'Indeed, I have,' Gwen acknowledged with

quiet dignity, while maintaining such remarkable control over her emotions that the gentleman who turned once again to study her could not help but admire her self-restraint. 'And you need not summon my maid, sir. I assure you I've no intention of causing you or myself embarrassment by falling into a swoon. I should much prefer that you return to your seat and explain to me what happened to Jane. Was she yet a further casualty of the influenza epidemic that has been sweeping through the county in recent weeks? I have learned from the doctor that half his patients have fallen victim at some time or other, and sadly not all have survived.'

Instead of resuming the chair opposite, Joss took up a stance before the hearth. 'Believe me, Lady Warrender, I wish I could confirm that it was so.' There could be no mistaking the deep regret in his voice now. 'Miss Robbins's death could not be attributed to natural causes.'

He paused to reach down for the glass of burgundy he had placed on the table by his chair, and tossed it down in one fortifying swallow, before adding, 'She met her end whilst out walking in Marsden Wood.'

For several long moments it was as much as Gwen could do to stare up at him, as she at last began to recall with frightening clarity elements of that conversation she had overheard between this gentleman and his friend in a certain posting-house in Bristol. Then, maintaining that admirable control, she asked bluntly, 'Are you trying to tell me, sir, Jane Robbins was murdered?'

Almost a week passed before Gwen could even attempt to bring herself to come to terms with the fact that her surrogate sister had died in such horrible circumstances; and in the days that followed she discovered a deal more about Jane's demise than Jocelyn Northbridge had seen fit to impart.

It was from her newly appointed housemaid, a mine of local opinions and gossip, salacious or quite otherwise, that Gwen learned that Jane had by no means been the only female in recent years to meet her end in Marsden Wood. Although a little reticent at first, the good doctor too had been persuaded to reveal certain other salient facts surrounding the deaths, and Jane's in particular. From the local vicar, Mr Harmond, one of the few people whom she had agreed to see during this time of deep depression and sorrow, Gwen had discovered the identity of the person who had ensured that Jane had at least received a decent burial and had not been placed in a pauper's grave.

'What a complex gentleman Mr Northbridge is, Gillie,' she remarked, as she led the way out of the churchyard, having at last brought herself to visit the grave. 'A mass of contradictions! He even went to the expense of buying a decent headstone.'

Unbeknownst to Gwen, Martha Gillingham had thoroughly approved of Mr Northbridge from the moment he had insisted they make the return journey in his own carriage, after that one and only visit to his home.

'A very solid, dependable sort, I should say, Miss Gwennie.'

'Yes, and beneath that brusque exterior, he's surprisingly kind and considerate too.' She managed a weak smile, the first to curl her lips in days, as memory stirred. 'One might not suppose just how kind he can be on first making his acquaintance.'

'I think he's what's termed a man's man, Miss Gwennie. He doesn't look the type to stand any nonsense.'

Gwen readily agreed with this viewpoint, even though she knew it could be a big mistake to make snap judgements about people. After all, hadn't she been guilty of doing precisely that, after their unfortunate encounter in a certain crowded posting-house? Whether or not she could ever bring herself to really like him, perhaps only time would tell. But at least she experienced no lingering animosity towards him whatsoever. How could she after the respect he had shown towards her dearest Jane?

'I must write, thanking him for his kindness, and offering to reimburse him for the expense he has incurred paying for Jane's funeral. I don't suppose for a moment he'll accept any money from me. But the least I can do is offer.'

'Well, it looks as if you'll be able to do so in person,' Martha announced, as they turned into the driveway. 'Because, unless I'm much mistaken, that's his carriage standing there at the front door.'

As she had instantly recognised the comfortable equipage too, Gwen didn't delay, once she had dispensed with her outdoor garments, in joining her unexpected visitor in the front parlour.

Standing over six feet in his stockinged feet, Jocelyn Northbridge was an impressive figure by any standard, and in the confines of a parlour that was only moderately proportioned he seemed more imposing than ever. Yet, strangely enough, as she moved towards him, hand automatically outstretched in welcome, Gwen felt not one iota intimidated by his superior height and breadth. In fact, the opposite was true—she felt oddly reassured to see him standing there before her hearth.

'Do make yourself comfortable, Mr Northbridge,' she cordially invited, once he had released her hand, after the briefest of clasps, so that she could indicate the most robustly made chair, the one that was sure to withstand his weight. 'May I offer you some refreshment? I came across numerous bottles of a very fine burgundy whilst I was inspecting the cellar shortly after my arrival here.'

She was well aware he was studying her every move during the time it took to dispense two glasses and rejoin him at the hearth. Fortunately the short walk from the local church had done something to restore her healthy bloom, even if it could not disguise the fact that a total lack of appetite in recent days had resulted in weight loss, a circumstance that wouldn't escape his notice, as very little did, she strongly suspected.

This was borne out by the exaggerated upward movement of one dark brow when she placed the two crystal vessels down on the table between their respective chairs. 'Breaking with tradition on this occasion, Lady Warrender, and imbibing in the forenoon, I see,' he quipped. 'I'm relieved to discover you're prepared to make adjustments from time to time to suit various occasions, and are not bound by monotonous convention or routine. Such persons swiftly become bores.'

Gwen came to the conclusion in that moment that if one wished to rub along with Mr Jocelyn Northbridge even just tolerably well, one must swiftly make allowances for his somewhat acerbic manner and forthright opinions. In view of the fact that she was very much beholden to him at the present time, it wasn't too difficult a decision to reach to do precisely that.

Which was perhaps just as well, for when, a second or two later, she attempted to thank him for the consideration he had shown in dealing with Jane's funeral, he interrupted with an expletive of impatience, dismissing her offer to reimburse him with a wave of one large, yet surprisingly shapely hand.

'Kindness doesn't enter into the matter, ma'am,' he continued in the same blunt manner. 'I had been assured by Miss Robbins herself, when she applied for the post, that she had no close relatives living. Consequently, when the tragedy occurred, I felt duty bound, as she was in my employ at the time, to deal with the matter personally.' He paused to sample the dark liquid in his glass, favouring the remaining contents a moment later with a look of decided approval. 'Needless to say I was oblivious to your close association, otherwise I would have taken the trouble to write apprising you of the tragedy. I happen to know she corresponded on a reasonably regular basis with someone residing in the capital, but could find no clue as to this unknown's direction among her effects.'

'That would undoubtedly have been Mr Claypole of Messrs Claypole, Claypole and Featherstone. Many of the letters Jane and I wrote to each other during my first years away from this country went astray. But when Percival and I visited Italy in more recent times, Mr Claypole the younger was kind enough to undertake the task of forwarding the letters, which resulted in many more eventually reaching their respective destinations.'

'I found no letters among her belongings, ma'am. Which, incidentally, I've brought with me today. I thought you might like them.'

Gwen felt moved by the gesture. 'That was kind of you, sir. I thank you.'

He didn't attempt to throw her gratitude back in her face this time. He merely watched as she sampled the fine wine with what appeared to be a deal less appreciation than he himself had done.

Acutely conscious of this continued close scrutiny, Gwen turned her head slightly to stare down at the burning logs in the hearth, thereby offering him a prime view of a small, tip-tilted nose and slightly protruding upper lip.

'Since learning of Jane's tragic demise, I've discovered she was by no means the only female to have met her end in this Marsden Wood.'

No comment was forthcoming. Undeterred, Gwen added, 'The daughter of a wealthy farmer is believed to have been yet another casualty. She, so I have been led to believe, was murdered some few years ago. There has been a further body unearthed, so I understand. Apparently it was too decomposed for any definite identification to be made. Although, because of a bracelet found close to the body, and remnants of clothing, it is strongly supposed she was none other than a local corn merchant's daughter who disappeared last summer. Whether she suffered the same fate as Jane was, I'm reliably informed, impossible to ascertain. But it is strongly suspected that she too was violated…a fact you chose to withhold from me, Mr Northbridge.'

He didn't attempt to deny it. Instead he cursed,

long and fluently under his breath, before demanding in the blunt, dictatorial manner to which
she was becoming increasingly less resentful,
'Who have you been talking to...? The local
sawbones, I'll be bound!'

Without experiencing the least need to resort to
profanity, Gwen returned the compliment by not
attempting to prevaricate, either. 'Dr Bartlet was,
eventually, a deal more forthcoming than you
were, sir, certainly. As was my new maid, Annie,
a veritable fount of local knowledge. And no
mean judge of public opinion, I might add.'

'Is she, by gad!' He was decidedly unim-
pressed, as his next words proved beyond doubt.
'And what good has it done you to discover all
the unsavoury facts surrounding the death? It was
enough for you to learn you had lost a good friend
in such a fashion without learning every last
sordid detail.'

Gwen favoured him with a searching stare, and
easily detected a look of concern lurking behind
the sparkle of annoyance in those dark eyes. 'I
believe you were trying to be kind in sparing me
the unsavoury facts, sir. But let me assure you,
I'm no child. My husband always did his utmost
to protect me, but he never once attempted to
prevent me from increasing my knowledge of the

world. I'm fully aware of what Jane must have endured before she was strangled.'

One expressive brow rose at this, betraying his scepticism, but he refrained from comment, leaving Gwen to rise to her feet and go over to the window, whilst the silence lengthened between them.

'What's of most concern to me now is what's being done to bring the murderer to book.' She swung round, catching a guarded look, not untouched by guilt, flickering over his strong and decidedly aristocratic features. 'From what I've discovered thus far, no one has been charged with the crimes, though several likely suspects have been named.'

'Sheer gossip, more often than not stemming from some personal dislike or grievance,' he returned, totally dismissive, before running impatient fingers through his thick, slightly waving dark hair. 'Of course enquiries were made about Miss Robbins. And the other women, too. But nothing ever came to light. No one ever came forward admitting to having witnessed the tragic incidents. In point of fact, no one has ever come forward with any relevant information at all, as far as I'm aware. And as far as Miss Robbins is concerned—no one, myself included, even saw her leave Bridge House. Her absence wasn't discovered until the evening, when she failed to go down to the kitchen for her dinner, and so a maid took a tray up to her room.'

The lines across his forehead grew more pronounced, making him appear more forbidding than ever. 'Naturally I instigated a thorough search of both house and grounds. But it was dark by that time, so there was no possibility of widening the search. Her body was discovered two days later by a man called Furslow, Lord Cranborne's gamekeeper.'

Gwen found these disclosures both interesting and puzzling at one and the same time. 'Was Jane in the habit of wandering about the countryside when the mood took her?' she asked, thinking him a very generous master in allowing his employees so much free time.

He wasn't slow to set her straight on the matter. 'Of course not! Not unless she undertook to take her charges out for some fresh air,' he answered snappishly. 'If her intention was to walk any distance, she was, at my insistence, always accompanied by a male servant, footman or groom.' His expression relaxed markedly and his voice became noticeably less caustic, too, as he added, 'Miss Robbins was extremely conscientious. She more than met my expectations. My wards improved in every respect under her charge.'

Although he continued to stare directly across the room in her general direction, Gwen gained the distinct impression he was seeing quite a different aspect. 'It just so happened that my wards were among the first to succumb to the recent, widespread influenza outbreak. I took what precautions I could to ensure my entire household wasn't afflicted by giving instructions that my old nursemaid was the only one to attend the sickroom until the girls were over the worst of it. Miss Robbins undertook to help me catalogue the books in my library during that period. But even so she was left with plenty of free time on her hands. Unfortunately, the weather naturally being so inclement at that season of the year, she rarely left the house.'

The cleft between his dark brows deepened once again. 'If my memory serves me correctly the girls were well on the way to a complete recovery, and Miss Robbins had decided to recommence lessons, at least in part, the very next day. Maybe she decided to take full advantage of the last of her free time by taking a walk, and went further than intended.'

As she had done little travelling about since

her arrival in Somerset, Gwen was unfamiliar with the area, and frowned as she attempted to recall the countryside she had passed through on that one and only visit made to Bridge House. 'Is this Marsden Wood situated close to your home, sir?'

'It's about a mile and a half or so away, and lies to the south-east of my property.'

Gwen took a moment to consider what he had disclosed thus far. Jane, she clearly recalled, had been an avid walker years ago, and the mile-and-a-half hike would have meant nothing to her, a mere stretch of the legs, as it were. Even so, choosing to explore a wood in the middle of January did seem rather odd behaviour for someone of Jane's sensible inclinations. Surely she would have been more likely to have explored the shelves in her master's library for a suitable read than have run the risk of returning to Bridge House with skirts and boots caked in mud, after an exploratory stroll in a wood? And what was so interesting to view there at that season of the year? Furthermore, would she deliberately have gone against her employer's express wishes and gone there alone? The answer came hard on the heels of the question—no, she would not, unless she had a very good reason for doing so. Odd...yes, it all seemed decidedly odd!

Suddenly aware that she was being, yet again, avidly studied by her forthright visitor, and that she was in the gravest danger of being accused of the sin of neglect, she apologised. 'My only excuse, sir, is that I'm finding it immensely difficult to come to terms with my dearest friend's demise, and my thoughts remain in turmoil. All the same, I must detain you no further, and must thank you again most sincerely for your help in the matter and for ensuring I received those personal effects.'

'Wrong on all counts, ma'am,' he returned, once more catching her completely offguard and surprising her by his response. 'I've been of no help to you whatsoever. Yet, I expect that'll change. And quite swiftly now you've set up home here.' He took a moment to stare about at what for him had once been very familiar surroundings. 'Warrender would have expected no less from a close neighbour and friend, even though we saw nothing of each other in recent years. And rid your mind of the nonsensical notion you're importuning me. I've never permitted anyone to do that since leaving Oxford. But what you have singularly failed to do, ma'am, is refill my glass. It's stood empty for the past five minutes, and I'm far too much of a gentleman to help myself.'

'Now that I simply can't believe!' Gwen retorted before she could stop herself. The resulting bark of masculine laughter instantly vanquished her slight feeling of pique at what she had deemed unnecessary strictures on her skills as a hostess, and she found herself willingly complying with his request.

'Without wishing to appear rude, why do you suppose you could be of service to me, sir?' she asked, having decided to maintain this mode of plain speaking, at least when solely in his company, which she didn't envisage would be so often that her powers of restraint would suffer as a result.

'Well, for a start, ma'am, I can assist you in acquiring a half-decent carriage,' he answered, after taking a moment to sample the contents of the refilled glass. 'If you're to continue residing here, and I assume that's your intention, you can't carry on making use of that antiquated bone-shaker of a vehicle. Old Percival used to ride most everywhere. Much preferred the open air. So that vehicle served his needs on the few occasions he was obliged to use it. But it won't serve yours, most especially if you're to put off your blacks in the near future. Which I assume you intend to do, as you've been widowed nine months now, by my reckoning. No one would expect you to mourn for ever, no matter how fond of old Percival you were. It's high time you thought of resuming a normal life, enjoying yourself a little and making and receiving visits.'

It was on the tip of Gwen's tongue to tell him to mind his own business, that she was more than capable of organising her own life, but checked at the last moment.

If the truth were known, it had indeed been her intention to go into half-mourning. Learning of Jane's tragic demise had persuaded her to remain in her blacks. Yet now, quite suddenly, she began to experience a change of heart once again. After all, what benefit would come of just mourning Jane? Her time and energy would be put to better use in attempting to discover who was responsible for the loss of her dearest friend, because it seemed that no one else had troubled unduly to do so.

The smile she bestowed upon her visitor induced him to blink several times before finishing off his wine in one fortifying swallow. 'I should consider it a very great favour, sir, if you would assist me in finding a suitable equipage. It is indeed my intention to go out and about a good deal more from now on.'

Evidently having decided to bring his visit to an

end now, he rose to his feet. Gwen did likewise, forestalling him as he made to cross to the door by asking the identity of the local Justice of the Peace.

'Lord Cranborne,' he enlightened, before favouring her with a decidedly suspicious look. 'What makes you ask?'

Seeing no earthly reason why she should keep her intentions secret, she said, 'Because I assume he is the very person to consult if one wishes to discover precisely what is the current situation with regard to uncovering the identity of the Marsden Wood Murderer!'

Chapter Three

Jocelyn Northbridge numbered among the select few who were never denied admittance to Cranborne Hall, the principal seat of the Earls of Cranborne for centuries past. Nevertheless, the butler, highly trained and a stickler for adhering to accepted codes of conduct, requested the visitor wait in a small room off the main hall as a matter of course, before showing him into his master's favourite retreat on the floor above a few minutes later.

The Earl, not attempting to hide his delight at this unexpected visit by one of his most well-respected and, in his considered opinion, sagacious of neighbours, rose immediately from behind his desk. More than happy to set aside estate matters for the time being, he drew the gentleman, whose reputation for selecting fine wines was second to none, across to the hearth and awaited judgement on what he himself considered a superior claret.

'Well?' he prompted when his welcome visitor, after sampling the liquid, merely held up his glass to the light, the better to study its contents' deep rich colour. 'Come, a little honesty, my friend. Isn't it one of the finest you've ever tasted?'

Joss, never one to be pressed on matters of real importance, considered for a moment longer before nodding approval, and then immediately afterwards destroying his host's understandable satisfaction by adding, 'But certainly not the best tipple I've sampled this day.'

'What?' His lordship regarded the younger man as though his neighbour had taken leave of his senses. 'You're bamming me!'

'Not at all, sir,' Joss assured him, setting the glass to one side. 'And that, in part, is why I'm here.'

'Aha!' His lordship was all avid attention. 'Got yourself a new vintner, have you, and are willing to share the rogue's fine stocks with an old friend?'

Joss wasn't slow to set his lordship straight on the matter. 'Not quite, no. What I have acquired is a new neighbour. And one who's shown re-markable judgement in selecting wine. A very fine palate, I should say…for a woman, that is.' He paused for a moment to stare blindly up at the portrait of the decidedly ill-favoured, though much missed, late Countess taking pride of place above the hearth. 'Possibly the result of that time spent in Italy, I should imagine.'

'And the name of the rare specimen?' his lordship prompted, amused by the dry tone, and not just a little intrigued as well.

'Old Warrender's widow.'

In all probability it would have been at this juncture that his lordship's interest in the unknown female would have swiftly begun to wane, had it not been for the odd flicker he detected, just for an instant, in his visitor's eyes. He didn't waste time in attempting to speculate on what the look might have denoted. If, however, it was a silent admission to a definite interest in the woman, then it would have been the first Northbridge had ever betrayed, at least in his lordship's presence, for it was a well-known fact that his highly respected neighbour held all too few of the fair sex in high esteem.

One of the rare exceptions was, in fact, none other than his lordship's favourite niece. A handsome young woman, with a fine figure and a quick mind, Anthea Kershaw appeared to be, on the surface at least, the ideal partner for a gentle-man of Jocelyn Northbridge's stamp. His lordship was very well aware that his youngest sister, Lady Florence Kershaw, had, for several years, nurtured the fondest hope of just such an alliance. Indeed, he himself wouldn't have been averse to such a match, for he was as fond of this particular niece as he was his own sons, if not a deal fonder in many respects. Notwithstanding, he was not altogether sure that Anthea would make the ideal wife for his estimable neighbour. If the girl had one failing, it was a tendency to be a trifle too refined, a little too conciliating, and therefore would do almost anything to avoid confrontation. She would undoubtedly allow Northbridge his way in more things than would be good for him, with possible disastrous consequences.

His lordship regarded his companion steadily, as Joss, clearly in a world of his own that day, continued absently to contemplate the portrait of the late Countess.

'Well, come on, Northbridge,' he urged, after a further moment's silence. 'What's the widow like? I seem to remember hearing someone mentioning once that she was young enough to be Warrender's daughter.'

'Ha! Granddaughter, more like!' Joss returned with brutal frankness.

'Good gad, the old dog! And is she pleasing on the eye?'

Surprising his lordship somewhat, Joss took a long moment to consider. 'Not a beauty, no, at least not in my humble opinion,' he revealed at last. 'But well enough. Got what I'd call a sweet face. Damned disarming little thing, though,' he went on, his heavy frown descending. 'Turns out she was well acquainted with that governess I employed. She's not at all happy nothing's being done to track down the killer.'

'You know we did all we could,' his lordship returned, far from annoyed, though slightly nettled by the accusation. 'Spoke again to all the usual suspects, but no fresh evidence came to light. No one heard anything; no one saw anything. Even had an extra word with my gamekeeper. I know Furslow's not liked by most hereabouts. He's been a prime suspect in many people's minds from the start, especially as the first girl was discovered only a matter of weeks after he came to work for me. What is more, there's no denying he has something of a reputation where women are concerned. But there's absolutely nothing to link him with these murders. In fact, the opposite's true. Several people have come forward to swear he was else-where, attending a prize fight or cockfight, when at least two of the women were first reported missing.'

'True enough,' Joss was forced to agree, his heavy frown still very much in evidence. 'But that doesn't alter the fact that more could have been done…should have been done to find the person responsible.'

His lordship watched, appalled, as his guest, quite without warning, tossed the remainder of his wine down his throat and rose abruptly to his feet. 'Good gad, Northbridge! That's no way to treat a wine of that quality!'

Ignoring the stricture, Joss began to pace up and down, resorting for the second time that morning to running impatient fingers through his hair as he did so. 'That damnable female's got under my skin, so she has!' he at last admitted, coming to a halt in the middle of the room. 'Just as I was on the point of departure, she came straight out and said that had any one of the victims been some highborn lady, no effort would have been spared. And damn it, Cranborne, you can't deny the chit's right! Then, when I attempted to persuade her not to interfere, she totally floored me with the response. Asked if I'd just sit back and do nothing if a friend of mine had been murdered. And the truth of the matter is I'd move heaven and earth in an attempt to uncover the killer.'

'So, what are you asking me to do?' his lordship prompted, when once again his visitor relapsed into a brooding silence. 'If you're asking me to start fresh enquiries, I don't honestly believe it would do much good.'

'No, I was thinking more on the lines of bringing in someone from the outside, an ex-Runner who has for some years now undertaken private commissions. I happen to know he successfully aided a very close friend of mine in locating the whereabouts of his errant wife. Seemingly he's extremely discreet. Furthermore, he has the knack of blending in, of going about a community without arousing suspicion, inducing people to reveal more than they might otherwise have done to someone they knew to be in authority. I could send an express to London, requesting my good friend Merriot Markham engages this person on my behalf—if you've no objection, that is?'

'Not in the least, dear boy,' the Earl agreed, urbanity itself, 'providing you don't keep me in the dark if any information is uncovered.'

'Understood,' Joss responded.

Deciding it was time to bring the visit to an end,

he made his way across the room. As he reached the door, he bethought himself of something else, however. 'You don't happen to know if young Gilmorton's still contemplating disposing of that new carriage and pair in order to pay those gaming debts?'

'Can't see him managing to do so otherwise, as his father steadfastly refuses to come to his aid this time. Why? Surely you're not thinking of making him an offer?'

'Not for myself, no. But I promised Warrender's widow I'd look out for a decent carriage and pair for her. And I'll do it too!' A look of rock-hard determination momentarily gripped Northbridge's features. 'But that's all I intend to do for the confounded woman!' he declared vehemently. '

His lordship smiled to himself as the door was closed none too gently by the departing visitor. 'I wonder now,' he murmured, taking his time to savour the remaining contents of his glass, 'how long it will be before our friend finds himself breaking that vow?'

Three days later Gwen had once again taken up the day-to-day running of her household. It wasn't that she had recovered swiftly from the loss of her friend. Nothing could have been further from the truth. Jane was never absent long from her thoughts, and she once again returned to the forefront of Gwen's mind the instant she had finished discussing the dinner menus for the following week with her now, thankfully, fully re-covered housekeeper.

'Before you go, Mrs Travis,' she said, forestall-ing the servant's immediate departure, 'are you by any chance acquainted with the housekeeper at Bridge House?'

'Why, yes, ma'am! Known Mrs Brice for a number of years. We both took up our posts at about the same time, though she's a good deal older than me. Always exchange a word or two after the Sunday service, we do, and if we happen to bump into each other in town when doing the marketing.'

'Sounds a pleasant, friendly sort of woman, Travis. Is that so?'

'Indeed, yes, ma'am,' she readily agreed. 'Not a gossip, you understand,' she added. 'And very loyal to her master, she be. Mind you, not much goes on at Bridge House she doesn't know about.'

Precisely what I was hoping to discover! Gwen thought, before her acute hearing picked up the sounds of an arrival, even though she was in her favourite retreat, the snug little parlour tucked away at the back of the house.

She watched Mrs Travis hurry out, and was astonished when the housekeeper returned a few minutes later to inform her that Lady Florence Kershaw and her daughter were now awaiting her in the much larger front parlour.

'Ordinarily, ma'am, I should have shown such visitors into the drawing room, it being the best room in the house. Except, as you know, you gave strict instructions no fire be lit in there until the chimney's been swept, and I thought it would be a mite on the chilly side, even though it's almost April.'

'You did quite right, Mrs Travis,' Gwen assured the slightly flustered housekeeper.

Clearly she was unused to inviting such high-ranking persons to cross the threshold, and Gwen couldn't in all honesty say she was in the least surprised. The late Sir Percival Warrender, having enjoyed a distinguished military career, had undeniably been well respected. His standing in the area would undoubtedly have been reasonably high. All the same, he had been no aristocrat, merely the son of an affluent gentleman. So why had his insignificant little widow been so singularly honoured?

Amazed though she was, Gwen didn't feel in the least overawed, simply because she had benefited from that recent, close association with one of the most endearing and unorthodox high-born ladies who had, over the years, rubbed shoulders with several crowned heads of Europe.

Consequently Gwen was able to greet her unexpected visitors with all the quiet dignity expected of a young widow, but without experiencing the least trepidation, while at the same time successfully concealing her natural curiosity.

On entering the comfortable, though undeniably faded, front parlour, Gwen experienced on odd mixture of surprise and slight disappointment. She didn't quite know what she had been expecting to find awaiting her, but she supposed she would have imagined two members of the most influential family in the county to make rather more of an impressive spectacle.

Lady Florence was undeniably dressed in the height of fashion. Sadly the prevailing mode ill suited her thickening figure. The colour puce made her appear slightly liverish, and the ugly turban-styled bonnet did absolutely nothing to improve the strong-featured, aristocratic lines of a face that had long since lost any slight claim to beauty.

Her daughter, on the other hand, neither favoured her mother in looks, nor in stature. Taller than average height, and slender, Anthea Kershaw had been blessed with a good complexion; and although her features were regular, one would have considered her handsome rather than pretty. There was no denying either that her plain, unadorned gown suited her very well, and was undoubtedly of good quality. Nevertheless it was clearly the achievement of some competent seamstress and not the creation of a top London modiste, of which Gwen had seen numerous examples during her sojourn in the capital earlier in the year.

She was instantly drawn to the younger woman as much by the warmth of a full-lipped smile as the completely unaffected manner. As things turned out, it was none other than Miss Kershaw herself who gave the first inclination as to why Gwen had been honoured by the visit, once initial pleasantries had been exchanged:

'I understand from my uncle that you were well acquainted with the latest unfortunate female to meet her end in Marsden Wood?'

'That is true,' Gwen confirmed, realising in an instant from whom Lord Cranborne must have attained this information, while in the next

moment wondering just when Mr Northbridge
had paid a visit to his illustrious neighbour and,
more importantly, why.

It might have been purely and simply a social
call, during which he had just happened to
mention there was someone in the neighbour-
hood who wasn't prepared to sit back and allow
matters to rest. But even if this was so, his
lordship, surely, would hardly feel so discomposed as to deem it necessary to send two close
female relations to pay a visit on the person who
just might stir up something of a hornet's nest?

Thrusting the various puzzling possibilities to
the back of her mind to mull over later, Gwen went
on to explain the close bond she had enjoyed with
Jane Robbins. Although both visitors expressed
sympathy, Lady Florence wasn't slow to change
the subject in an attempt to discover more about
Gwen's life, her parentage and family history.

She betrayed a degree of surprise, not untouched by approval, when she learned that
Gwen's father had been a member of the old and
very distinguished Playfair family heralding from
Derbyshire; and that her mother had borne the
name of one of the most influential families in the
county of Shropshire before her marriage.

'So your mother and one of my dearest friends,

Constance Blanchard, that was, must have been related in some way. First or second cousins, perhaps?' Lady Florence suggested, after taking a few moments to work out the possible relationship. 'An excellent old family, the Blanchards. No title, of course, but worthy, all the same.'

Gwen was just silently debating whether or not to reduce drastically her standing in this aristocratic visitor's eyes by revealing that her mother had not, in fact, come from the wealthy branch of the Blanchard family that owned a good portion of land in the county of Shropshire, when she was forestalled by Miss Kershaw, who took advantage of the temporary lull in the conversation by returning to the subject of the recent murders.

'I mentioned to Uncle Charles only the other week that it's getting to the stage where it's unsafe for a female to walk anywhere unaccompanied.'

'And I sincerely trust, Anthea, you would never consider doing such an outrageous thing!' Lady Florence exclaimed, looking appalled at the mere thought. 'Nor Lady Warrender, for that matter,' she added, seemingly having already judged that there was, surprisingly, little difference in age between the young women. 'A female must always adhere to accepted rules of behaviour, no matter how respectable her status.'

'Very true, my lady,' Gwen readily agreed, not knowing whether to feel amused or nettled by this quite unnecessary reminder of good conduct. 'But you must remember that the majority of women in the land are not nearly so fortunate as we three. They cannot afford the luxury of maid-servants or companions to bear them company whenever they choose to venture forth. Indeed, most are obliged to do so in order to survive.'

'And they should be able to do so without fear of being attacked,' Anthea Kershaw put in without hesitation, her views on the subject seemingly in complete accord with Gwen's. 'Furthermore, Mama, I have no intention of dragging along a re-luctant maidservant whenever I wish to take a breath of air in the park. I would far rather have Felix to bear me company. And one could hardly consider him an ideal companion. Why, on every occasion we've ventured into the wood, he's relapsed into a world of his own, quite oblivious to my presence. And do remember a goodly portion of the wood forms part of the Cranborne estate. Up until now all incidents have taken place in that far area, where people may roam quite freely. But there's no saying, if there should be more attacks, in what area they might take place.'

'Oh, Anthea, dear, pray do not!' her mother implored, appearing genuinely distressed. 'I do not know from where you get these callous notions and dark thoughts.'

The smile that pulled at one corner of Miss Kershaw's mouth for once was not pleasant, and a decidedly uneasy, almost troubled, look appeared momentarily in her eyes as she said, 'It's undoubtedly inherited, Mama. A family trait, wouldn't you say?'

The speed with which Lady Florence changed the subject took Gwen so completely by surprise that it was a few moments before she was able to respond to the question directed at her.

'No, ma'am, I have no plans to spend any time in the capital this spring.' She chose not to add that, although it wasn't beyond her means now to do so, she had no intention of needlessly wasting money by enjoying the unlimited pleasures the capital had to offer in an attempt to alter her widowed state. 'I fully intend to go into half-mourning and socialise a little from now on. But I've more than enough to occupy me here for the present,' she added, glancing about her. 'The house is sadly in need of refurbishing, and bringing up to date. I sometimes think I've been swept back into the past century when I walk through these rooms. Most all the furnishings, as you've possibly observed, are quite antiquated.'

'If that is your objective, then, yes, you will have much to occupy you for the foreseeable future,' Lady Florence agreed, rising to her feet, a clear indication that she had every intention of bringing the visit to an end. 'Nevertheless, I sincerely trust you are not so busy that you cannot dine with us, before we make our yearly trip to the capital next month. I shall ensure you receive a formal invitation, Lady Warrender. If nothing else, it will offer you the ideal opportunity to recommence your socialising by meeting a few of your neighbours.'

It will offer me a great deal more than that, Gwen silently acknowledged, well pleased by the unexpected visit and the chance it would soon present to become acquainted with the local Justice of the Peace.

It wasn't so much the formal, gilt-edged invitation card, which was delivered by hand the following day, that brought Gwen such gratification as the totally unexpected appearance on her driveway of a bang-up-to-date lightweight carriage, pulled by a superb pair of matched greys. Most surprising of all was that the carriage was being tooled by none other than Annie's eldest brother, Ben, a circumstance of which Annie herself demanded an immediate explanation the instant she had accompanied her mistress outside.

'Don't work for the blacksmith n'more, Annie. Works for Mr Northbridge now,' he revealed, looking well pleased with the change of situation. 'Leastways, I reckon I do,' he amended, 'if Lady Warrender, 'ere, ain't too keen to take me on.'

Gwen wasn't quite sure what to make of this, and didn't attempt to hide her puzzlement. 'I'm sorry. Ben, I'm not altogether certain I know precisely what you mean.'

'It's this way, ma'am. Mr Northbridge seemed to s'pose you'd be in need of a groom, 'im not 'aving a good word to say about the man you've got now. Said as 'ow 'ee weren't up to tooling a donkey, let alone a decent pair of 'orses. Besides, 'im being a lazy b—'

His sister's warning cry was sufficient to remind Ben to mind his language. Gwen had, however, already grasped the general drift, and couldn't say she was unduly surprised by her affluent neighbour resorting to colourful language. Nonetheless she felt the situation needed some clarification, so didn't hesitate to take advantage of the big brother's presence for the time being at least.

Delaying only for as long as it took to collect a cloak, put on a bonnet and secure Gillie's services, Gwen then set out on what she considered was the most comfortable carriage ride she had experienced in her entire life. Cushioned by thick and luxurious velvet upholstery, she felt not the slightest rut, and arrived at Bridge House in a surprisingly short space of time feeling hugely satisfied with her latest acquisition, completely uncaring as to the amount of money that would be required to reimburse Mr Northbridge, and more than ready to forgive and forget any past grievances she might still have retained with the man himself.

Unfortunately she was denied the opportunity to offer her personal thanks, but wasn't unduly dejected to discover the master of the house away from home, for the information was relayed by none other than the housekeeper, who showed no unwillingness in allowing the visitor to step over the threshold in order to write a note.

Gwen soon found herself in what was surely Mr Northbridge's private sanctum. Smelling faintly of leather, cigars and fine old brandy, the room was a representation of its owner's personality—solid, reliable and wholly masculine.

Settling herself behind the desk, she easily arrested the housekeeper's immediate departure by saying, 'Please don't rush away. It won't take many moments just to scribble a few lines… It's Mrs Brice, isn't it?'

'Why, yes, ma'am!' she responded, appearing surprised.

'I wish to thank you for ensuring that Jane Robbins's belongings were safely packed away until such time as your master was able to dispose of them. Did you know I was a particular friend of hers?'

'The master did mention it, ma'am, when he gave orders for the box to be brought down from the attic.' She was quiet for a moment, then, evidently feeling she ought to say something further, added, 'All very sorry we were, ma'am. Miss Robbins was a real nice young woman. There wasn't a servant here who didn't think well of her.'

Even though Gwen was much moved by the tribute, simply because she believed it had been totally sincere, not uttered merely as a formality, her mind was working rapidly in order to turn the conversation to her advantage, and maybe uncover something, anything, that might offer a clue as to why Jane had lost her life on that particular day in January. Was it simply a case of being in the wrong place at the wrong time? Or had she, perhaps, arranged to meet someone in secret, which would necessitate in her having to venture forth alone?

The latter was unlikely, and yet anything was possible, Gwen decided, striving to keep an open mind as she said, 'Yes, dear Jane always attempted to get along with people, no matter their station in life. I cannot recall anyone who didn't like her. She was both trustworthy and hardworking. And so sensible too! That's why I cannot understand what could have possessed her to go out walking on what I'm reliably informed was such a damp and dismal day, by herself and in such a lonely spot.'

Mrs Brice wasn't slow to agree. 'Truth to tell, ma'am, it surprised us too. Never mentioned to anyone she meant to go out. Which was most odd, not like her at all. She'd always let one of the staff know, even if she was just going for a walk in the garden. And she was never late for meals. Always so considerate to Cook, she was.'

'Perhaps something had upset her, and it slipped her mind,' Gwen suggested, and watched a slightly troubled expression flit over the house-keeper's face.

'Now, it's strange you should say that, ma'am. Because, unless I'm much mistaken, it were on that very day the young parlourmaid happened to catch sight of Miss Robbins coming along the passageway from the nursery. Said as how she looked upset, red eyed and sniffing, and whisked herself into her room without speaking. But I don't see as how she could have been upset, because she was fine earlier when I spoke to her, and I know for a fact she was looking forward to beginning lessons with the girls again the following morning.

'She'd done wonders with those girls, ma'am,' she went on to reveal, her mind seemingly locked in the past, 'especially Miss Amy, who can be something of a handful at times. Both Miss Mary and Miss Amy had grown right fond of her, so they had. So I can't see as how a visit to the nursery to see them would have upset her. No, I think it's much more likely she'd picked up a touch of the influenza herself, and maybe thought to walk it off that afternoon.'

'Or maybe she'd agreed to meet someone, and chose Marsden Wood so that the assignation wouldn't be witnessed,' Gwen suggested, and then watched as Mrs Brice's expression of gentle concern changed at once into a decidedly guarded look.

She easily guessed the reason for the slight withdrawal. 'I'm not suggesting for a moment that Miss Robbins's behaviour was in any way improper,' she assured the servant. 'I suppose I'm just trying to think of some reason why she should have taken it into her head to visit such a place alone, when she knew of its unfortunate reputation.'

The explanation evidently satisfied Mrs Brice, because she visibly thawed. 'That I couldn't say, ma'am. But what I can tell you is Miss Robbins never had any callers…followers, as you might say. And never received any letters, at least none that weren't picked up in a proper manner from the receiving office, with the master's own. And she received a few of those during the many months she were here.'

'And yet there were none among her belongings, Mrs Brice,' Gwen reminded her, but the housekeeper didn't seem in the least discomposed, and merely shrugged thin shoulders.

'All I can tell you, ma'am, is I saw to it all Miss Robbins's belongings were packed away into that there box.'

'Just as I assured you myself not a week ago,' a deep voice from behind the housekeeper drawled.

Strangely enough Gwen wasn't in the least embarrassed by the master of the house's unexpected appearance, even though she detected slight irritation in his voice and an accusing flicker in the depths of his deep-set dark eyes, which betrayed clearly enough that he knew she had been attempting to glean what information she could from his housekeeper.

'Did you enjoy your ride?' she asked casually, after a brief inspection of the riding garb that suited his large frame very well.

'I always do.'

After dismissing Mrs Brice with the briefest of nods, he came sauntering across to the desk, and whisked away the piece of paper upon which Gwen had been writing before she realised his intention. 'Yes, a very neat hand,' he remarked judiciously, before tossing the letter back down in a decidedly indifferent manner and without the least reference to its contents. 'And do you ride, Lady Warrender?'

'Infrequently and indifferently, sir,' Gwen answered with no little amusement. 'I cannot imagine why people should suppose I've enjoyed a privileged existence thus far. Yes, my husband was a man of means, which enabled him in his latter years to travel extensively, and I've been fortunate enough to live in relative comfort since I married. But people are inclined to forget, or are unaware, that I was merely the daughter of a country parson. Not a totally impoverished one, it's true. But neither could my father squander sums of money on unnecessary luxuries, such as the keeping of horses for pleasure only.'

A recent memory drew a smile to her lips. 'Lady Florence Kershaw seemed to suppose I'd even enjoyed London Seasons in my youth. I cannot imagine from where she might have obtained such an absurd notion...unless it was from you.'

If he detected the slightly accusing tone, he certainly betrayed no sign of it, as he went over to the table on which several decanters stood. 'Ahh, so you've received a visit from the county's most celebrated hostess, have you. I'd be interested to know what you made of her. Did she drag her daughter along by any chance?'

'She did. And I'm forced to admit Miss Kershaw left me with a very favourable impression. Her mother less so,' Gwen admitted. 'Lady Florence was pleasant enough, but I detected a certain reserve in her, and a degree of snobbery too. Which is only to be expected, I suppose.' She frowned slightly. 'I gained the distinct impression she had a specific reason for honouring me with a visit, and it had little to do with merely being sociable.'

'Probably went to see you at her brother's behest.'

Gwen managed a look that was both mocking and accusing at one and the same time. 'Ahh! So you did let him know I was intent on doing something about these unsolved murders.'

'Yes, warned him you'd probably turn out to be an infernal nuisance to us both. Now, come over here to the fire,' he went on, with an abrupt change of subject, 'and tell me what you think of this wine. And don't give me any of that missish nonsense about it being before noon, so you'd prefer to decline!'

Gwen found herself automatically complying with what was undoubtedly a command, and smiling too at the dictatorial tone he had suddenly chosen to adopt. It was most strange, but for some obscure reason she hadn't found it even remotely irritating.

'Very palatable indeed,' she opined, after sampling the contents of the glass he had handed to her.

'Yes, it is,' he agreed. 'But it still isn't as good as that drop I had over at your place t'other day. Wish

I knew where that old rogue of a husband of yours managed to lay his hands on such a fine stock.'

'Well, I just might be able to help you there,' she responded, much to his surprise. 'Percival was a very patient, methodical man. That's perhaps why during his last months he was so successful in searching through piles of earth in order to uncover the smallest of artefacts. I came across a stack of accounts and household bills going back years when I was in the attic the other day. I dare say the name of the supplier will be lurking in there somewhere.'

'I shall be for ever in your debt, ma'am, if you can lay your hands upon it,' he vowed, looking very well pleased at the prospect.

'Just as I find myself in yours,' she returned, wondering why the smile he was bestowing upon her should have evoked such a pleasurable tingling sensation upon differing areas of her skin. 'I came here with a purpose, sir. I insist you tell me how much…to the exact penny, mind you…I am in your debt!'

He didn't pretend to misunderstand. 'I'll look out the bill of sale and let you have it in a day or two.'

'And in the meantime, what am I supposed to do with the coachman you've seen fit to engage on my behalf?'

He appeared surprised. 'Take him on, of course, unless you've some objection, though I don't see why you should have. You're already employing half the dratted Small family, as it is. So one more should make no odds.'

She chose to ignore the sarcasm. 'But aren't you forgetting I already employ a male servant, Mr Northbridge?'

Joss regarded her as he might have done some half-witted child. 'You don't seriously suppose Manders is capable of handling a spirited pair like those greys? Good gad, girl! He's half-blind, riddled with arthritis, not to mention an idle loafer. Get shot of him!'

'I can't do that!' Gwen was appalled by such a callous suggestion. 'I know the female members of my household haven't a good word to say about him. And I gained the distinct impression from my man of business, Mr Claypole, that he has never been favourably impressed, either. But Manders has worked at the house most all his life, so Percival must have been satisfied with him at some time. Besides which, he must be nearing sixty. Where would he get another position at his time of life?'

'Well, put him out to pasture, then, along with that old nag of Percival's you still keep.' A bark of decidedly callous laughter rent the air. 'Or, better still, send 'em both down to the knacker's yard, and have done with it!'

'What a suggestion!' Gwen returned, half-laughing, certain in her own mind that he would never treat his own servants with such callous in-difference. 'I shall just have to find him some other work.'

Joss tutted. 'If you're not very careful you'll gain the reputation of being a soft touch. Then you'll have every beggarly scoundrel for miles around at your door expecting a handout, you goose!'

Ignoring the insult, Gwen gave a start. 'Why, how very clever of you, Mr Northbridge! I'd been thinking seriously about doing something about that. You've suggested the very thing!'

After a despairing glance, Joss tossed the contents of his glass down his throat, wondering what he could possibly have said to make his increasingly highly companionable neighbour appear so animated, not to mention so adorably feminine.

Chapter Four

It must have been just about two weeks later when Gwen had become firmly convinced that her comings and goings were being followed with some interest

At first she hadn't taken much notice of the stocky individual with the piercing eyes whom she had glimpsed on a couple of occasions when she had just happened to be strolling down the main village street. It was only when she had spotted him hanging round street corners on two successive visits to the local market town that it had begun to occur to her that his frequent appearances seemed just too much of a coincidence.

None the less she had had no intention of overreacting, or allowing her imagination to run wild, and had decided to keep her suspicions to herself. Thankfully, her sensible approach was rewarded on her very next visit to the busy market town, during which she caught no sight of the unknown stalker whatsoever.

After retracing her steps to the White Hart Inn, where her smart new carriage awaited her, Gwen was gripped by a sudden whim, invoked in part by a guilty conscience, and gave instructions to her latest employee to take a detour and return to the village by way of the narrow road that skirted Marsden Wood.

Possibly as a direct result of the visit made by Lady Florence and her daughter, Gwen had received several morning callers during subsequent days. These visits, coupled with the improvements she intended making to her new home, had occupied much of her time. Notwithstanding, her friend's tragic demise had never once left her thoughts entirely. Consequently she hadn't hesitated in asking one or two pertinent questions of various people, and was now in possession of some interesting facts concerning the grisly happenings in recent years, which hopefully might help her to uncover the identity of the killer.

Neither a determination to succeed, nor a fear of failure crossed her mind as she called out to her new groom to stop the carriage in roughly the location where, she had been reliably informed, Jane had been found.

After alighting from the carriage, she experienced no qualms whatsoever over taking those first steps into that area of countryside that would soon be extensively carpeted in a certain shade of blue common to that most prolific of woodland flower. Already evidence that spring had well and truly arrived could be seen almost everywhere.

How very different the woodland must look now, she mused, compared to when dearest Jane had made her fatal last visit. There was reason enough for exploring now, when everywhere was bursting with new life, fresh and green. So different from dreary January, so cold, depressing…lifeless. If only the reason behind that tragic visit could be unearthed, it might provide a starting point, she ruminated, a moment before she came to a sudden stop, and watched a stocky figure approaching along one of the many tracks.

For one heart-stopping moment Gwen thought it might be none other than the very person whom she had suspected of watching her movements in recent days. They were much alike in both height and build, and both dressed in rough working clothes, but there the similarities between them ended. Although she hadn't been offered the opportunity to study the suspected stalker closely, she felt sure, from the few glimpses she had caught of him thus far, that there had been no lascivious twist to his mouth, no leering gleam in his eyes. Moreover, he was a good many years older than this ogling stranger, whose extensive knowledge of the opposite sex was evident in the assessing glance he cast over her figure as he came to a stop a mere few feet away.

Her judgement of him was equally swift. He definitely wasn't the type of man with whom any virtuous female of sense would choose to find herself alone. Furthermore, had it not been for the fact that she was fairly certain her burly young coachman could still glimpse her through the trees or, if not, definitely hear her if she called, Gwen might have beat a sensible retreat. None the less, she did take the precaution of taking a step or two away when the unpleasant leer faded marginally as he bade her a cheery 'good day'.

He then cast her slender form a further insultingly lingering look before adding, 'Dangerous place, these woods, ma'am. Ain't wise to linger 'ere on yer own.'

'I'm not on my own, my groom awaits me, yonder,' she assured him, gesturing towards the road. 'He'll come quickly enough, should I call, Mr—er—?'

'Furslow, ma'am…just Furslow.'

The name instantly struck a chord of memory. 'You're Lord Cranborne's gamekeeper, are you not?'

'Aye, ma'am.'

'And am I right in thinking it was none other than your good self who discovered the body of the unfortunate woman who recently lost her life in these woods?'

'Aye, ma'am. That I did. But it weren't round 'ere. It were further back that-a-way.' He gestured with his head in a certain direction, his leering smile returning. 'I can show you just the spot, if you've a mind to see it for yerself.'

Curious though she might be, Gwen wouldn't have needed to think twice about declining the offer had not the sound of further approaching footsteps caught her attention. She swung round, and was astonished to discover a tall, familiar figure bearing down upon them.

His thunderous expression was proof enough of his mood, even before he demanded though gritted teeth, 'What the devil do you suppose you're doing here, woman!'

Although she would have liked to think she

was a most composed person for the most part, Gwen would have been the first to admit that it wasn't totally unknown for her to give way to displays of ill humour herself on rare occasions. All at once she felt more than just a faint stirring of her own temper, and only the gamekeeper's continued presence persuaded her to maintain a firm control. Even so, she was determined to leave the new arrival in no doubt that she wasn't best pleased with the over-familiar and needlessly forceful attitude he had taken it upon himself to adopt with her.

'I am here, Mr Northbridge, because I choose to be.' Raising her chin, she eyed him defiantly. 'And a most fortuitous first visit it has been too, as I met up with Lord Cranborne's gamekeeper here, who, as you well know, was none other than the person who came upon Miss Robbins all those weeks ago. He was on the point of showing me precisely where she was found. Perhaps you'd care to accompany us?'

Appearing as though he were attempting to swallow a mouthful of horseshoe nails and, in consequence, uttering nothing further, Jocelyn Northbridge followed deeper into the wood. Only after the gamekeeper had pointed out the exact spot where the governess had been found did he part his tightly compressed lips to ask Furslow what he was doing in this area of wood, which lay way beyond the boundary of the Earl's estate.

'Merely taking advantage of a shortcut, after the—er—business I had in the village.'

As Joss could guess the nature of the business—which, unless he was much mistaken, was of a highly personal nature involving the local landlord's over-friendly young spouse—he refrained from probing further into the game-keeper's activities, and merely suggested that he make all haste to the area of the wood he was supposed to be patrolling.

Surprisingly enough Furslow didn't attempt to argue, even though his employer's well-respected neighbour had no authority over him whatsoever. He merely satisfied himself by casting a last insolent glance in Gwen's vicinity before setting off in the direction of his employer's land.

Jocelyn watched his departure for a few moments before swinging round on his heel, the lengthy tirade he had been mentally rehearsing not even coming remotely close to passing his lips as he saw the look of desolation in cornflower-blue eyes.

'Come along, Gwennie Warrender, ' he gently urged. 'Those fine horses of yours have been left standing quite long enough.'

Then, without further ado, he tucked her arm through his and led her away, surprisingly enough without meeting the least resistance. She was like a subdued child who had indeed just been severely reprimanded. Only he was well aware she wasn't feeling in the least chastened, merely deeply saddened by visiting that very poignant location.

Again he felt the strength of that protective instinct within him stir. Determined to draw her out of this mood of deep despondency, he said, 'I would have thought you'd have had more sense than to go wandering off with a man of Furslow's stamp. And what have your featherbrained actions achieved, eh? Answer me that! Nothing but doom and gloom!'

The ploy worked better than he could have hoped. Even though she made no attempt to withdraw her arm, the glint of annoyance that he hadn't failed to observe a short time earlier was most definitely back in her eyes.

'Since first making your acquaintance I have borne much from you in impudence, Mr Northbridge. But let me make this quite clear, here and now—if you wish amicable relations to continue between us, you will curb the infuriatingly overbearing attitude you occasionally adopt towards me. Furthermore, you shall henceforward desist in the use of unnecessary and strong invective when speaking to me, most especially when in the presence of others.'

For answer he patted her hand approvingly, before saying, much to her further irritation, 'That's better! Don't like to see you looking so down in the mouth. Doesn't suit you! Not that you could have expected to feel any differently, I suppose.' He tutted. 'Damned silly notion, if you ask me, wanting to see that place. Bound to have had an effect upon you, silly girl.'

The display of sympathy was so unexpected that Gwen was left nonplussed for several moments, before deciding that a continued show of pique might prove her best form of defence, until she'd come to terms with the astonishing discovery that Jocelyn Northbridge had a much wider streak of tenderness and understanding running through him than she had hitherto supposed.

'A foolish whim on my part it might have been,' she conceded, maintaining quite beautifully a curt tone. 'But rid your mind here and now that I could ever be featherbrained enough to accompany that womaniser anywhere. I only agreed to view that terrible place because you'd turned up.'

It was only then that his unexpected appearance struck her as odd, and she frowned up at him.

'What brought you into the wood in the first place?'

His look of exasperation was almost comic. 'What do you imagine brought me in here, you goose!' Joss retorted, conveniently forgetting her strictures of a few moments before. 'I sometimes take this route home when I'm tooling my curricle, and in no hurry. Naturally I recognised your carriage pulled just off the road, and discovered from young Ben you'd gone traipsing off on your own.' His look of staunch disapproval was all at once more marked. 'And why isn't your maid with you? Let me tell you, you'll very quickly earn yourself a reputation of being fast, my girl, if you continue to visit the local town unaccompanied, as you did this morning.'

'And how do you come to know that?' she demanded, swooping down on this interesting disclosure, like a sparrow hawk in sight of easy prey. 'And don't you dare to try to tell me Ben informed you of it, because I'm positive it wouldn't enter his head, unless specifically asked.'

He suddenly seemed to find the toes of his topboots of immense interest, 'One gets to hear about these things, don't you know? As a matter of fact, I was in town myself this morning,' he disclosed.

'I didn't see you. Who told you I'd been there?'

His evident reluctance to offer an answer immediately ignited an interesting possibility in her mind. 'You've had me followed, haven't you? That man…that thickset, stocky individual who resembles an ageing pugilist—he works for you, doesn't he?'

His dark eyes suddenly glinted with unholy amusement. 'I'd like to know from where you gained knowledge of prize-fighting, my girl.'

'Don't prevaricate!' Gwen scolded, steadfastly refusing to be drawn, and he found himself, surprisingly, relenting.

'Very well. I did hire Stubbs. He's an ex-Bow Street Runner, if you must know. But he isn't here, ostensibly, to follow you. I engaged him to see if he could uncover anything about the unfortunate events hereabouts. Though I did ask him just to keep an eye on you whilst I've been away in recent days visiting my sister Alice.'

Gwen was so startled to discover this surprising fact about her neighbour that she almost gaped up at him, her thoughts having spun off at a tangent. 'You've a sister!'

'Well, don't look so surprised! Sisters do crop up from time to time, even in the very best of families. I've five of 'em, as it happens,' he disclosed, frowning very heavily now. 'All older than me and all equally tiresome and feather-brained, though I suppose Alice, who's closest to me in age, is the best of the bunch. At least she's not for ever plaguing me to visit her like the others. Pity she weren't born a boy. I'd have liked a brother.'

Gwen couldn't prevent a very wicked smile curling her lips. 'That explains a great deal, Mr Northbridge.'

He regarded her in evident suspicion. 'And what precisely do you mean by that, may I ask?'

'I did wonder from where your dislike of my sex stemmed. It did cross my mind that you might possibly have suffered a disappointment in youth, which soured you. But then I decided it was much more likely you were just born an out-and-out misogynist.'

'I don't dislike women,' he refuted, feeling surprisingly miffed, even though the very same accusation had been levelled at him on scores of occasions and by numerous people in recent years. 'At least I don't dislike you,' he amended. 'But damned if I know why I do like you so much, as you've caused me a deal of bother since your arrival here.'

So surprised was she by this disclosure that Gwen didn't think to question the accuracy of the entire declaration. Their timely arrival back at the roadside gave her a few seconds in which to recover from the shock. Unfortunately her momentary confusion also offered her forceful companion the opportunity to indulge in what seemed to come quite naturally to him—namely, taking control. He ordered her coachman to return home so that she had little choice but to accompany him in his very smart racing curricle.

'And don't worry about the proprieties,' he adjured, helping her to scramble up into the seat. 'It's quite in order for you to ride in an open carriage, without burdening yourself with a female companion.'

'I'm not completely ignorant of the rules governing correct behaviour, Mr Northbridge,' she assured him, her mind having quickly recalled one of his earlier strictures. 'The reason I didn't take Gillie with me today is because she's busy making new curtains for the parlour.'

'Yes, I'd heard you'd been spreading your blunt about quite freely among the local tradesmen,' he remarked, giving his fine horses the office to start the instant his young tiger had sprung up on the perch at the back. 'You certainly know how to make yourself popular, I'll say that for you.'

She half-suspected some hidden meaning, but

chose not to dwell on the possibility, and merely admitted, 'That wasn't my intention. But I see no reason to travel far and wide when there are perfectly good craftsmen to be hired locally. Besides which, I'm in something of a hurry to refurbish the drawing room and front parlour.'

'Why the urgency?' he asked, displaying a surprising interest.

'I would have thought, Mr Northbridge, that since you have visited the house recently, the reason would have been perfectly obvious,' she returned, amusing him by the dryness of her tone. 'The rooms are positively shabby! I feel ashamed each time I ask someone to step into the front parlour.'

He tutted. 'A typically feminine reaction!'

'Well, I am typically female.'

'No, you're not,' he countered. 'You've a deal more fortitude than most. That's one of the reasons why I like you so much, I can only suppose.'

Gwen could feel the heat rising in her cheeks. She felt inordinately pleased by the compliment, but couldn't for the life of her understand why this brusque gentleman's approbation should mean so much.

'So, you intend to do more entertaining from now on,' he remarked, when she seemed intent on surveying the landscape in stony silence. 'Good thing, too! Hope you intend putting off your blacks before Cranborne's do on Friday. Can't have you sitting at such an illustrious table resembling a dashed crow!'

This brought her head round as he had suspected it might. 'Yes, I heard you'd accepted the invitation,' he said, gauging her thoughts with uncanny accuracy. 'I'm invited, too, by the way, so I'll collect you in the carriage on the way. Pointless both of us travelling there separately. And don't worry about the proprieties, I'm collecting the vicar and his wife en route too. They're both friends of mine, so you'll be adequately chaperoned. Not that you need to concern yourself unduly when you're with me.'

But Gwen wasn't so sure. She had the feeling their relationship had moved on a good deal further from that of generally affable acquaintances. For one thing, he seemed to suppose she would be willing to fall in with his wishes without consultation. It would have been quite understandable had she felt angry by this quite brazen interference in her life. The trouble was, though, she didn't even feel a spark of annoyance, and for the second time in the space of a few minutes she was left attempting to understand these peculiar reactions.

* * *

By the time she had arrived at Cranborne Hall on Friday evening, Gwen was firmly convinced she had managed to put her odd relationship with Jocelyn Northbridge into some kind of perspective. Having had no contact with him whatsoever since their meeting in Marsden Wood had certainly been beneficial. She had been able to face him again a short while earlier without feeling in the least self-conscious in his company, certain in her own mind that the evident interest he had taken in her well-being stemmed from nothing more than an honourable gentleman's attempts to assist the widow of an old and valued neighbour.

What an infuriating enigma the man could be on occasions! Gwen mused, glancing down the table to discover him in earnest conversation with Anthea Kershaw, and appearing, on the surface at least, most contented. A mass of perplexing contradictions was what he was, she decided. One moment infuriatingly overbearing, the next touchingly thoughtful, he succeeded in keeping one guessing just how he would behave next. That evening his manner towards her from the first had been impeccable, the perfect gentleman escort. All the same, she refused to be lulled into a false sense of security. Chances were that, should she ever be foolish enough to drop her guard, Mr Jocelyn Northbridge would floor her with a cutting body-blow when she was least expecting it!

'Our mutual acquaintance, Mr Northbridge, appears in remarkably good spirits this evening.'

The unexpected observation caught Gwen completely off guard, forcing her instantly back to the present, and obliging her to acknowledge, at least silently, that she had come perilously close to committing the sin of ignoring completely her closest dinner companions. Which would have been a grave solecism indeed, as she had been placed next to no less a personage than the Earl himself.

Having something of a suspicious nature, Gwen couldn't help wondering if there could well be some ulterior motive for her being so privileged. Truth to tell, she had half-expected his lordship to broach the subject of Jane Robbins and request she leave well alone, allowing the authorities to do their work. Surprisingly enough, though, he hadn't attempted to do so thus far, and he had been given ample opportunity. So why had she been so favoured?

'He does indeed, my lord. I believe I'm right in thinking he knows your niece quite well,' Gwen answered, feeling she must at least attempt to keep the conversation going as he was honouring her with his full attention.

'Very. They've always rubbed along remarkably well together, possibly because my niece isn't easily shocked. Northbridge's manner is somewhat blunt on occasions, as you've possibly already discovered for yourself. I'm afraid he's sometimes guilty of not always making allowances for the company he's in.'

'How true!' Gwen returned, smiling wryly. 'But I'm of the opinion his admirable qualities far outweigh his less favourable traits. So, like your niece, I suspect, I tend to overlook the defects for the most part.'

'Good for you, Lady Warrender!' His lordship regarded her with evident approval. 'Northbridge is a fine fellow, and an honourable one to boot. I can think of no one I'd rather have beside me if I were ever in a tight spot.'

Praise, indeed, Gwen mused, concentrating briefly on the course laid before her, whilst the Earl's attention was once again claimed by the vivacious matron on his left. She then turned to the gentleman on her right who had roused himself from a rapt contemplation of the salt cellar set within his reach to announce,

'Rather a fine piece, that! Nice lines, don't you agree, ma'am?'

Although she considered it a privilege to be placed next to his lordship at table, Gwen couldn't view having his lordship's younger son in such close proximity in a similar vein.

A young man of about her own age, of average height, of average build, and with no facial feature worthy of note, he was a gentleman quite easily overlooked. There was about him too a definite faraway look that gave one to suppose that for the most part he lived in a world of his own, where he was wholly content to allow every aspect of day-to-day life to pass him by. This, coupled with a seeming disinclination to indulge in any form of small talk, made his unexpected observation even more surprising.

Gwen assumed the remark must have been addressed to her, as the lady seated on the Honourable Mr Felix Lucas's other side had, almost from the moment she had taken her seat, wisely refrained from attempting to engage the Earl's son in conversation.

'Indeed it is, sir,' Gwen agreed, managing to preserve her countenance. 'But, then, all the silver on the table is very fine.'

'Is it?' He betrayed a degree of surprise.

'Hadn't noticed. Don't notice very much, ma'am…well, not those sorts of things, at any rate. Everyone tells me I've a shocking memory. And it's true, I suppose,' he continued, after appearing to consider the point. 'Don't remember people too well. Names and faces are a complete blur for the most part. But I've no difficulty in remembering the names of flowers or recognising birds.'

Gwen would have been quite happy to leave the discussion at that and allow Mr Lucas to drift back into his own private world had not his remarks struck a chord of memory. 'I recall your cousin mentioning to me that you spend time in Marsden Wood. Is that where you study birds and flowers?'

He nodded. 'Yes. In fact, I often go there. Even in the winter one can glimpse the most unexpected things.'

Gwen regarded him with renewed interest. 'Really? What sorts of things, Mr Lucas…? People, perhaps, wandering about?'

'Oh, no, ma'am. Don't often see people. Good thing, too!' he opined, looking more animated than she had seen him thus far. 'Folk never look where they're putting their feet. Criminal it is. Absolutely shocking!'

'What is, Mr Lucas?'

'The way some people trample willy-nilly over wild flowers. Rare ones, too, some of 'em! No appreciation of real beauty, some people haven't, ma'am.'

When his attention then returned to the food on his plate, Gwen suspected he considered his social duties at an end, and no further conversation would be forthcoming. But what little he had revealed had been worth discovering, at least up to a point.

There had been an unmistakable hint of resentment in his voice for a few moments, which bordered on dislike. He definitely preferred flora and fauna to his fellow man. He had given the impression too that he resented the presence of others, especially in Marsden Wood. Hardly sufficient reason for a normal person to take it upon himself to reduce the population, she reasoned. Trouble was, though, one would hardly consider Felix Lucas as precisely normal. But a murderer…?

Considering the matter, she raised her eyes, and was surprised to discover a pair of a darker and completely different hue regarding her keenly from further down the table. As usual she found it difficult to assess just what was passing through Jocelyn Northbridge's mind, though she suspected there was a suspicion of amused sympathy lurking in those rich brown depths; a suggestion too, perhaps, that he didn't envy her at least one of her close dinner companions. She might have been happy at this juncture to keep an open mind where the Earl's younger son was concerned, but she thought it might be interesting to discover precisely what her frequently abrasive yet surprisingly considerate self-appointed protector thought of Felix Lucas, and made a mental note to broach the subject at the first opportunity.

It might have surprised Gwen to discover that Joss, in fact, held Felix in much higher regard than he did the Earl's more popular elder son, who spent most of his time in the capital indulging in a variety of hugely expensive pastimes, none of which redounded to his credit. Yet, at the same time, his partiality didn't blind him to the younger brother's faults.

Unless one was prepared to concentrate on a subject that was of particular interest to him, and there were precious few of those, holding a reasonable conversation with Felix was an uphill struggle. All the same, Gwen appeared to have succeeded reasonably well thus far, and didn't seem wholly displeased to be seated next to someone who could hardly be described as the most stimulating orator. To be fair, though, he was hardly shining in that particular department himself that evening.

For some reason, which escaped him completely, he found himself enjoying the evening less and less as time went on. Lady Florence, a hostess of immense skill, had taken great pains as usual to place him beside two members of the opposite sex for whom he had a degree of respect. The vicar's wife, a lady of sound common sense, had earned his approval quite swiftly after her husband had acquired the living, and they had taken up residence in the local village. Lady Florence's amiable daughter had from the first also been a firm favourite with him. Yet for some obscure reason this evening not even Anthea's lively and sensible conversation could check the ever-increasing feeling of dissatisfaction that had plagued him since his arrival at Cranborne Hall, though he sincerely believed he had managed to disguise the fact remarkably well thus far.

A short time later, Joss experienced no regret whatsoever at losing both charming dinner companions, when Lady Florence gave the signal for the ladies to rise from the table, leaving the menfolk to their cigars, and to mull over the evils besetting the world.

He discovered himself caring even less when Lord Cranborne, deviating from the norm, chose not to linger over the port, possibly because he too was finding the conversation unprofitable and highly tedious. In fact it wasn't until crossing the hall in order to rejoin the ladies that Joss began to experience a return of the animation he had felt earlier in the evening, when first setting out for the Earl's residence.

Surprisingly enough, it was none other than Felix himself who first detected the sweet melodic sound emanating from the drawing room. Stopping dead in his tracks, thereby very nearly causing the gentlemen closely following to cannon into him, Felix put his head on one side and stared up at the lofty ceiling, as though expecting to catch sight of some rare species of songbird.

'Delightful! Quite delightful!' he exclaimed, betraying a rare show of enthusiasm for someone who usually allowed most happenings to pass quite unnoticed. 'Ain't Anthea singing, I'm sure.'

Joss was equally certain, for he had a pretty shrewd idea of precisely who had by that time succeeded in capturing every single gentleman's attention by the rendition of an unknown ballad, sung in faultless Italian and in a clear soprano voice that was truly without flaw.

Consequently it wasn't astonishment he felt when he led the way into the drawing room to witness Gwen seated at the pianoforte, holding her audience spellbound by the peerless performance, but an overwhelming sense of pride, just as though he himself had nurtured such a rare gift in one of his own womenfolk.

Not unduly surprised by her refusal to remain at the instrument to entertain them further, when the rendition had come to an end, Joss made sure he was the first to reach her side, and drew her over to one of the unoccupied sofas.

'You are full of surprises, Gwennie, my girl,' he said, quite deliberately taking the liberty of using her first name whilst she was too confused and embarrassed by the continued applause to take issue with him. 'Why on earth did you never mention you'd such a wonderful singing voice?'

Her look of impatience was proof enough that she was rapidly recovering her poise. 'It isn't something one brings up in everyday conversations.' She raised one hand in a dismissive gesture. 'Oh, I shan't indulge in insincere modesty. I sing well enough, and can hold a tune. But my voice is nothing when compared to my late mother's. Many was the time we used to sing out in church when there was only a small congregation. I think dear Papa preferred those Sundays when there was a poor attendance, just so that he could have the pleasure of hearing her sing.'

'Hearing you both, I'm sure,' he said, relieving a passing footman of two glasses of champagne. 'You even succeeded in capturing young Felix's attention. No mean feat, my dear, believe me! He was gazing up as though expecting to catch sight of a nightingale fluttering about the lofty hall.'

'Well, he's surprisingly astute, then, because in point of fact I was singing a little-known Italian folk song about swallows. Happens to be one of my favourites.' Her smile was unexpectedly replaced by a thoughtful frown. 'What do you make of the Earl's younger son, sir? More to him than one might at first suppose, wouldn't you say?'

'Clever girl!' Joss took a moment to sample the contents of his glass. 'He can be hard work, unless one manages to get him on a subject that interests him. And you'd be hard pressed to hit upon one of those, I might add. But he notices far more than one might suppose. He seems vague, but don't be fooled by that vacant expression of his. I swear he deliberately adopts it when he wishes to be left alone. He's not lacking intelligence either, believe me. I much prefer him to his brother, who's little more than a pleasure-seeking wastrel in my opinion. I must be truthful and say, though, I wouldn't go out of my way actively to seek the companionship of either of 'em.'

As her self-appointed protector continued to appear, to her at least, in an unusually convivial mood that evening, Gwen took advantage of the opportunity to ask his opinion of several other people present, including the Earl himself.

Only too willing to oblige, Joss placed one arm along the top of the sofa behind her, and settled himself against the comfort of its padded fabric in a highly relaxed attitude that couldn't possibly be feigned, and which drew no little attention from several people present.

The Earl himself raised a brow, while his sister's drew together in evident disapproval, and his niece merely surveyed the highly companionable couple with no small degree of interest.

Anthea had known Jocelyn Northbridge well for a number of years. Yet she couldn't bring to mind one occasion when she had seen him looking so at ease with himself and the world at large.

'I wonder,' she murmured before turning to her companion. 'Felix, dear, what did you think of Lady Warrender?'

'Who?' he said, his expression vague.

'Oh, never mind, dear. Doubtless I'll discover what I want to know when I return from my sojourn in the capital.'

Chapter Five

Considering she was kept busy throughout the following week, Gwen couldn't perfectly understand just why she was plagued by a steadily increasing discontent. Issuing instructions to the workmen, whom she had employed to effect necessary repairs and redecorate the house, and helping with numerous tasks herself, certainly meant that she was never at a loss to find something to occupy her. All the same she was forced silently to own that witnessing the front parlour and drawing room being transformed into elegant salons in which one might feel justifiably proud to entertain any visitor was insufficient to arrest the ever-tightening grip of malcontent. Finally, she was forced to acknowledge the reason why she felt as she did.

With her home in such disorder, she had been

thankful she'd been called upon to entertain so few visitors throughout the week. Yet, the one person she would have been delighted to see hadn't even attempted to cross the threshold once since the night of the dinner-party at Cranborne Hall.

Just why Jocelyn Northbridge's non-appearance should disgruntle her so, Gwen was at a complete loss to comprehend. True, they had parted after the dinner party upon the very best of terms, both having enjoyed each other's company throughout the latter part of what had turned out to be a most convivial evening. It would also have been true to suggest that the much better understanding that had evolved between them was rapidly developing into a genuine bond of friendship, which on first making her neighbour's acquaintance Gwen would never have imagined possible. All the same, innate honesty forced her to acknowledge that Joss's absence didn't wholly account for the increasing melancholy. Even when she had discovered from Annie, just the day before, that he was in fact away from home at the present time, she had been unable to suppress a sudden surge of resentment, simply because he hadn't even taken the trouble to drop her a few lines to inform her of his intentions.

Yet why, for heaven's sake, should she imagine she had any right to be apprised of his movements? She shook her head in total disbelief, wondering at herself for harbouring such an illogical, not to say possessive, attitude. The fact remained, though, that she did feel aggrieved, and try as she might she didn't seem able to shrug it off.

The unexpected opening of the parlour door succeeded in drawing her immediate attention. All the same it was several seconds before she was sure the figure filling the aperture was not merely a figment of her own imagination, borne of tangled thoughts and absurdly possessive feelings.

Absolute confirmation that she was in full possession of her faculties came when that now familiar, attractive voice ordered, 'Stop staring at me as though I were a complete stranger, Gwennie girl, and go pour me out a drop of that excellent wine of yours! I'm absolutely parched.'

Thus adjured, Gwen found herself automatically complying with the demands, though not before favouring him with a disapproving frown at his continued over-familiar term of address.

Several times on the evening of the dinner party she had had occasion to chide him over his liberty-taking in addressing her in a way that only her father had hitherto done before. Needless to say her rebukes had fallen on deaf ears, and as she didn't suppose for a moment she would meet with any more success now, she merely asked him why she had been singularly honoured by the unexpected visit.

The thread of sarcasm didn't go unnoticed, and he cast her a searching look before happily sampling the filled glass handed to him. 'Why, missed me, did you?' Her lack of response, and sudden interest in a certain ornament on the mantelshelf drew a satisfied smile to his lips before he revealed the reason for his visit. 'The truth of the matter is, I'm in desperate need of your help, m'dear.'

After a moment's indecision she decided he was in earnest, and favoured him with her full attention once again. 'Why, whatever is wrong?'

'Mumps.'

'I beg your pardon,' she said, swiftly revising her former opinion. 'It isn't my advice you should seek, but that of a doctor. I know little about the malady, save that it can be prodigious nasty to someone of your advanced years.'

'I'll box your ears for you, my girl!' Joss threatened, sounding as though he'd enjoy the exercise, and instantly sending Gwen into whoops of laughter. 'I haven't succumbed to the infection, but three of my favourite sister's brood have—confound it!—the result of which means she cannot possibly have my wards to stay for the next week or so, as she promised to do when I approached her the other week.'

'Well, I'm sure she didn't infect her offspring on purpose,' Gwen pointed out, having quickly decided his sister, having sick children on her hands, deserved pity, not censure.

'That's all very well,' he countered, clearly not one iota appeased, 'but what am I supposed to do with the girls? I can hardly take 'em back to the seminary, though I don't suppose the headmistress would object in the circumstances. She's plenty of other full-time boarders at the school. But the fact is I promised the girls they could have a change from school life for a week or so in the spring, and I feel as if I'm breaking my word.'

His heavy frown descended, clear evidence of his increasing annoyance. 'Unless I'm prepared to give rise to gossip, I can't have them to stay with me. It doesn't matter so much about Amy, of course. She's only ten, still a child, after all. But Mary's turned fourteen, which, if I know anything, would be bound to set malicious tongues a-wagging. Apart from my housekeeper, who has more than enough to occupy her without playing chaperon, there isn't a female in my household capable of taking care of the girls. Lady Kershaw would certainly have come to my rescue, but as I'm sure you're aware, she's already on her way to the capital with Anthea. So you see, Gwennie, I was wondering if…'

She didn't hesitate to comply with the request he suddenly seemed genuinely reluctant to make. 'Of course, I'll be delighted to have them to stay! When might I expect them?'

'They're here now,' he astounded her by revealing. 'They're waiting outside in the carriage.'

Appalled, Gwen rose at once to her feet and headed towards the door. 'Oh, Joss, how could you be so thoughtless! They're bound to feel they're not in the least welcome. Did you suppose for a moment I'd be so heartless as to refuse your request?'

'On the contrary,' he assured her softly, easily reaching her before she had chance to leave the room, and smiling down at her with such affectionate warmth that she thought for a moment her knees were in imminent danger of buckling. 'Angel that you are, I felt sure you would come to my aid. All the same, having recalled during the journey here your intention to begin the many improvements to your house this week, even I, arrogantly presumptuous creature that I am on occasions, thought it only fair to offer you the opportunity to refuse.'

Thankfully a dismissive wave of her hand was sufficient response. Which was perhaps just as well, because Gwen was very certain she dared not trust her voice.

Fortunately, two days later, when Jocelyn returned to the house to fulfil the promise he had made to take her and his wards on a trip to visit Wells Cathedral, Gwen felt she had her occasionally wayward feelings well under control once more. She greeted him with just the right amount of warmth, borne, she was persuaded, merely of genuine friendship.

More important still, she had managed with quite remarkable ease to break down those barriers of shyness which, understandably, her young guests had felt on first making her acquaintance. Both girls now showed remarkable ease in her company, most especially Mary, who was only too willing to allow her young sister to ride in the curricle with their guardian so that she could bear Gwen company in the carriage.

'I'm sure your guardian will be fair and take

you up beside him on the homeward journey,'
Gwen remarked, as she watched Joss giving his
horses the office to start in order to lead the way
out of the drive.

'Oh, if Amy wishes to return in the curricle, I
shan't mind. I'd prefer to travel with you.'

Although she felt a degree of satisfaction at
having her company so avidly sought, Gwen experienced no small degree of surprise as well,
simply because she had discovered already that
both girls simply adored their guardian.

Jocelyn Northbridge, surprisingly enough, had
proved to be most indulgent during the time he had
been solely responsible for the girls' welfare. Both
Mary and her younger sister had, seemingly,
always addressed him affectionately as Uncle Joss,
even though he was no blood kin. He had been, in
fact, a close friend only of their deceased father
who had, like so many others, given his life for his
country at Waterloo. Their mother, tragically, had
died soon afterwards, giving birth to a stillborn
child. Losing both parents in quick succession had
undoubtedly been a grievous blow. Yet both girls
appeared to have overcome their tragic loss, and
seemed remarkably well adjusted, a circumstance
for which, in Gwen's considered opinion, their
guardian must take most of the credit.

'And I shall be happy to have you bear me company,' Gwen assured her young companion. 'I know I shall miss you both when it's time for you to return to school.'

She received a shy smile in response, further proof, had she needed it, that Mary was definitely more reserved than her lively younger sister who was bidding fair to becoming something of a beauty in a few years.

It was doubtful that Mary would ever equal her sister in looks. She was by no means plain. On the contrary, her features were regular, and her complexion was good, giving one every reason to suppose that she would undoubtedly blossom into a handsome young woman. There was also a quiet dignity about the elder sister, of which Gwen privately approved, that made the girl appear older than her fourteen years.

'From what you've told me already, I've gained the distinct impression both you and your sister have settled in very well at the seminary. I assume, therefore, neither of you will object to returning next week?'

'Oh, no,' Mary assured her. 'Amy and I have made some friends there already.' She frowned slightly. 'But, given the choice, I would have preferred to remain with Uncle Joss, except I don't think I could like any governess as well as I liked Miss Robbins.'

All at once Mary gave a guilty start, and her face turned a deep crimson hue as she hurriedly stuttered an apology. Gwen was quite nonplussed by the girl's sudden change of demeanour and demanded an explanation.

'Uncle Joss particularly asked us not to mention Miss Robbins, as she was a good friend of yours, and he thought you might be upset. You're not, are you?'

Although not prepared to lie, Gwen wasn't slow to reassure. 'Jane Robbins was like a sister to me, Mary. We grew up together. And it's true I was…still am deeply upset over her death, most especially by the manner of her passing. But I think it's a big mistake not to talk about those we have cherished and lost. Also, it gives me a great deal of satisfaction to know that you and Amy were so very fond of her too.'

'Oh, we were,' Mary confirmed, thankfully looking a deal less troubled now. 'She was so kind to us. And always encouraged us to talk about Mama and Papa.'

'Yes, she was always so very understanding. And so sensible, too.' Gwen leaned back against the comfort of the upholstery, her mind's eye seeing too clearly that certain spot in Marsden Wood where her dear friend had met her untimely end.

'That's why she must have gone there to meet someone… Why else? Surely she would never have gone there alone, otherwise.'

Gwen wasn't aware she had spoken her thoughts aloud, until she noticed her young companion staring at her in puzzlement. 'I'm sorry, Mary, merely thinking aloud,' she admitted, before a thought suddenly occurred to her. 'Did Jane…Miss Robbins often go to Marsden Wood?'

'We went there a few times throughout the spring and summer last year. Amy didn't like it much. Said it was too far to walk. But I liked to go. We used to take our sketch pads and draw the flowers. Miss Robbins's sketches were really good. Even Mr Lucas told her her attention to detail was excellent.'

'Mr Lucas…? Mr Felix Lucas, the Earl of Cranborne's son?' Gwen's attention was well and truly captured now. 'Did you sometimes meet him in the wood?'

'We saw him there once or twice,' Mary admitted, 'but not always.'

'Did Miss Robbins arrange to meet him there? Were they friends, do you suppose?'

'Oh, no, I don't think so,' Mary answered, after a moment or two's quiet reflection. 'Miss Robbins always spoke whenever she saw him, but never for very long. She never spoke to the other man, though. I don't think she liked him very much. Whenever she saw him coming along one of the tracks, she always made us pack up our belongings and we left.'

'And do you know who this other man was, Mary?'

She frowned. 'I'm not sure. But I think Miss Robbins said once he was Lord Cranborne's gamekeeper.'

She would never have gone to the wood to meet him, of that Gwen felt absolutely sure. And judging by what Mary had revealed, Jane tried to avoid him whenever possible. Furthermore, Jane would never have formed a friendship with Felix Lucas either. And it was stupid of her to have supposed she might!

Gwen could only wonder at herself for harbouring such a foolish notion, if only momentarily. The trouble was, she tended to forget that she and Jane had inhabited completely different worlds since leaving the quiet country vicarage in Hampshire. She had married a well-respected gentleman of means, and in consequence had risen up the social ladder. Jane, on the other hand, having felt obliged to make her own way in the world, had lived a totally different lifestyle.

During those years Jane had been employed at that seminary near London, Jane would, naturally, have associated with other teachers. During the last eighteen months of her life, her companions would have been the Bridge House servants, and maybe one or two others who, like herself, were obliged to earn a living.

Gwen's eyes narrowed speculatively as she stared at an imaginary spot on the soft blue upholstery. So who could Jane have arranged to meet that day? If only she could discover that! A distinct possibility was someone with whom Jane had become acquainted from the local town—a librarian, perhaps, or a clerk in an office.

After a further few moments' intense thought, Gwen shook her head sadly, finally accepting it was fruitless to speculate. 'Oh, Mary! If only I knew why your governess took it into her head to go to Marsden Wood that day…if only I knew the identity of the person she went there to meet!'

All at once the young girl seated beside her seemed to find the skirt of her gown of immense interest, and began to pleat the material with decidedly unsteady fingers.

'Do you know something, child?'

'I—I don't think she went to meet anyone,' Mary at last revealed, though she continued to stare steadfastly down at her lap. 'I think she went out because she was so upset…because of what happened to the letters, you see?'

This instantly struck a chord of memory. Hadn't Joss's housekeeper said something about Jane leaving the nursery looking upset? Furthermore, there had been no letters among Jane's belongings, Gwen reminded herself, which she had thought strange at the time. Jane, she felt certain, would have retained each and every letter received during their long separation.

'What happened to Miss Robbins's letters, Mary?' Gwen asked gently. Attaining no response, she added, 'Of course, you need not tell me if you do not wish to do so. And I shan't press you. But I should dearly like to know.'

If anything, poor Mary became more disturbed than before, twisting her hands together nervously, while still resolutely refusing to look in Gwen's direction.

'It—it isn't that I don't wish to tell you, Mrs Warrender. It—it's just that I don't want to get…anyone into trouble.'

Gwen wasn't slow to comprehend fully, and

couldn't help but admire such sibling loyalty, even as she said, 'I perfectly understand why you wish to protect your sister, and can only promise, Mary, that whatever you do tell me will go no further.'

Gwen thought her pledge had fallen on deaf ears, until Mary very slowly raised her head. What the girl then evidently perceived in a pair of cornflower-blue eyes was assurance enough.

'It happened while we were recovering from the influenza,' she at last revealed. 'Amy was bored, and so slipped along the passageway to see Miss Robbins. She wasn't in her room. Amy said she was about to leave, when she noticed the bundle of letters, tied up with ribbon, on the shelf above the hearth.'

At this juncture Mary paused to gnaw at her bottom lip again for several moments, clearly finding the confession no easy task. 'We often saw Miss Robbins smile or chuckle when reading her letters. Amy thought they must contain funny stories, and so decided to take them back to the nursery with her to cheer us both up. She reached up for the bundle, only it slipped out of her hand into the grate, dislodging some of the coals and wood. Even before she could try to pick them up again, she heard someone coming along the passage, and so hid behind the curtain. Amy said the maid came into the room, cursed when she saw the smouldering mess in the grate, and put everything on to the fire, including the letters. By the time the maid had left, there was nothing Amy could do except…'

'Except confess what she'd done,' Gwen finished for her. 'No, of course there wasn't.'

She sighed. In many ways those letters were Jane's only links with the past—full of memories, hopes for the future, and so many shared thoughts. Naturally she would have been deeply upset, and had possibly gone out for a walk to calm herself down, for she would have known their loss had been purely and simply an accident.

'Amy didn't mean to do it, Mrs Warrender,' Mary reiterated, as though reading her thoughts.

Gwen managed a reassuring smile. 'There's a deal of difference between mischief and malice, Mary. Miss Robbins would have appreciated that too. Thank you for telling me.'

By the time they had reached their destination, and had enjoyed a satisfying luncheon in one of the town's more popular inns, Gwen felt sure that the easy relationship she had enjoyed most especially with Joss's elder ward had been fully restored.

She was determined to keep the promise she

had made and not breathe a word of what she had discovered. Unfortunately, that didn't prevent her mulling over what she had learned and drifting off into her own private world a little too frequently, a circumstance that one member of the party wasn't slow to observe.

'Either the architectural splendour of this structure before us has singularly failed to impress you,' Joss remarked suavely, as they paused in their stroll along one of the paths so that they might study more closely the magnificent façade. 'Or you are finding my presence so irritating at present that you're doing your level best to ignore my very existence in the hope I just might favour my wards with my undivided attention.'

His eyes flickered with a distinctly challenging gleam, as he deliberately reached for her hand, and tucked her arm through his. 'I'm not easily rebuffed, my girl,' he warned. 'Nor am I gentlemanly enough to receive my *congé* with a good grace. You'll need to become a deal more inhospitable if you wish to be rid of me.'

Had he uttered anything so outrageous at the start of their association, Gwen would have been mortified to think she'd been guilty of the sin of rudeness or neglect. Now, however, she had grown quite accustomed to his blunt turn of phrase, and his strictures this time didn't even induce a guilty hue to touch her cheeks.

Instead, she merely favoured him with a syrupy smile. 'My dear Jocelyn, should I ever wish to be rid of your presence, you will be left in no doubt of it whatsoever.'

For answer he threw back his head and barked with laughter, quite uncaring that by so doing he succeeded in making them the focus of interest of those Cathedral visitors nearby.

'That's my girl!' he uttered, patting her hand approvingly, as they set off in the direction of the Bishop's Palace in an attempt to bridge the distance between themselves and his wards. 'If there's one thing I cannot abide it's a missish female. Which thankfully you're not!' His smile could not have been more winning. 'So, what's wrong? You've been unusually quiet since we arrived here. Are you finding having my wards to stay too much at the present time, with all the work being done at the house? If so, say so. I'll quite understand.'

'Not at all,' she assured him so promptly that he didn't doubt the sincerity of the answer. 'They're both delightful girls, and I'm enjoying their company very much.'

'I gained the distinct impression from Amy you

were rubbing along together famously. She was singing your praises throughout the entire journey here. Quite tedious I found it, I can tell you,' he lied.

She chuckled readily at this, but he wasn't fooled for a moment into thinking all was well with her now. 'Come, what's put your nose out of joint? I know there's something troubling you.'

Although still doggedly determined to keep the promise she had made by not revealing Amy's fateful actions on that tragic day, Gwen had no intention of repaying Joss's many acts of kindness towards her with a mouthful of lies. 'I've been thinking about Jane. I'm positive now she didn't go out that day specifically to meet someone. Which, I suppose, will make it more difficult to unearth her killer. Although I do happen to know that Furslow crossed her path on more than one occasion.'

His expression betrayed instantly that he was not best pleased. 'And from whom did you glean this snippet, may I ask?'

No response was forthcoming. One, however, wasn't necessary. 'My wards, I'll be bound! I distinctly told them not—'

'Now, Joss,' she interrupted without hesitation, determined to set him straight on the matter. 'Neither of them deliberately disobeyed you. It was I who encouraged Mary to speak about Jane. I was much moved by the depth of the girl's affection for my friend. During the conversation I discovered those few facts which I've already related.' She frowned slightly as she glanced up at him, a thought suddenly having occurred to her. 'I know they must have been deeply upset by the loss of their governess, but I'm rather surprised you chose not to question them more closely at the time.'

'As neither of them even knew she'd left the house, I saw little point in doing so. Furthermore, I was fairly certain myself that she hadn't gone out to meet someone. No one, according to my servants, ever came to the house asking for her.'

'No, your housekeeper assured me she hadn't any—er—followers, as she phrased it. And, as I've already mentioned, I don't imagine she went to Marsden Wood for the sole purpose of meeting someone. It just isn't the sort of place one would choose for a rendezvous in the month of January. It's much more likely she had something on her mind.' Determined to keep to the truth as far as she could, she added, 'Possibly me.'

'And why should she have had you on her mind?'

Here she knew she would need to be extra careful, simply because he was staring at her so intently. 'Because I'd written to her at the beginning of the year, apprising her of my arrival in the capital, and my intention to take up residence in my late husband's home within a matter of weeks. She was no fool. She would have known that sooner or later I would broach the subject of her living with me.'

Dark brows rose sharply. 'Oh, so you weren't above attempting to deprive me of an excellent governess!'

Neither the severity of the tone, nor the disapproving look bent in her direction fooled Gwen for a moment. 'Absolutely not.'

The assurance was accompanied by such a wickedly arch grin that Joss found himself laughing again. 'You're a minx, Gwen Warrender. But an honest one.'

'I always try to be,' she responded, staring directly ahead. Then, with an abrupt change of subject, she added, 'Mary also revealed that, besides the gamekeeper, the Earl of Cranborne's younger son also crossed Jane's path in Marsden Wood.'

He shrugged. 'Well, all I can do is to reveal to Stubbs what you've told me when next I see him. But I don't suppose for a moment it will lead anywhere.'

She looked back up at him at this. 'I can understand you thinking that where Felix Lucas is concerned. He doesn't strike me as a very likely suspect, either, though I'm not prepared to disregard him completely at this juncture. But the gamekeeper's a different matter entirely, surely?'

Joss wasn't so sure. 'Furslow's an out-and-out womaniser, Gwen. No one can argue with that. He's also been known to treat women roughly if they should happen to prove a nuisance and start pestering him. But no woman has ever come forward and claimed she was unwilling and he forced himself on her. Seemingly certain members of your sex find him devilish attractive and encourage his advances. And he's quite brazen about his conquests. His association with various women hereabouts have all been conducted quite openly. There's a vast difference between a rogue and a womaniser, and a rapist and murderer.'

He had a point, and she readily acknowledged it before saying, 'But you will pass on what I've told you to…Stubbs, is it?'

'Of course.'

'And will you share what he discovers with me?'

His response this time was not so prompt, but eventually he said, albeit begrudgingly, 'Very well. But only on condition you promise me you'll keep well clear of that wretched wood yourself.'

Gwen readily agreed, never supposing for a moment that any circumstances could possibly arise that would result in her ever wishing to return.

Chapter Six

The girls' return to the seminary brought an immediate cessation to Joss's frequent and impromptu visits to the house. During the days that followed Gwen almost managed to convince herself that it was the company of the girls she missed so very much, that the house was much too lonely and quiet without Amy's frequent chortles, and the elder sister's surprisingly mature conversations. Eventually, though, she was forced to own that it was their guardian's companionship for which she truly pined.

Discovering from that wellspring of local knowledge, Annie Small, that he had, in fact, after depositing his wards in Bath, taken it into his head to travel on to the capital induced Gwen to suppose his absence from the locale wasn't likely to be of short duration. After all, gentlemen of Mr Northbridge's stamp, who possessed status, not to mention funds enough to indulge themselves without restraint, received numerous invitations. Hence, they could remain for the duration of the Season if they were so inclined.

Notwithstanding, miss him though she did, Gwen possessed strength of character enough to channel her thoughts, for the most part, and energy into overseeing the remaining alterations to the house, and putting into effect certain other changes, which included allocating extra tasks to at least one member of her outdoor staff.

By the time May was almost over, Gwen was highly satisfied with the progress made. The house was all but completed, each and every room brightened with the latest fashions in wall-coverings, and modernised with a number of new and tasteful furnishings. The outside, too, if not wholly transformed, was vastly improved. The clinging ivy had been removed from the house walls, the driveway and paths were now free of weeds, and most of the flower beds, having been tidied and restocked, were at last beginning to bring welcome splashes of colour to the once-neglected garden.

The sudden overzealous application of the door-knocker brought her out of her moderately satisfying reverie with a start. Then the clearly annoyed and much missed voice demanding to know her immediate whereabouts instantly drew a smile to her lips, which not even the glowering look of disapproval she received moments later could dim.

Rising from her chair, she moved across the room, arms outstretched, to greet her very welcome visitor. Her hands were instantly captured and held against the lapels of a beautifully tailored dark blue riding jacket. There was a definite softening about the finely chiselled lips, even though the deep furrow between his dark brows remained, as a demand to know why the devil she had taken to keeping ferocious creatures in the stable yard, where they could easily unnerve prime horseflesh, not to mention disconcert unsuspecting visitors, was forcefully uttered.

Enlightenment dawned almost at once. 'Oh, you must be referring to our gander, Clarence.' She tried to appear contrite, but failed quite miserably. She then compounded the unsympathetic display by gurgling with laughter.

'He must have waddled up the lane from the little home farm we've created in the large paddock,' she explained, once she was able. 'He's not so bad with any of us now. Settled in quite nicely, in fact. But he still isn't too good with strangers. Attacked you, did he?'

'Yes, the blighted thing! Caught me in the breech, just after I'd dismounted. Mind, I took my revenge, right enough, by clipping it across the bill with my crop,' Joss admitted, betraying a certain grim satisfaction.

'Oh, well, sit yourself down, do…if you're able, that is,' she invited, more successful this time in containing her mirth, 'and I'll pour you wine.'

Gwen joined him in a glass, which more often than not she did since coming to know him a good deal better, no matter the time of day. 'How was your trip away?' she enquired, once he had made himself comfortable in his favourite chair, the one that for some obscure reason she simply couldn't bring herself to replace during the extensive refurbishment of the parlour. 'Was London bustling with life?'

'Oppressively so! Glad to get shot of the place, if the truth be known,' he admitted, surprising her somewhat.

'Well, why go there in the first place if the Season's no longer to your taste?' Gwen returned, not unreasonably.

His lips were instantly curled by a rather enigmatic smile. 'Just wanted to keep an eye on—er—certain parties, as you might say.'

Intrigued though she was, she experienced the strongest suspicion he wouldn't divulge more should she be foolish enough to attempt to satisfy her curiosity. So, she merely enquired after his wards.

'Fine, once they were back in the seminary with their friends.' Joss favoured her with one of his prolonged and thoughtful looks. 'Weren't too keen to leave here, as you're probably aware. Quite taken with you, Gwennie, my girl.'

Having been totally unsuccessful in curbing his use of this over-familiar form of address, she had long since ceased to waste her breath in profitless remonstration, and merely admitted, 'I have missed them very much. It's a great pity they both feel they wouldn't be happy with another governess.'

'Understandable, though,' he returned softly, once again revealing the compassionate side of his nature that was for the most part adequately concealed behind his more usual blunt manner. 'Still, they may yet change their minds,' he went on, once again falling into that easy camaraderie they had enjoyed before his sojourn in the capital. 'Not that Mary's in need of a governess any longer. Wouldn't have sent her to the seminary in the first place, except I thought it would be wrong to part her from her sister. I shall possibly broach the subject of a permanent return to Bridge House next year, when I fully expect my domestic arrangements to have undergone—er—something of a change.'

Barely giving her time to assimilate what he had said, Joss rose to his feet, tossing off his wine as he did so, before demanding he be shown her recently acquired livestock.

Gwen required no further prompting. She was well pleased with her choices of domestic fowl and animals, and readily accompanied him down the lane to the larger paddock, where Manders quite literally ruled the roost.

'And surprisingly conscientious he is too,' Gwen revealed, when Joss had inspected the sow and her large litter, the goat pen and the various other wooden structures that housed hens, geese and ducks. 'He showed real enthusiasm constructing the hen houses. And looks quite smug when he arrives at the kitchen door with a basketful of eggs. Must come from his starting life as a farm boy, I suppose.

'And look at Clarence, too,' she urged, after failing to elicit a response. 'Now he's with his

Clara he's much more contented, not in the least aggressive.'

'Mmm. I suppose it's true enough that some females have an effect on the male of the species, and not always a detrimental one at that,' he conceded, surprising her somewhat, before changing the subject by inviting her to dine at his home the following week.

As this was the first formal invitation she had received, she didn't need even a moment to consider. 'I'd love to,' she admitted. 'Any particular reason?'

In his usual familiar fashion, Joss entwined her arm round his as they strolled back up the lane towards the stable and outhouses. 'I'm having a friend to stay, and I'd very much like you to make his acquaintance. I'll invite the Harmonds, Anthea and her mother, of course, if they've returned from the capital by then, and maybe one or two others. So you'll be adequately chaperoned.'

She refrained from quizzing him over his continued efforts to preserve her good name, and merely, out of politeness more than anything else, requested the identity of his future house guest. Then it was as much as she could do to preserve her countenance, before finally coming to a decision.

'Unless I'm much mistaken,' she remarked, with only the barest trace of unsteadiness in her voice, 'that is the gentleman you address as Merry.'

'Why, yes! His real name's—' Stopping dead in his tracks, thereby obliging her to do likewise, Joss favoured her with yet another of those penetrating looks. 'How the deuce did you discover that? You're not already acquainted with Merriot Markham, are you? If so, he quite failed to mention it whilst I was in the capital.'

'We've never been formally introduced,' she answered, enjoying herself hugely. 'Doubt I shall even recognise him, as I've seen him only once in my life before, and then only briefly.'

'Where…London?'

'No, Bristol.'

Joss regarded her with keen interest now, simply because he was almost sure his good friend had not travelled into the West Country since staying at Bridge House during the latter part of the winter. 'When and where in Bristol, may I ask?'

'Early March in a certain crowded posting-house,' she revealed, eyes dancing with the wicked enjoyment she didn't attempt to conceal. 'Just prior to setting eyes on your friend for the first time, I bumped into the most ill-mannered wretch

I've ever had the misfortune to meet, who later had the temerity to suggest my hair wasn't natural.'

Joss fixed his gaze on the glossy brown locks, with the abundance of burnished-copper threads streaking through them. Then just the merest flicker of memory stirred. 'Confound it! I knew there was something about you,' he confirmed, experiencing a degree of satisfaction, even though the image his mind's eye was managing to conjure up remained decidedly hazy. 'Yet for the life of me I can't recall details of our very first encounter. Why on earth didn't you admit we'd run into each other before, when you first visited Bridge House all those weeks ago?'

'Because it didn't redound to my credit, that's why,' Gwen admitted, scrupulously truthful. 'You berated me for not looking where I was going. With some justification, I might add.'

The laughter in her eyes gave him every reason to suppose that she had long since forgiven any rudeness on his part. Then he was surprised to witness the lighter mood ousted in an instant by the unmistakable shadow of grief.

'I should have realised back then,' she revealed softly, 'that something terrible had happened to Jane. I overheard you and Mr Markham discussing the tragedy. Yet not once did it occur to me that two complete strangers could possibly be discussing someone I knew. So very foolish of me! All the pointers were there, including one alluding to your name. I clearly remember him calling you Pont.' She shook her head. 'Bridge, of course… Northbridge. Jane mentioned you several times by name in her letters, and always most favourably. Yet I foolishly forgot everything you discussed almost immediately after I left that inn.'

Joss felt the tremor run through her, as though she were giving herself a mental shake, a moment before she moved away, and smiled up at him with that wickedly impudent grin he had grown simply to adore.

'And may I call you Pont, now that we have become such friends?'

Without conscious thought he reached out to trace the outline of her jaw with the gentlest of feather-light touches. 'I sincerely hope, my dear, that we are now on the brink of becoming a deal closer than mere friends.'

The speed with which she stepped away would have given anyone observing from some hidden corner to suppose that he had just dealt her a vicious slap across the face, and her expression of combined shock, not untouched by fear, might only have confirmed an unprovoked physical assault.

'Oh, you must return to the house with me before you leave,' she said in a husky, rushed tone, clearly borne of embarrassed confusion. 'I've managed to locate the bill from that vintner you are so desperate to patronise.'

And with that she hurried on ahead, leaving Joss in something of a quandary. That he had overstepped the mark was patently obvious. What wasn't so clear to him at the moment was how he was going to rectify his blunder. Worse still—how on earth was he supposed to conduct himself towards her from now on?

The servants at Bridge House were always pleased to wait upon Mr Merriot Markham, a gentleman of clean habits who made few demands on their time. His visit on this occasion was doubly welcome to the higher-ranking servants at least, for both the housekeeper and butler had noticed their master had seemed un-usually withdrawn in recent days. Disinclined to leave the confines of his library for any length of time, he had ceased to pay morning calls or receive visitors, and his face wore a perpetually troubled look.

The arrival of the very amiable Mr Markham did indeed succeed in lifting, almost at once, the unusually morose atmosphere pervading the house. Nevertheless, gentlemen who have enjoyed an agreeable association that has spanned decades, not merely years, were never slow to detect the slightest change in a close friend's temperament.

Mr Markham proved that he was no exception, when he asked, quite without warning, 'What's troubling you, old fellow?'

Pausing in the act of refilling their glasses, Joss shot a glance across the room at where his good friend sat sprawled at his ease in one of the comfortable winged-chairs, before finishing his task and rejoining his guest. The mocking glint he then couldn't fail to detect in a pair of grey eyes was sufficient warning that to deny any feelings of concern would be futile, so he didn't attempt to try.

'I didn't realise I had become so transparent.' Joss smiled ruefully as he studied the liquid in his glass, surprisingly experiencing no disinclination to share the very personal matter that had plagued him constantly during the past days. 'I thought I'd maintained an adequate degree of affability since your arrival this afternoon, Merry.'

'You could never be accused of being a particularly garrulous person, Pont. But even so, you've never had the least difficulty in playing the genial host. The difference this time is that the affability during dinner seemed slightly artificial, a little too forced to be considered wholly sincere to someone who knows you so very well.'

Once again Joss didn't attempt to refute the accusation, and merely said, 'You've succeeded in lightening my mood, Merry. Be sure of that. But I doubt even you could instruct me in how to proceed in a certain very delicate matter.'

His shout of laughter could not have held a more self-deprecating ring had he tried. 'For a supposed man of the world, I've made a hopeless mess of it all. And a great many people would undoubtedly say it's no more than I deserve.'

'You'll never hear me say that,' was the prompt response.

'I know that, old friend. But the fact remains that where affairs of the heart are concerned, I'm a complete novice. I've never been in love before, you see. Never wished to be either, come to that. Always considered the condition a weakness best avoided by any man of sense. Well, I've received my comeuppance for my scornful and unfeeling attitude over the years. And it's knocked me completely off balance.'

Had his mind not been so wrapped up in his own personal concerns, Joss might have taken more notice of the sharp intake of breath emanating from the other side of the hearth. As it was, it took him almost a full minute to digest the question that immediately followed the tiny sound, and even then he thought he must have misheard.

'Anthea…?' he echoed. 'What the deuce has Anthea to do with anything?'

'But—but, I thought…perhaps…you'd at last asked her to marry you, and she'd refused,' Merry answered, looking slightly puzzled himself now. Nevertheless Joss wasn't slow to recognise the glint of hopefulness lurking behind the bewilderment.

'You're a damnable fool, Merry!' he proclaimed in his usual no-nonsense fashion. 'I told you three years or more ago that I'd never offer for Anthea Kershaw, fond of her though I've always been. And I'm damnably sure if I were to ask for her hand now she'd have sense enough to refuse. It might have been different at one time,' he went on, after a moment's consideration. 'But she's no longer so influenced by her mother's wishes as she once was. Thank the Lord! She'll decide the type of man she wishes to marry. But she won't wait for ever. So be warned!'

Merriot's eyes positively glowed with renewed hope after hearing this. 'You—you really think there might be a chance for me, then?'

Joss glanced ceilingwards. 'I despair of you sometimes, Merry. Truly I do! For a man of sense, you can be damnably obtuse on occasions.' He regarded his closest friend in amused exasperation. 'Look how Anthea behaved towards you during your last visit here in the winter—friendliness itself! Look how she treated you in London recently. Any fool could see she actively sought your company above any other's, including mine.'

It appeared that Mr Markham was having some difficulty in coming to terms with these astounding revelations, as his next words proved. 'Even though I know you said you wouldn't offer for her, I always thought you'd end up doing so, you know. I suppose that's the main reason why I never attempted to further my own interests.'

'Then do so now,' Joss urged, rising to his feet to rest one muscular arm along the mantelshelf and stare down at the empty grate. 'Anthea and I wouldn't suit… There's only one girl for me.'

'But who?' Merriot prompted, when his friend looked as if he were about to relapse into a brooding silence.

'Old Warrender's young widow. I told you about her when I was in London, remember?'

Merriot was puzzled, and it clearly showed. 'I

recall your mentioning she'd settled in the area, right enough. I also recall your saying something about her knowing very well that poor governess you employed who lost her life. But I never imagined for a moment your feelings went so deep. You concealed it mightily well, old fellow.'

'I'm not one to wear my heart on my sleeve, Merry. Besides…' Joss shrugged, straining the material of his impeccably tailored jacket across his broad shoulders as he did so '…I don't think I was so very certain myself of the depth of my regard for Gwennie before my recent stay in the capital, even though I was strangely drawn to her from the first. I only know I missed her damnably throughout my stay in town. Life simply wasn't the same with her so far away.' Smiling ruefully, he began to massage the nape of his neck, a habit he'd had from boyhood and practised when something was troubling him. 'Why, not even the expert attentions of my mistress could vanquish thoughts of the little darling from my mind.'

Merriot pursed his lips together in a silent whistle. 'My, my! She must be a perfect specimen of womanhood to have so captivated you. A pearl beyond price, no doubt.'

Joss wasn't slow to set him straight on the

matter in his customary blunt fashion. 'That she is not! She can be a damnably headstrong little minx when it takes her fancy! Careless of her own safety, not to mention infuriatingly contrary on occasions.' A surprisingly tender smile then erased completely the furrow between his brows. 'And an absolute sweetheart,' he finished softly.

'My, my, you have got it bad, old fellow,' Merriot murmured. Then, receiving no response, he swiftly decided a display of sympathy wouldn't be appreciated and settled on a more direct line. 'So, what happened, Joss? Did you propose to her on your return?'

'As good as.'

'And evidently she refused?'

'As good as.'

Merriot was quiet for a moment, before stating what he privately considered to be obvious. 'Evidently your feelings are not wholly reciprocated, old chap.'

'There you are wrong, my friend, because I'm damnably sure they are,' Joss countered, with such conviction that no one hearing the assertion could have doubted the truth of it. Certainly Mr Markham did not.

'If you'd have seen that sweet face of hers light up when I walked into her front parlour, after our few weeks apart, you'd know I wasn't being fool-hardy to believe she cares deeply for me.'

Sighing, Joss returned to his chair. There was no mistaking he was still troubled. Yet behind the look of lingering concern lurked a flicker of something that bore the hallmark of dogged determination.

'What has been plaguing the life out of me in recent days is how I'm to conduct myself from now on. And I'm beginning to believe increasingly that my best course is merely to treat her just as I've always done, while allowing her a little more time to adjust to the prospect of a totally different lifestyle at my side.'

Mr Markham wasn't so sure this was quite the right policy to adopt, which not only showed in his expression, but also in his voice as he asked, 'Are you certain that's such a wise course, in view of the fact that she as good as gave you your *congé*? I don't wish to put a damper on your enthusiasm, old fellow, but it stands to reason there's something about you she don't quite like.'

At this Joss gave vent to a deep rumble of laughter, the first he'd managed in days. 'Lord, Merry! There must be a dozen things and more about me of which she totally disapproves. And she ain't afraid to tell me so either, bless her little heart! She might be as innocent as a new-born babe in so many ways, but she don't lack courage or character.'

Once again Mr Markham appeared a little nonplussed. 'I don't see how she can be so innocent. Surely she must be about your own age. And a widow, to boot!'

Joss wasn't slow to set him right on the matter. 'I can give her almost ten years. Warrender was more than forty years her senior.'

'Great heavens! I never realised there was such a disparity in their ages.' Mr Markham's look of deliberation suggested strongly that his mind was waking up to certain very interesting possibilities. 'I look forward to meeting her.'

'I strongly suspect you'll be granted your wish tomorrow. I've invited her and a few others to dine here.'

'Are you sure she'll turn up?'

Joss gave the question a moment's consideration, and then smiled. 'Oh yes, she'll come, even though I strongly suspect she'll have given the matter some thought before finally making up her mind.'

It might have surprised Joss to discover just how close the one and only love of his life had come in recent days to dashing off a note refusing his invitation to dine. Time and again she had seated herself at the escritoire in the little back parlour, hand poised above a clean sheet of paper. Each time the outcome had been precisely the same. She had thrown down the pen in disgust, cursing herself for a faint heart, while stigmatising herself once again for reacting like an immature fool to the gentle advances of a man whose approbation she valued and whose companionship she had increasingly sought.

Yet, as she stepped down from the carriage, and entered that beautifully constructed Georgian home of the gentleman she now held in such high regard, Gwen was no closer to understanding what had prompted such a negative response in her. She only knew that, during the intervening days, she had experienced an increasing determination not to allow such an insignificant incident, a foolish misunderstanding, damage what for her had become a friendship necessary for her well being and future happiness.

Any slight misgivings she might still have been harbouring over the wisdom of her attendance that evening were immediately vanquished by the host himself. Joss came striding forwards the instant she entered the drawing room to capture her hand. He then took the time to introduce her to those few guests present with whom she was unacquainted, before escorting her personally in to dinner. It was perhaps unfortunate that it was at this point his attentiveness towards her ceased abruptly.

Although she quite understood why Lady Florence had been given the honour of sitting at the foot of the table, Gwen felt a strong sense of disappointment, not to say hurt, that Joss had seen fit not to choose her as one of his closest dinner companions. That privilege, as she realised quite quickly, had been bestowed upon the vicar's charming wife and Anthea Kershaw.

Finding herself placed between the very amiable Mr Markham and a retired Admiral of the Fleet, Sir Robert Rawlinson, Gwen managed to suppress her slight feelings of pique, at least during the early part of the meal, while she carried on an interesting discussion with the distinguished ex-naval officer, and a more lively discourse with the gentleman on her immediate left. Eventually though, their host's clear partiality for one of those ladies sitting closest to him caused the chagrin within to increase fourfold. Consequently she took the opportunity to escape, unnoticed, through the French windows, the instant the ladies returned to the drawing room, leaving the gentlemen to their port.

Lowering herself on to the stone wall of the

terrace, Gwen attempted to comprehend the collection of contradictory feelings warring within. On the one hand, she could appreciate just why Joss had paid Miss Kershaw such particular attention. They had been on friendly terms for a number of years, almost from the time Lady Florence had taken up residence, with her daughter, in the home she had lived in as a child. On the other hand, though, she couldn't quite understand, and certainly felt aggrieved over, why she had not received preferential treatment. After all, hadn't he as good as proposed marriage to her less than a week before? Had he been so piqued by her negative response that he had tried to punish her by dancing attendance upon Anthea? Or was he so fickle that he could transfer his affections to another woman so quickly, and without suffering the least pang of conscience? Worse, still, could it not have been a proposal of marriage he had come close to making at all, but something far less honourable?

'What the deuce are you doing out here alone?'

Gwen turned her head sharply to discover none other than the very being who was causing her such disquiet stepping out on to the terrace. Unfortunately his long striding gait brought him before her in a trice, thereby denying her sufficient time to compose herself, marshal her thoughts, or even settle her features into something less threatening than a darkling mask.

'Good God, girl! What's put your nose out of joint? You look fit to murder.'

Yes, you! Gwen longed to retort, but managed to check just in time and ask, in a semblance of an even tone, why he'd chosen not to linger over his port.

He regarded her in much the same way as he always did when he considered she had uttered something utterly bird-witted. 'Isn't it obvious? I wished to speak with you, that's why. Not had much chance to talk thus far this evening, have we?'

And whose fault's that! her baser self longed to retort. Thankfully she had managed to regain sufficient control over her wayward feelings by this time not to resort to needless displays of childish ill humour, though not quite enough control to disguise the lingering pique, as she said, 'We'd best not tarry long out here, otherwise we risk setting tongues wagging. And that would never do, now would it?'

Joss took a moment to study the firm set of a perfectly shaped feminine mouth and determined little chin, and drew his own conclusions. 'I hope you're not still brooding over the other day.' Although he spoke gently, there was an unmistakable edge of censure in his voice. 'It was too soon, I realise that now. We'll talk about it again when you're ready, Gwennie. What I want to discuss with you now is something altogether different. But not here, where we might be overheard. We'll stroll a while in the garden.'

Without offering her an opportunity to refuse, he drew her to her feet, entwined her arm through his, as was his wont, and escorted her down the stone steps to commence the stroll through the formal gardens. Yet for some obscure reason Gwen found herself automatically complying, like some well-behaved child who'd never think to disobey. And worse, she was revelling once again in the comfort this tall man's close proximity always brought her. To have repulsed him never for an instant crossed her mind. From the first it had never once entered her head to do so, she reminded herself. Was it really any wonder, then, that he had assumed she would be agreeable to a much closer association when she had, with that one recent exception only, always welcomed his gentle advances?

Joss asking what she thought of his friend instantly gained her attention. 'I thought him most charming,' she responded without hesitation. 'I disclosed the first time I ever saw him. He thought it highly diverting.'

'Yes, I did notice him in a high state of amusement on several occasions throughout dinner, you baggage!' Joss retorted, but she knew he wasn't really annoyed, as his next words proved. 'I'm glad you got along so well, because I could do with a little assistance in a certain matter concerning him.'

As it was evident he still retained her full attention, he didn't delay in explaining. 'He's sweet on Anthea, would you believe? Has been for years, great chump! But never attempted to further his interests, because for some obscure reason he seemed to suppose I entertained designs in that direction myself.'

'Well, that's hardly surprising, given your behaviour towards her this evening!' Gwen retorted before she could stop herself, and then watched a slow, hugely smug smile soften his features.

'Jealous, were we?' No response was forthcoming. 'Well, that's promising, at any rate,' Joss added, highly satisfied. 'And in more ways than one. Lady Florence wouldn't have been slow to note my seeming preference for her daughter's company either.'

'And why should that please you?' Gwen

asked, while silently cursing herself for revealing so much of her own feelings in the matter.

'Because, my darling idiot, if she continues to suppose I might be interested in her daughter, she might be more inclined to overlook Merry's frequent visits to the Hall during the next few weeks, thereby granting him and Anthea the opportunity to spend time together.'

'You devious rogue!' Gwen scolded, but for all the good it did she might as well have saved her breath, for his only response was to laugh appreciatively. She then bethought herself of something else. 'Would Lady Florence be so opposed to the union, do you suppose?'

'I wouldn't go as far as to say that exactly,' Joss answered, after giving the matter due consideration. 'I think she'll come round to it in the end, especially when she finally accepts I'm not in the running, as it were. After all, Merry's hardly a pauper. He's been remarkably shrewd in his business ventures over the years, and could certainly offer Anthea a comfortable existence, if she's sense enough to take him.'

Gwen wasn't perfectly certain what he was trying to convey by this. 'Do you think there's a chance she might not?'

Once again Joss chose to mull the question over

for a moment before saying, 'I think they need more time together, certainly. I don't doubt Merry's feelings. Anthea's, though, I'm not so certain of. She likes him well enough. More than just likes him, I strongly suspect. But she's turned four-and-twenty. She's received several offers in the past, and refused them all. And not, let me assure you, because she hoped to receive a proposal from me. Of that I'm firmly convinced.' Joss frowned, genuinely perplexed. 'Yet there's something that's persuaded her to remain single up until now.'

Gwen was at a loss to know what course to recommend. She and Anthea had hardly been granted the opportunity, as yet, to form even a lukewarm friendship, so the exchanging of confidences was unlikely to take place for some little time, if ever. 'So how can I help?'

'You can enable them to see a little more of each other, without arousing the darling mama's suspicions, by holding a dinner party in—say— a week or two. It's high time you did so, anyway,' he continued, as dictatorial as ever. 'And you've no excuse not to. The house is all in order now.'

Whether it was the romantic setting of the beautifully constructed rose arbour surrounding them, the heady scent of the flowers themselves, or the mere fact that their wonderfully close association had, blessedly, not been damaged by foolish misunderstanding, Gwen didn't know. She only knew no thought of refusing him entered her head.

'Of course I shall,' she answered at once, and as a reward had her hand raised and pressed against masculine lips in very much the grand manner. Only this time she felt not the least trepidation at the more intimate contact, nor the least desire to put any distance between herself and her self-appointed protector.

Chapter Seven

'I think I'll have a change from the silver-grey gown I wore when dining at Cranborne Hall that time, and at Bridge House last week, and wear the new lavender silk this evening instead, Gillie. And the pearls,' Gwen declared. 'Rather daring, perhaps, for someone who's yet to complete a full year's mourning. But hardly the height of dissipation, either, in view of the fact that I'm holding a small, private dinner party, where cards will be the only entertainment on offer. Besides which, the only person who might possibly have cast a disapproving eye over my attire won't now be attending.'

'True enough. Yet in one way, Miss Gwen, it's a shame Lady Florence did contract that chill,' Martha pointed out, as she helped her mistress don the chosen raiment. 'It's made the place-settings a little difficult for you to arrange.'

'There, I'm forced to agree with you. It wasn't so bad when Anthea suggested Felix take her mother's place, because I'd already included the Harmonds' eldest daughter, Caroline, on the invitation I sent to the vicarage. Mr Lucas's presence would have balanced the numbers quite nicely. But when Anthea dropped me a line, asking whether I'd be kind enough to include her brother Ralph also, I knew it would leave an odd number at table. But what could I do? It was too late to invite anyone else. And it would have been churlish to refuse. Apparently he turned up at the Hall the day before yesterday, quite without warning, for a very brief stay, little realising, I suppose, that his mother was feeling a touch under the weather, or that his uncle, the Earl, was away for a few days visiting friends. I suppose Anthea thought her brother would have a poor time of it with her and Felix out for an entire evening.'

'Must be very fond of her brother to consider him so much,' the maid suggested, while securing the string of pearls about her mistress's slender neck. 'Has Miss Kershaw any other brothers or sisters?'

'Just the one sibling, I believe,' Gwen confirmed, frowning in an effort to remember what she had learned about the Kershaws since her arrival in the county.

She had seen Anthea on three occasions since the evening of Joss's dinner party: twice in the company of Joss himself and Mr Markham, when they had called whilst out enjoying morning rides; and once when Anthea had accompanied her mother on a round of social calls. So naturally they had come to know each other a good deal better and, in consequence, Gwen might have expected to discover more about the Kershaw family. Yet, strangely enough, this had not turned out to be the case. Although Anthea was always most amiable, and would converse easily on a wide range of topics, she had rarely alluded to any member of her immediate family.

'It's strange, Gillie, but now you come to remark upon it, I cannot in all honesty recall Anthea ever mentioning her brother once. I believe it was Lady Florence who revealed she had a son. If my memory serves me correctly, he's four or maybe five years his sister's senior, and in the army.' She frowned more deeply. 'Or is it the navy? Oh, dear, I cannot recall. Nor who told me, for that matter. I dare say I shall discover more about him this evening. It just so happens I've placed him next to me at dinner in the fervent hope he'll prove a better conversationalist than that cousin of his. I've been forced to place Felix on my other side to spare the vicar's daughter. She's only just begun to join her parents on social occasions, so I didn't wish to dash what confidence the poor girl might already have acquired by seating her beside someone as retiring as the Earl's younger son.'

Later, however, much to her intense surprise, Gwen was forced to revise her opinion and silently admit that of her two closest dinner companions, she favoured the company of Felix Lucas, whom she had succeeded in engaging in conversation on several occasions during the meal.

It wasn't that she had taken Anthea's brother in dislike. On the contrary, in form, at least, most women, she felt sure, would have considered him a fine specimen of manhood. His physique, shown to advantage that evening in a smart dress uniform, was wonderfully proportioned. He, like his sister, was undoubtedly good looking, if in a darkly saturnine sort of way. There was nothing wanting in his address whatsoever. If anything, his manners were impeccable.

Yet there was something about him that Gwen didn't quite like, didn't quite trust. Perhaps, she mused, it was simply that in recent months she had grown so very appreciative and approving of someone whose manners and language frequently left much to be desired.

Raising her eyes, Gwen instinctively fixed her gaze on the gentleman seated at the opposite end of the table. At that moment he was holding the clergyman's charming daughter in conversation, and, judging by the girl's animated expression, he was doing a sterling job of keeping her entertained. Which, of course, in no way surprised Gwen. Joss had his faults, not least of which was a tendency to speak his mind a little too forcefully on occasions. None the less, he had many fine qualities, too, the most surprising, perhaps, being his innate ability to win the confidence of the young. She had seen him often enough in the company of his two wards to be sure that he knew precisely how to deal with innocent young misses, and not cause them the least embarrassment.

She then focused her attention on the female on Joss's right, who had been happily conversing with the vicar for quite some time. A few days before, when she had learned that Lady Florence wouldn't be attending, Gwen had considered placing Anthea next to Mr Markham. Now, however, she was glad she had resisted the temptation to play Cupid to the pair who appeared to be rubbing along together remarkably well without any outside interference. At least Ralph Kershaw couldn't return to the Hall with crumbs of gossip to spill into his mother's lap concerning his sister. Perhaps she was doing him a gross injustice to suppose for a moment that he might stoop so low as to play the tale-bearer. All the same, unless she came to know him a good deal better, she would prefer to err on the side of caution where the dashing Major was concerned.

Notwithstanding, this resolve did not deter her from accepting his invitation to take a stroll round the garden later that evening, once she had four of her guests settled round a table, enjoying a game of whist, and the other three happily conversing.

'Believe me, Major Kershaw, I wouldn't have been so eager to accept your invitation had you asked me several weeks ago.'

He gazed down at her searchingly, as though probing for some hidden meaning. 'Forgive me, ma'am, I do not perfectly understand. Are you trying to suggest you are nervous in my company? If so, we can remain close to the house.'

'Not at all, Major. Besides, I only need raise my voice for someone to hear, so there's absolutely no reason for me to feel anxious,' she assured him. 'No, what I was referring to was the state of my garden.' She glanced across at one secluded corner, where work still needed to be done. 'It's far from perfect now, but a few weeks ago it was in a sadly neglected state. At least I no longer feel ashamed to stroll along the paths with a guest.'

'It's most charming,' he responded, though she wasn't perfectly certain whether or not he was being totally sincere, as he didn't seem to be taking much notice of his surroundings, keeping his gaze for the most part on her. 'I understand from my sister you came to live here only a few months ago.'

'Yes, that's correct. Sadly, my husband and I never resided here together.'

As he seemed genuinely interested, Gwen was happy to reveal that directly after their marriage had taken place, her husband had taken her to Yorkshire to stay with his brother and his wife. They had remained throughout the spring and summer of that year, using her brother-in-law's home as a base and travelling extensively about the north country, and even venturing some distance into Scotland, before eventually journeying to Liverpool in order to board a ship bound for America.

'Initially Percival was against the idea of my accompanying him on a trip that he had been planning for quite some time. He wanted me to come here. But I managed to persuade him to take me along.'

Whenever she thought of her late husband, Gwen found herself smiling a soft, reminiscent smile, and it was no different this time. 'You see, Major, I'd never, ever travelled more than five miles from my home before I married Percival. And I was so eager for adventure.'

The man beside her drew his brows together. 'Am I right in thinking that your husband was in America in 1775, fighting for his country, ma'am?'

'Yes, bravely and loyally. And was honoured with a knighthood when he eventually sold his commission and retired from the army,' Gwen confirmed. 'But that doesn't necessarily mean he agreed with the stance his country adopted in that particular conflict. In fact, his sympathies were with those in the New World. Several of his comrades remained out there. One of his closest friends married a rich merchant's daughter, and it was with this family that we stayed for almost two years. We travelled a good deal too, before finally boarding a vessel bound for Spain, and then England. Of course, we did from time to time learn of the happenings in Europe. But it wasn't until after we had arrived at Cadiz that we discovered Napoleon had been exiled on Elba.'

Once again Gwen's lips were curled by that soft, reminiscent smile. 'One would have imaged that a gentleman well into his sixties would have had enough jaunting about the world by then. But not Percival. On a whim he decided not to return to England, but to get passage on a merchant ship bound for Naples, where he swiftly made contact with one of his oldest friends, an Italian nobleman he had met many years before in London in his youth. Within a short time the Conte had sent his carriage to convey us to his beautiful home a few miles further down the coast.'

Gwen's smile slowly faded as she recalled vividly that time spent in Italy. 'The Conte persuaded my husband to make the visit an extended one, simply because he considered that, at their time of life, travelling great distances would soon be beyond them both. I raised no objections, simply because it granted me the opportunity to travel to some wonderful places with the Contessa, whom I swiftly grew to adore. But I shouldn't have been so selfish. I should have realised…should have kept a closer watch on him, I suppose, when Percival began to betray more than a mild interest in his friend's passion for archaeology. Both he and the Conte spent hours together happily excavating the remains of an ancient villa unearthed in one corner of the estate. The Conte, of course, although of a similar age, was accustomed to the hot Italian sun; Percival was not. As the months passed, he began to tire more easily, sleep for longer. But he wouldn't stop accompanying his friend almost every day. Eventually, though, his heart could no longer stand the strain.'

'So, you then came back to England alone and settled down here,' the Major said after a few moments' silence, his voice bland, quite without any emotion.

'To be truthful, I had nowhere else to go.' Gwen shrugged. 'I could have stayed in Italy, I suppose. The Contessa, too, was many years younger than her husband, though some twenty years older than me. As I mentioned, we had become very close. I think she eventually began to look upon me as the daughter she'd never been blessed to have. But I wanted to return. You see, Major, there was someone here I was desperate to see again… Sadly I was denied the reunion for which I had longed. Unbeknownst to me, she died a week or two after my arrival back in this country, whilst I was in London, sightseeing, acquiring a new and warmer wardrobe, and dealing with my late husband's business affairs.'

The Major's dark brows drew together momentarily. 'Would I be correct in thinking that your friend was none other than the young woman who was found in Marsden Wood earlier this year?'

He might have been remarking on a topic of no more moment than the weather, so impassive did he sound. Yet Gwen felt neither aggrieved nor surprised by this evident lack of emotion. After all, it was highly unlikely that he had even met Jane Robbins, she reasoned, so he could hardly be expected to feel the least pang of sorrow at the passing of a stranger.

'Yes, that's correct, Major.' Gwen couldn't suppress the sudden swell of resentment. ' And the murderer still goes unpunished.'

'You sound bitter, ma'am. And with good reason, as she was a friend of yours.' He stared straight ahead, his expression totally unreadable. 'But maybe he is not wholly to blame for his actions. Not all women are as innocent as they seem. I have recently been in the north with my company, dealing with several instances of civil unrest. One of my young officers was lured down an alley by a female and hacked to death by a gang of ruffians. No, not all women are so innocent, ma'am.'

'Perhaps not, Major. But let me assure you, Jane Robbins was not of their number. She was a gentle soul, and didn't deserve to die in such a terrible way.'

'Forgive me. I was forgetting she was a personal friend of yours. My sister did tell me as much before we set out this evening.' His smile was distinctly crooked. 'My years in the army have left their mark, I'm afraid. I've seen more than my share of hardship and death during those three long years I spent across the Channel. Perhaps I have become inured. Indeed, some might say that I have been guilty of inflicting much suffering myself.'

'All in the line of duty, I sincerely trust, sir?' No response was forthcoming, so Gwen changed the subject by asking how long he intended to remain at the Hall.

'Oh, only until tomorrow. Then I'm off to Horse Guards for a spell, before I enjoy a further spot of leave, most of which will be spent at my home near Portsmouth. But I plan to return here at the end of July for the annual summer ball. I sincerely hope I shall have the pleasure of seeing you there, Lady Warr—'

Major Kershaw broke off abruptly, his hand instinctively reaching for the hilt of his sword, as an aggressor appeared from behind a shrub directly in front of them. Honking loudly and wings flapping, Clarence looked eager to do battle with the unknown soldier, until Gwen intervened. Raising her arms, she shooed the gander back towards the path leading to the large paddock.

'Manders couldn't have secured the latch on the pen properly. Clarence isn't usually out at this time. I sincerely hope he didn't unnerve you, Major. He can still be something of a Tartar with strangers, I'm afraid.'

'Soldiers are trained to deal with the unexpected, ma'am.' Although he smiled, there was absolutely no softening in the contours of his face. 'Permit me,' he added, helping her to reposition the silk shawl that had fallen from her shoulders whilst dealing with the gander, and in so doing inadvertently scratched her upper arm with the signet ring he sported on his left hand, causing her to wince slightly.

'It's nothing, Major, merely a scratch,' she assured him, glancing briefly at the instrument of pain, before her attention was drawn to the tall figure bearing down upon them. 'Oh, dear, have you come out here to remind me that I'm guilty of neglecting the majority of my guests for far too long?'

'Not at all. It's Kershaw, here, I'm after, not you,' Joss responded bluntly, before turning his attention to her companion. 'Anthea is wishful for you to partner her in the next game of whist.'

As the Major didn't delay in responding to the request, Gwen waited only until he was out of earshot to ask, 'What do you think of him, Joss?'

He didn't answer immediately. Instead, he secured her arm in his usual fashion before continuing to stroll along the path. 'He's never given me any reason to dislike him, my darling. All the same, I've never looked upon him as a friend, as I do his sister. Why do you ask?'

She shrugged. 'No reason, really. It's just that I've never heard anyone talk about him much. I cannot recall Anthea once mentioning him, until she sent me that brief note asking if I'd be kind enough to include him in the invitation this evening. And I suppose I just wondered why she's never discussed him.'

'I don't think they're particularly close,' he revealed, after giving the matter a further moment's thought. 'But that's nothing unusual, after all. Siblings are not always bound to be so very fond of each other. Look at me! I'm a prime example of someone with that outlook. Wouldn't care a jot if I never saw any of mine again, with the possible exception of Alice, that is.'

The look of staunch disapproval he received didn't come even remotely close to causing him to suffer pangs of conscience, or upsetting his train of thought for that matter. 'And I think Anthea might possibly still harbour a degree of resentment over the fact that her brother obliged her and her mother to leave the family home some seven years ago by inviting his mistress to stay, once it became legally his property.'

'Really?' This very interesting snippet succeeded in capturing her attention in a big way. 'I'd be the first to acknowledge that I'm nowhere near as well versed as you undoubtedly are in such matters, Joss. But I understood that any gentleman possessing a modicum of sensibility would at least attempt to keep his *amours* well hidden from the female members of his immediate family, and not flaunt them quite openly.'

'Certainly the vast majority of my friends do so,' Joss disclosed, with only the slightest twitch at one corner of his mouth to betray his amusement at the faint thread of censure he clearly discerned in her voice. 'But I should be a liar to suggest that all gentlemen follow such hard-and-fast rules,' he added, candid as always. 'Whether through cold indifference, or lack of funds, some men are guilty of doing absolutely nothing to conceal the—er—more personal aspects of their lives.

'However, to do Kershaw justice,' Joss went on, when his delightful companion wisely refrained from comment, 'he was very young at the time, merely one and twenty. I believe I'm right in saying he did come into his father's property at that time, but not the majority of the money left to him by his sire. That he didn't inherit until three or four years ago, when he attained the age of five and twenty. So let us be charitable and suggest it was possibly a combination of youthful high spirits and lack of funds, not callous indifference, that induced him to invite a mistress to the family home, if only for a relatively short period of time.'

Gwen frowned as something else rather odd occurred to her. 'You are the first person to mention anything about Anthea's father in my hearing.'

Joss looked nonplussed for a moment, then shrugged. 'Well, it's unlikely Anthea remembers very much about him. She must have been four, or five at most, when he lost his life at the Battle of the Nile.'

Gwen was even more surprised to discover this.

'He was in the Navy? Great heavens! I wonder why his son didn't follow his example, and go to sea?'

'I've no idea. All I can tell you is that he was with the Provost Marshal's lot out in the Peninsula during the latter years of the Campaign. Spent some time in France, I believe, and was also at Waterloo. Earned himself the reputation of being thorough, a stickler for duty. Not one to show much sympathy towards deserters, from what I've heard.'

A string of highly colourful oaths, loudly voiced, was instrumental in preventing any further discussion about the Kershaw family taking place that evening. Both Gwen and Joss swung round and were as surprised as each other to discover none other than the Earl of Cranborne's normally mild-mannered younger son striding purposefully towards them, his expression for once anything but vague.

'Dash it, Lady Warrender!' Mr Lucas exclaimed, acute annoyance clearly writ across his unremarkable features. 'Protect your property from intruders you might wish to do, but you could at least have the common courtesy to warn guests of the dangers lurking in your grounds. A body might easily suffer a serious injury. That confounded creature deserves to have its neck wrung!'

Joss might have found Felix's encounter with the gander highly diverting, but Gwen wasn't in the least amused. After requesting Joss to see the highly disgruntled Mr Lucas back inside the house, she set off to look for the miscreant, but abandoned the task after only a brief and singularly unprofitable search, a decision she was destined to regret bitterly.

Joss realised all was not as it should be the instant he walked his mount round the back of the house to the small stable the following morning, and handed his sturdy bay hack into Ben Small's very capable hands.

'What's amiss, lad?' he asked, when he failed to receive the groom's usually cheerful greeting. 'You've a face like a wet afternoon.'

'It's the mistress, sir. Can't bear to see 'er so upset.'

Joss was instantly alert. 'What's wrong? What's happened?'

'It's that damned fool, Manders, sir!' Ben spat on the ground, clearly revealing his opinion of the elderly servant wasn't so far removed from that of his sister's. 'Should 'ave come to me and young Joe when he couldn't find the dratted goose. But no, he 'as to go up to the 'ouse to tell the mistress. And it were she that found it. It were over by the bushes, yonder—head off, slashed to bits it were, sir. Now, I asks you, who'd do a thing like that?'

Joss was perplexed too. 'It's hard to imagine any normal person behaving in such a fashion, unless of course it was pure malice, an act of revenge.'

'But no one from round 'ere would do summat like that, sir. The mistress be well liked by the village folk. Always uses locals when she needs work done, and they're obliged to her for it an' all, I can tell you.' Ben sounded sure of himself. 'I ain't saying we're all saints in these parts. There be those that'ud not think twice about doing a spot of poaching, especially when times are 'ard.'

'True enough, but from what you've told me, this was no poacher's work. He'd have wrung its neck, no doubt, and carted it off in a sack, not hacked it to bits, and left it to rot,' Joss wasn't slow to point out. 'Keep your eyes and ears open. You never know, whoever it was might be back. And it would appear he's a particularly nasty piece of work.'

Joss was concerned, and it clearly showed in every strong contour of his face as he strode across the small yard towards the house. By the time he entered the front parlour, however, he had himself well in hand, his expression giving nothing away, except perhaps a flicker of satisfaction at being in the company of the woman he was determined to marry. The same could not be said for Gwen. She took one glance across the room, a moment after the door had opened, and her vision quickly blurred with the tears she could no longer suppress.

'Oh, my darling girl,' Joss murmured, opening wide his arms, and then closing them about the slender woman who hadn't needed to think twice about finding solace in his tender embrace.

Resting her head against the great barrel of his chest, Gwen wept silently for a few moments. Even when she was well on the way to regaining her poise, she experienced not the least desire to break free from that gentle, loving hold.

'All my fault,' she murmured. 'All my wretched fault. I should have remembered I'd given Manders the evening off. I should have continued searching for Clarence myself.'

'And neglect your guests…? I don't think so,' Joss countered, ever the pragmatist. 'Your only fault is that you'd grown too fond of the wretched creature. He'd never have ended up in the pot at Christmas, or at any other time, if I know anything.'

Smiling in spite of the fact that she was still deeply saddened, Gwen had to own to the truth of it. 'Yes, foolishly, I suppose, I'd come to look upon him as a pet. He was such a character, Joss. Besides being a wonderful watchdog.'

'And that, my darling girl, could well have been his downfall,' Joss pointed out, before taking the liberty of burying his lips in the soft chestnut locks.

Still Gwen experienced not the least desire to break free. If anything, she clung to him more tightly, with every passing moment regaining her strength from his seemingly bottomless reserves, and surprisingly relishing this lengthy, more intimate contact too, a contact that she was seriously beginning to believe she might possibly have craved almost from the first.

'You think he surprised an intruder, came hissing out from his hiding place in the shrubbery, and was silenced with that first fatal slash to his neck? Yes, yes, that's certainly a strong possibility, because none of the servants seem to have heard anything,' she acknowledged. 'But why continue slashing at his body in…what must surely have been a kind of frenzy? A simple poacher wouldn't have done so.'

Receiving no response whatsoever, Gwen raised her head to find him staring down at her, his eyes softened by a renewed look of tenderness. Then, very slowly, he lowered his head and covered her mouth with his own so gently that she experienced not one single moment's alarm, only a desire to respond by raising one arm to place a hand against his face.

'You're a witch, Gwennie Warrender,' he husked into her hair when finally he reluctantly withdrew his mouth from hers. 'God, how I love you, body and soul! Believe me when I tell you I've never come even remotely close to loving any woman as I love you.'

If it had been Joss's underlying intention to take her mind off the unfortunate discovery of the morning, then he had succeeded quite splendidly well. He had also succeeded, even after what had occurred between them, of restoring her composure to such an extent that she saw little benefit in prevarication, or attempting to pretend that he had taken advantage of her in a moment of weakness. Quite simply he had not.

'And I love you, Joss…I do, so very much.'

There, it was out! She had admitted it at last, so naturally, so easily, that she knew it must be true, and possibly had been for some little time. Yet even though she now silently acknowledged the certainty of her own feelings, those niggling doubts persisted.

Easily disengaging herself from his gentle hold, she took a step away. 'What I'm not so certain of is whether I wish to marry again.'

His shout of derisive laughter was so unexpected, it almost made her start. 'Don't talk such flummery to me, my girl!' Joss barked, like some strict tutor easily catching a pupil in an outright lie. 'You never have been married. At least, not in the full sense,' he rectified in the next breath so that she could be in no doubt that he was under any illusions about her first union, and then watched as she swung round and went across to stand by the window.

Joss took a moment to pour out two glasses of wine before joining her where she had sought refuge the instant he had touched upon the more private aspects of her first union. The telltale maidenly blush was there for anyone to see. Yet he didn't permit her evident embarrassment or reluctance to discuss such a personal matter deter him from discovering something that had puzzled him almost from the beginning of their acquaintance.

'Why did you marry Percival Warrender, Gwennie?' He handed her one of the glasses, and then watched her sample its contents gratefully. 'These so-called marriages of convenience do occur, I know, for various reasons. But how convenient could it have been for you to look after someone old enough to be your grandfather?'

This drew a reluctant smile to her lips. 'Oh, come now, Joss! You know yourself that, although he might not have been in the same healthy state as a strapping youth, Percival was not infirm, and there was absolutely nothing amiss with his mental faculties either. And what you might possibly be unaware of is that the disparity in our ages didn't seem such an impediment to me. My father was a good many years older than my mother, almost twenty.'

Gwen took a further fortifying sip from her glass before at last admitting to something that she had only ever revealed to one other person before. 'The only reason I was happy to marry Percival was because I believed that by doing so I could attain what I wanted. I was a naïve little fool to suppose that I could achieve my objective through the marriage.'

Joss was puzzled by the tone of self-disgust clearly discernible in her voice. 'You're not trying to suggest you married him for money? If so, I won't believe it for a moment!'

Gwen raised her hand once again to caress his cheek. 'Thank you for that, at least. But the truth is, Joss, my reason for doing so was very nearly as mercenary.'

She removed her hand to place it against her own forehead, as the foolish decision she had made so many years ago came back once more to taunt her. 'I'd turned nineteen when I agreed to marry Percival. I truly believe the original notion for me to do so was my father's, not Percival's. But I don't want you to suppose for a moment that I was coerced into the union. The decision was entirely my own, and made entirely for the wrong reasons.'

This time when Gwen had recourse to her glass, she finished its contents in one swallow, something Joss had never witnessed her do before, and something that was testament to her present troubled state of mind.

'Three years before, when I was sixteen, I not only lost my mother, but Jane Robbins also. She decided that, having reached the age of eighteen, it was time she made her own way in the world, and so attained a post in a seminary near London, whilst I remained at the vicarage and kept house for my father. Two years later it became clear that my father was seriously ill. He had the wasting disease. Knowing he had months, not years left to live, he wrote to Percival. They had been boyhood friends, and had kept in touch throughout their lives, though they saw each other only rarely in latter years. I had met Percival on three previous occasions when he had visited the vicarage. I liked him. I looked upon him as a very amiable, elderly gentleman. So when it was suggested he take care of me, and would settle me here in this house, while he travelled to America, I agreed to marry him.'

A sigh escaped her. 'I wrote to Jane, so pleased with myself for having enabled us to live together once again, and not merely see each other on rare occasions. She'd have no need to earn a living any longer, I wrote and told her. We could live the carefree life we'd enjoyed as children. You knew her, knew the high standards she set herself. Needless to say, she wasn't best pleased. She wrote back, begging me not to marry for such an absurd reason, and assuring me she was content with her life as a teacher.' Gwen gave vent to a further heartfelt sigh. 'But it was too late, I'd already done the deed.'

Raising her head, Gwen took a moment to stare across the front garden at where Joe had created a particularly colourful bed of summer flowers.

'Many times since, though, I've wondered whether I would have married Percival had I known what Jane's reaction would be. But I had married him, and I was determined to make the best of it. Living here without my girlhood friend held no appeal, and so I managed to persuade Percival to allow me to accompany him on his travels. And that was something I never regretted. He was very good to me, so very kind, like some indulgent great-uncle, and I was very content with life with him. My one regret is that I was unable to bring him back here to a final resting place in the churchyard. But it was impossible. The hot Italian sun does not permit bodies to remain above ground for long.'

'I don't suppose for a moment he would have cared very much,' Joss suggested, after digesting everything he had learned. 'He spent so little time here. He was always off somewhere or other, visiting friends.'

He slid an arm about her trim waist, once again gratified when she made no attempt to draw away. 'But he would have cared very much about what happens to you. So, what I propose to do is respect your widowed state and allow you your full year's mourning. We can announce our betrothal on the evening of the summer ball at

Cranborne Hall, then marry at the end of the following month.'

For answer Gwen rested her head against his chest, very content to place her future well being in such capable, loving hands.

Chapter Eight

The instant Joss departed Gwen didn't ponder over what she felt certain would be a wonderful future at the side of the man she had grown so quickly to love. Instead, her thoughts turned to the past, most especially the recent past, and the grisly discovery of that morning.

Her groom, Ben, had hinted that it was unlikely to have been the work of a poacher. Gwen was inclined to agree with this viewpoint. Yet Clarence had surprised someone, and if not a poacher...?

Apparently, the night before, Manders had returned a matter of ten minutes or so after the last of her guests had departed. He had noticed nothing untoward, even though he had passed close to the very spot where the gander had met his end. Given, though, by that time it was quite dark and, more importantly, Manders had spent most of the evening propped against the counter in the village inn, supping ale, and had been, by his own admission, not perfectly sober, one couldn't place too much reliance on anything he said, and Clarence might already have been dead by the time Manders had sought his bed.

But if so, surely one of the guests, or one of their grooms, would have noticed at least the feathers strewn across the edge of the driveway? Gwen reasoned, then shook head, perplexed. Perhaps the only thing about which one could be absolutely certain was that whoever slew Clarence had come armed with a sharp-bladed weapon that he had been prepared to use if challenged.

As if by a natural progression of thought Gwen couldn't help speculating on the reason why someone, carrying a deadly weapon, had entered her garden in the first place, if not to gain access to the paddock to acquire a duck or two, or maybe one of the sow's litter. Manders had checked that morning, and had already confirmed all was as it should be. The only other possibility that immediately sprang to mind was a robber, intent on breaking into the house.

Gwen took a moment to stare round the recently refurbished front parlour. It was true to say that there were a few very pretty ornaments dotted about, and in other rooms too, for that matter. It was also true to say that she owned one or two pieces of jewellery worth purloining, and some fine items of silverware. But there were plenty of houses hereabouts that offered far richer pickings: Bridge House, to name but one! So what had drawn such a violent rogue to her mediocre dwelling? More importantly, was he likely to return? Most disturbing of all—would he be willing to wield a knife against anything or anyone who stood in his way?

The sounds of an arrival didn't allow her to dwell on these disturbing possibilities, as a moment or two later Annie was showing Miss Kershaw and her cousin into the room, both of whom had willingly agreed to dispense with unnecessary formality the previous evening.

'We came to thank you for a most enjoyable evening,' Anthea said, accepting Gwen's invitation to take a seat, and then staring across the room at her cousin, who was already gazing absently out of the window. 'Did we not, Felix?'

It was a moment or two before he seemed to grasp the fact that someone had addressed him. 'What...? Oh, yes, I should say so. Jolly enjoyable affair!'

Appearing slightly bewildered, as though not

quite knowing precisely where he was, or why he had come, for that matter, he seemed quite different from the evening before, Gwen mused. His behaviour then had been almost bordering on normality, for once surprisingly alert to what had been going on around him. Furthermore, he had been downright annoyed after the episode with Clarence.

'Be truthful, Felix. You didn't enjoy yourself so much,' she reminded him, keeping her voice light, almost teasing. 'At least not when you had that unfortunate encounter in the garden, remember?'

For a moment it seemed that he definitely did not recall, then his vague look was swept away by an expression of decided animation. 'By Jove, you're right! I'd clean forgotten all about it. Attacked by a confounded goose, Anthea, would you believe? Quite unnerved me, I can tell you.' He bent as severe a look as a man of his decidedly mild disposition could muster in Gwen's direction. 'Hope you've got the wretched creature safely locked up today.'

He was either the most consummate actor who ever drew breath, or completely innocent of committing the grisly deed, Gwen decided, her every instinct persuading her to take the latter view, and acquit him of all blame.

'You're perfectly safe, Felix,' she assured him, deciding, in the next moment, not to reveal the gander's demise, but to ask, instead, if either of them had seen anyone suspicious loitering near the gates, or in the lane beyond, when they had left after the dinner party. 'You see, one of my servants is certain he disturbed someone attempting to break in last night,' she lied.

Miss Kershaw was the first to respond. 'Oh, dear, how dreadful! Well, I certainly didn't see anyone at all, until Ralph caught up with us. Unfortunately I cannot ask my brother. He left for London first thing this morning.' She turned to her cousin. 'Did you notice anything untoward, Felix?'

'No, can't say as I did,' he eventually roused himself to answer, his attention having been drawn by this time to the folder lying open on the table by the window.

Her mind having quickly picked up on something Anthea had innocently revealed, Gwen was hardly aware of Felix's response. Nor was she aware that he was now avidly scrutinising the highly detailed water-colour paintings, contained in the folder, that had been drawn by Jane Robbins during the spring and summer of the previous year.

'Do I infer correctly that your brother didn't accompany you and Felix in the carriage, Anthea?'

'No, he always rides whenever possible.'

'Yes, so did my late husband,' Gwen recalled. 'Must be something peculiar to army men, I suppose.'

'Not in Ralph's case,' Anthea countered. 'He cannot abide confined spaces, never could. When he was a child he couldn't bear even having the curtains drawn about his bed.'

'That's perhaps why he chose a career in the army in preference to one in the navy,' Gwen suggested. 'I've done a fair bit of travelling by sea myself, and know there's a vast difference between above and below deck.'

'That ain't the reason he chose the army,' Felix unexpectedly announced, thereby revealing that he wasn't always so oblivious to what was taking place around him. 'He hates the sea, always suffers from seasickness. Told me so himself. Said how he dreaded his father ever coming home on leave, on account of his sire forcing him, at a ridiculously young age, to put to sea in a rowing boat, no matter the weather. Cruel it was, if you ask me. No wonder Ralph's such a dark one now, keeping himself to himself for the most part, and allowing few people to get close to him.'

Gwen found this most interesting, and turned

towards Felix's cousin in the hope of learning a little more about her brother's relationship with their father. Anthea, however, was maintaining a stony silence, staring resolutely down at the hands in her lap, and so Gwen once again favoured Felix with her attention, only to be startled a moment later when he declared,

'I've seen these before. By gad, I know I have! The woman in the wood, that's who drew them!'

These revelations thrust everything else from Gwen's mind. She was on her feet and across the room in an instant, Anthea herself not far behind. 'These were drawn by my friend Jane Robbins.' No one possessing a ha'p'orth of sensibility could have mistaken the thread of urgency in her voice. 'You remember her, don't you?'

'Such marvellous attention to detail!' Felix declared, staring at one sketch in particular. 'Distinctly remember telling her so myself.'

'Yes, dear, I'm sure you're right,' Anthea said coaxingly, having easily guessed the reason behind Gwen's eagerness. 'It's a very pretty— er—cowslip indeed.'

Felix regarded his cousin in a mixture of disgust and dismay. 'It's an orchid, Cousin.'

'Yes, dear, of course. How very foolish of me!' Anthea swiftly apologised, if a trifle unsteadily.

'But you remember the woman who drew it, don't you?'

'Just told you so, didn't I!' Felix returned so testily that Gwen thought it prudent to intervene.

'Perhaps what you don't recall, though, Felix, is the lady who drew these fine pictures was a very good friend of mine. She was murdered in the wood earlier this year.'

'By gad, yes! Recall Anthea mentioning something about it, now. But never realised it was that particular female. Dashed pity!' Felix announced, appearing as though he meant it too. 'Nice woman. Looked where she was putting her feet, not like most of 'em.'

By this time Gwen was as sure as it was possible to be that Felix wasn't responsible for the tragedies in Marsden Wood. He was undoubtedly a more complex character than one might suppose on first making his acquaintance, as Joss himself had intimated, and there was no denying his vagueness concealed quite wonderfully well the more passionate side to his nature. Yet she had the distinct impression his basic instinct was to protect and preserve, and she suspected that it extended beyond the flora to be found in woodland areas.

Seemingly Anthea held this view too, for she made no mention of his activities, and merely asked if he had ever come across others traipsing the woodland paths, a question that surprisingly roused his ire yet again.

'Well, of course I do! Dashed silly thing to ask, Anthea,' he said testily. 'You know yourself most everyone at the Hall, including the servants, goes into the wood at some time or other, never caring where they put their dratted feet. And my brother's the worst offender of all, curse him! Lawrence never pays a visit these days without a pack of mindless cronies in tow. The Lord only knows what mayhem they cause in the woods. They're a law unto themselves. High time Father put his foot down, if you ask me!'

To see Felix in a rare passion for the second time within twenty-four hours wasn't without its amusing side. Nevertheless, he had spoken no less than the truth. Marsden Wood's unfortunate reputation hadn't deterred a great many people, surprisingly of both sexes, from continuing to venture there for whatever reason. Trying to uncover the one man whose sole purpose for stalking woodland paths was anything but innocent seemed a forlorn task.

Gwen continued to harbour this woefully defeatist attitude until two days later, when a missive was placed in her hand, the direction scrawled in a bold and clearly masculine hand. As far as she could remember she had seen no examples of Joss's handwriting, and yet she was certain it was from none other than her future husband, even before she broke the seal to read: *Be ready within the hour. Wear something suitable for riding, a habit if you have one, N.*

'Upon my word! Would you just look at that now!' Gwen exclaimed, waving the missive in the air. 'Seen absolutely nothing of him since Saturday morning, and now he has the crass nerve to send me curt notes making demands on my time, without so much as a by your leave!'

Martha Gillingham headed towards the wardrobe, thereby hiding her appreciative smile from view. As far as she knew, she was the only member of the household privy to her young mistress's intention of becoming Mrs Jocelyn Northbridge, and she could not have been more delighted by the news.

'Well, Miss Gwen, you know my views on Mr Northbridge. He's a fine man, and I truly believe you'll mellow him in time. You've maybe made a start already and didn't know it,' she suggested. 'All the same, his nature being what it is, you'll never change him completely. And I don't think you'd want to, neither, if you're honest with yourself.'

Gwen couldn't help smiling at this shrewd judgement, but refrained from comment, and merely requested that her sadly outmoded riding habit be unearthed from whatever dark niche it happened to be occupying and receive a good brushing down.

Sadly, though, not even the maid's expert attentions could disguise the fact that the cloth, if not precisely moth-eaten, was sadly worn in several places. Nor could Gwen rid herself of the uncomfortable feeling that there was a decided odour of mustiness clinging to her person, as she descended the stairs to answer the imperious application of the front-door-knocker herself later that morning. A moment later, however, any lingering resentment towards the caller, or misgivings about her appearance were swept away at the sight of the most beautiful grey mare she had ever set eyes on.

'Oh, where on earth have you been hiding this beauty?' Gwen demanded to know, as she stroked the horse's sleek neck gently. 'You never ride her, surely, Joss! She's not up to your weight.'

'True enough. But she's easily up to yours.

Which is just as well as she belongs to you now,' he surprised her by divulging. 'That's where I've been for the last couple of days—collecting her and bringing her back to Bridge House. Look upon her as an engagement gift, the first of many I intend bestowing upon you.'

The loving smile he received before she stood on tiptoe to brush her mouth against one corner of his was reward enough for his trouble. 'If you continue to behave like this in public, you're not likely to keep our betrothal a secret for very much longer, my sweet life. Most especially as you were just observed by your wickedly grinning maidservant, standing there at the parlour window, not to mention one of my grooms, awaiting us at the gate.'

'And we're not likely to keep it a secret if you continue to shower me with gifts, either. Really, Joss, you mustn't.' No one, least of all the man staring avidly down at the sweet face he had grown to love above any other, could have failed to recognise what was clearly mirrored in lovely blue eyes. 'You are all I want.'

Conveniently forgetting his prior warning, he took her in his arms, albeit only briefly as his powers of restraint were increasingly being sorely tested these days, before tossing her effortlessly into the saddle.

'Well, my darling, you certainly don't possess Anthea's excellent seat,' he remarked, judiciously, after a brief assessment of her abilities, 'but at least you're not as ungainly as a few pounds of vegetables jostling about in a sack.'

Although she accepted the criticism with good grace, Gwen couldn't resist countering with, 'I should be relieved, I suppose, to discover that your eyesight hasn't suffered as a result of our close association. All the same, I could have hoped that experiencing that most tender of emotions might have induced you to temper honesty with a little diplomacy on occasions, most especially in your dealings with me.'

'Don't try to flummery me, my girl!' Joss returned in a flash. 'I know you too well. You wouldn't respond to insincere flattery. And you'll never receive any from me. You can't be outstanding at everything. Be satisfied with that angelic singing voice of yours. Besides which, I'd much prefer to have you entertain me in my drawing room, sat at the pianoforte, than galloping expertly beside me across a hunting field. Although,' he added, after a moment's consideration, 'I don't suppose it would take much effort to improve your style.'

Wisely Gwen refrained from comment this

time, and asked instead where they were bound. 'Not Bridge House, surely?'

'Yes, I've arranged for that ex-Runner, Stubbs, to be there, as he dropped me a line, suggesting a meeting.' Joss wasn't slow to observe his companion's faintly apathetic look. 'What's the matter? You expressed a desire to make his acquaintance not so very long ago,' he reminded her.

'Yes, I know I did.' Gwen couldn't prevent a sigh escaping. 'But I can't help feeling now, after something Felix said the other day, that I've embarked on a hopeless quest,' she admitted. 'A great many people visit Marsden Wood, and for various reasons. How on earth are we going to find the one, among so many, responsible for the murders?'

'Not by giving up so easily, that's for sure. Let's discover what Stubbs has to say before becoming too disheartened, shall we?' Joss suggested, and with that he gave the mare a hearty slap on its flanks, sending her into a brisk trot, the result of which had them at Bridge House in a very short time.

As arranged, the ex-Bow Street Runner was awaiting the master of the house in the library. There was an empty glass at his elbow, which Joss didn't hesitate to refill with brandy at the same time as he poured out two glasses of wine.

Once he had Gwen settled comfortably in a chair, he took up a stance before the empty hearth, and came straight to the point of the meeting in his no-nonsense fashion. 'So, what have you to tell us, Stubbs? Have you managed to uncover anything at all during the weeks you've been down here?'

'Not as much as I would've hoped, sir,' he freely admitted, reaching in his pocket for a decidedly worn, leather-bound notebook. 'But a few interesting details have come my way, which I'd like to share with you.'

He paused in order to consult his notes. 'The first girl found was farmer Barton's eldest daughter. Now, as you know, sir, I approached him for work, as you suggested, and he were only too willing to take me on, especially after I'd told him what I'm really about. Very useful, he's been, sending me over this way to make deliveries. I'm getting quite friendly with a few of the locals. Your man Manders, to name but one, Lady Warrender.'

Gwen couldn't help wondering what he thought of Manders, but refrained from asking, as the facts thus far uncovered were of far more interest to her.

'Young Mary Barton went missing in the

middle of August in 1815, and were found three days later. Last year in early July a corn merchant's daughter disappeared without trace. But a corpse unearthed a few days after your friend was found, Lady Warrender, is believed to be that missing girl, identified by a bangle she wore. Now they are the girls found. But three others have gone missing in recent years, all during the summer months. One, a flighty young wife of a farm labourer, was thought to have run off with the son of a local carrier. And as there have been one or two sightings of her in recent months in Bristol, I think we can safely leave her off the list. But the other two can't be accounted for, and so could well be further victims of the Marsden Wood murderer. The first to go missing was a Daisy Turner in the summer of 1812. The other, a simple farm labourer's lass, also disappeared in the late summer of 1815.

'So, we are looking at a time span of roughly five years, if the last two girls mentioned were indeed victims, with a gap of three years between the first and subsequent victims,' Joss reiterated. 'Do you consider the long interlude between the possible murders significant?'

'That I couldn't say, sir,' Stubbs responded. 'All I do know is, with the exception of Miss Robbins, all went missing or were murdered during summer months—July or August.'

'Which suggests what?' Gwen put in. 'Not someone local, but someone visiting the area occasionally?'

'It looks that way to me, ma'am,' Stubbs concurred, 'else, why do no females go missing at other times?'

Having digested everything thus far mentioned, Joss said, 'There's a horse fair held every summer on the outskirts of the market town, not so very far away from Marsden Wood. It attracts a good many folk, and not all of them are locals.'

'Aye, sir. I'd discovered that for myself,' Stubbs disclosed, 'and I think it would have been worth while looking into further, if it weren't that certain facts simply don't tally.'

The ex-Runner paused for a moment to refresh himself from his glass. 'The fair takes place every year in mid-August. Which ties in quite nicely with one of the deaths, and one missing girl. But not with the death and disappearance which took place in the month of July. And, of course, not with Lady Warrender's poor friend, neither.' Stubbs frowned heavily, clearly troubled. 'And it's not just that, sir. Those confounded trinkets 'ave got me right puzzled.'

'What trinkets would those be?' Joss queried, a little puzzled himself now.

'Them belonging to the victims, and left on 'em—a bangle on one, a ring on another,' Stubbs quickly explained. 'You know yourself, Mr Northbridge, that them kind of gatherings don't attract many from your station in life. You won't find prime horseflesh for sale at those fairs. No, it's workhorses and the like, sought after by farmers or tradesmen. And I can't help wondering why someone from that order would miss the chance of putting a few extra shillings in his pocket by leaving trinkets on his victims.' He shook his head. 'No, he'd take 'em with him, hoping to sell on later.'

'I think you have a point there,' Gwen announced. 'Don't you, Joss?'

'Possibly.' Clearly he didn't choose to commit himself at the present time, and there was a hint of wariness, too, in his expression as he asked, 'Would I be correct in thinking that you believe, Stubbs, we should be looking for someone not belonging to the lower orders?'

'I'm increasingly favouring that viewpoint,' he concurred. 'So I think it would be a grave mistake not to consider every event that takes place round about that time each year, don't you, sir?'

'You may be sure I'll give it some thought,' Joss returned, after holding the ex-Runner's penetrating gaze for several lengthy moments. 'Nor shall I hesitate to make contact if I should by the remotest possibility uncover anything of interest.'

'I was trusting you would, sir. And I'll do likewise, you may be sure. After all, neither of us would want a further nastiness taking place 'cause we didn't consider every angle.'

After delivering this final parting shot, Stubbs wasn't slow to take his leave. Joss, moving over to the window, watched the wily ex-Runner ride along the drive and disappear from view before saying, 'Well, that's certainly narrowed the field a bit, giving us both food for thought. And I trust it has successfully dispelled a little of your despondency too.'

'It's certainly done that,' Gwen admitted, joining him at the window. It was only then that she detected the deep lines furrowing his intelligent brow. 'What is it, Joss? What's wrong?'

'You heard yourself what Stubbs said. He doesn't think the perpetrator is someone from the lower orders.' His troubled sigh hung in the air for several moments. 'And neither do I. Nor do I believe it's likely to be someone from the middle classes either, as most work for a living, too. Miss

Robbins, and I suspect the others too, was attacked during the day, when most folk are at their labours. So who does that leave, Gwennie? Who isn't obliged to work from dawn till dusk in order to keep a roof over his head, and enough food on the table to feed his family? Who can afford to spend an hour or two during the daytime aimlessly wandering through the countryside, at leisure?'

'Yes, I see,' she responded softly. 'Someone from the privileged class, not unlike you, Joss.'

'Just so!' If possible, his expression was grimmer than before. 'And what event takes place each year at the end of July?'

It took Gwen a moment only to understand precisely to what he was alluding. 'The Cranborne Summer Ball… Oh, my God!'

Suddenly feeling the need for a little sustenance, Gwen returned to her chair in order to reduce drastically the contents of the glass of wine Joss had pressed upon her a short time earlier. 'Do you truly believe there could be a link?' she asked, still hoping against hope that it wasn't so.

Joss wasn't slow to dash them. 'Sadly, yes, I do. And, more importantly, so does that wily old demon, Stubbs. That's why he wants me to involve myself more. It wouldn't be so easy for him to move in the upper echelons of society.'

Even though she had wondered herself about one person closely connected to Cranborne Hall, Gwen still didn't want to believe it could be true. 'It's so hard to comprehend.'

'Let's consider the facts.' Taking the seat opposite, Joss could see at a glance that he held her full attention. 'Most of the women went missing around the time of the ball. It's now the beginning of July. In a week or two people will start arriving at the Hall, and some will stay on until September. The heir, to name but one, spends most of the summer at the ancestral pile, and never fails to bring several of his friends with him. Wastrels to a man!'

As Felix held much the same opinion of his brother's friends and, indeed, of Lawrence himself, Gwen was neither unduly surprised by the disclosure, nor surprised that Joss held a similar opinion, and she was forced silently to own that the forthcoming summer ball was likely to provide many likely suspects among the guests. Yet a niggling doubt remained.

'But Jane wasn't murdered in the summer,' she reminded him. 'Do you think her killer might have no connection with the Hall whatsoever?'

'More likely he has,' he returned without a moment's hesitation. 'You know yourself the grisly details. I was called upon to identify your friend, Gwen. I saw first hand what that fiend is capable of. Not only does he violate and strangle his victims, he also adds to their suffering by using his fists. You don't need me to tell you that what he leaves behind isn't a pretty sight. And the doctor assured me that young Mary Barton, who died in the summer of 1815, suffered exactly the same kinds of injuries.'

His grim expression was proof enough that he hadn't enjoyed the experience, that the image continued to prey on his mind. So Gwen tried to divert his thoughts slightly by saying, 'Correct me if I'm wrong, but I believe what you're suggesting is that whoever is responsible for the murders has been at the Hall in both winter and summer.' Gwen frowned slightly. 'But it would be wrong, surely, to assume that he's a permanent resident, or even a relative of the Earl's? He might be just a regular visitor, a close friend.'

'Quite possibly. And I'm hoping Jane Robbins's murder might well prove to be his downfall, simply because far fewer people stay at the Hall during the winter months. So when I get back, I'll pay a call on the Earl.'

'And don't forget that possible three-year gap

between the murders,' she reminded him. 'Stubbs seemed to think it might be significant. Do you?'

'It could be, yes,' he reluctantly agreed. 'But if I were to tell you that I didn't attend the ball myself during those three consecutive years, simply because I'd accepted invitations to stay with various friends up country, it proves that it would be wrong to point an accusing finger at someone simply because they weren't present during those years. There could be a dozen reasons for the three-year gap—the most obvious being that the killer came across no likely victim. Or that other victims have yet to be discovered.'

Joss was silent for a second or two in order for her to digest this very unpleasant possibility. 'All the same,' he at last continued, 'I will pay a call on the Earl when I get back to see what, if anything, I can discover. He'll not like it, of course, but I'm afraid he's going to have to face the fact that, if not exactly related to, he's possibly very well acquainted with the Marsden Wood murderer.'

For a moment or two Gwen pondered over what his lordship's reaction might be if, sadly, it did turn out to be true. Then she bethought herself of something else Joss had revealed.

'You're going away?'

'Yes, I'll be leaving at the end of the week.' He grinned wickedly across at her. 'Would love to take you with me, naturally. But as I cannot go jaunting about the country with you in a closed carriage without damaging your hitherto flawless reputation, and as I flatly refuse to saddle myself with a confounded duenna, I've decided to ask Merry instead. Like me, he's one or two matters requiring his attention in the capital. Also, I wish to see my wards before they embark on their summer vacation with my sister Alice.'

Gwen felt a definite twinge of disappointment. 'Oh, but I could have had them to stay with me, surely?'

'No, you couldn't,' he countered bluntly. 'You'll have far too much to do organising things for our wedding to concern yourself with entertaining my wards.'

He had made a very valid point, and she readily acknowledged it. 'Yes, I dare say you're right. It's high time I considered my trousseau. Perhaps I might prevail upon you to take a letter to a certain dressmaker in Bond Street, as you'll be staying in the capital. Business is usually slack at this time of year, so with luck she'll be able to make my gown and send it to me in ample time for the wedding.'

Although she knew she would miss him terribly, she tried to make light of their parting.

'And I dare say I can find enough to occupy me until your return. For a start, I might try to discover who was staying at the Hall last summer and at Christmas, and save you the bother.'

'No, you shall not!'

Uncaring that he had made her start by the abruptness of his command, Joss was on his feet, and forcibly drawing her to hers within seconds. 'Promise me, you'll not attempt to discover anything further.' Keeping a firm grasp of her arms, he administered a small shake. 'We're not dealing with a rational being here, Gwen, but a pitiless killer who wouldn't think twice about making you his next victim. Give him any reason to be wary, and he'll strike.' He paused, swallowing hard. 'And I couldn't bear to lose you, after waiting so long for you to cross my path. I would be inconsolable.'

Had she needed further proof of the depths of his feelings for her, she was being given it now. Easily disengaging her arms, she reached up to hold his face between her hands.

'Very well, Joss. I promise that whilst you're away I shan't go out of my way to discover anything further. But once you're back, and I can consult with you again, it will be a different matter.'

And with that he was forced to be satisfied.

Chapter Nine

Although she continued to find much to occupy her during Joss's absence, Gwen found herself all too often wondering what had truly drawn him to the capital at a time of year when vast numbers of those more privileged members of the human race were abandoning the metropolis, with all its unhealthy odours, for the sweeter country air.

Of course, she could quite understand that he wished to visit his tailor to place an express order for a new set of clothes for the wedding, even though this could easily have been arranged by letter, as she herself had done. Furthermore, as they had both been in complete accord in preferring a quiet and simple service, conducted here in the local church by their good friend, the Reverend Mr Harmond, they had spared themselves a colossal amount of anxiety in trying to organise a grand London affair in so short a time.

She could perfectly understand, too, that there were other things for him to arrange. To name but one, he wished to ensure everything was in readiness for a long autumn stay in his town house, where he intended to hold a ball to celebrate their union in order to invite those relatives and friends who would not be receiving an invitation to the marriage ceremony itself. He also had many arrangements to make concerning their sojourn in Italy during the forthcoming winter. So it was true there was much to occupy him. Yet she couldn't help wondering if there was another, very private motive for his visiting the capital.

Again she felt that gnawing sensation in the pit of her stomach. Jealousy was undoubtedly an unpleasant emotion, and one she hadn't experienced up until quite recently. She wasn't so naïve as to suppose that Joss had never kept a mistress. She wouldn't have been at all surprised if he still did, and that he had gone to London with every intention of paying her a visit. If it was to be the final meeting, the last before the termination of their liaison, then she could understand and forgive. But if not…

Setting aside her embroidery, Gwen went

across to the parlour window to stare out at the increasingly pleasing aspect of the vastly improved front garden, while that ever-recurring question tortured her mind. The answer yet again was not long in coming. No, she would not be willing to share Joss with another woman…ever!

To be fair, he had been consideration itself in recent weeks, his lovemaking going no further than the most gentle of caresses, Gwen reminded herself. He had never once taken advantage of any situation by attempting to lure her to a place where they would be completely alone. In fact, the opposite was true. He had ensured that there were always others nearby to come to her if she so wished, both here, at her own home, and at Bridge House. Why, even on those two occasions when they had gone riding together before his departure for the capital, he had always brought one of his grooms along.

Smiling ruefully, she could only wonder at herself for continuing to harbour such doubts about the man she proposed to marry. Almost from their first meeting everything he had done had been an attempt to cherish and protect. Was there any reason to suppose he would turn into an unfeeling monster simply because he had placed a gold band upon her finger? No, of course there was not! All she was suffering from was a rather nasty bout of premarital nerves, for heavens' sake!

The surprising sight of Miss Kershaw turning her mount into the gateway, accompanied by one of the Earl's grooms, succeeded in giving her thoughts a new direction. Although it would have been true to say that she and Anthea had rubbed along quite wonderfully well since Anthea's return from the capital early the previous month, this was the first time the Earl's niece had chosen to pay a visit alone, and Gwen couldn't help wondering what had prompted her to do so.

'Why, what a delightful surprise!' Gwen announced truthfully, when the visitor entered the room a minute or so later. 'I wasn't expecting any callers today.'

'I've not arrived at an inconvenient time, I trust?'

'Not at all! Gwen assured her. 'I'm having one of my lazy days, with no commitments whatsoever. Can I offer you some refreshment? A glass of ratafia, or Madeira, perhaps?'

When the latter was chosen without hesitation, Gwen was almost certain there was something preying on Anthea's mind, for as a rule her newfound friend never accepted anything stronger than a dish of tea when she came to call.

'And I think I shall join you,' she declared in an attempt to put Anthea, who had been wandering aimlessly about since entering the room, at her ease. 'And shall salve my conscience by blaming Joss for leading me into very bad habits. Though I notice,' she added, glancing at the mantel-clock, 'it wants only a few minutes to the noon hour, so perhaps I can forgive him on this occasion.'

This piece of badinage at least drew a weak smile to Anthea's lips before she finally made herself comfortable in one of the chairs. 'You and Joss are so wonderfully well suited. I thought so from the first. I'm so happy for you both.'

Up until that moment Gwen hadn't been sure whether Joss had confided in anyone his readiness to relinquish his bachelor state. It was clear now, of course, that he most definitely had. 'Who told you—Merry?'

'Yes,' Anthea admitted, all at once appearing guilty. 'Shouldn't he have done so? He didn't seem to suppose either of you would mind so very much, though he did make me promise not to spread it abroad, and I haven't.'

'No, I don't mind your knowing,' Gwen assured her. 'I think Joss is attempting to avoid too much fuss until the evening of your uncle's ball. Initially, though, I think his prime reason was to give me a little more time to consider before making the betrothal generally known.'

Anthea appeared surprised. 'Do you still need more time?'

'Not now, no,' Gwen admitted.

'You don't know how lucky you are to be so sure you're making the right choice.'

Gwen studied her visitor thoughtfully over the rim of her glass, before sampling the contents. 'Do I infer correctly from that that Mr Markham has proposed marriage, and you remain undecided?'

She hadn't been altogether sure what response she would receive to this direct approach to what was, after all, a very private matter. She had half-expected an outright denial, or at the very least a response that was totally noncommittal. Not for a moment did she suppose the enquiry would produce a bout of weeping.

Gwen was across the room in a flash and removing the glass of Madeira from Anthea's trembling fingers for safety's sake. 'Oh, my dear, whatever is wrong? Pressure is not being brought to bear upon you to accept Merry's proposal, surely?'

'Oh, no, no. Nothing like that,' Anthea admitted, once she had regained a little control. She even managed a watery kind of smile. 'If anything, I think a certain party will do a great deal to persuade me not to accept him.'

Gwen wasn't slow to comprehend, and decided to leave Lady Florence's views out of the matter for the present time. 'Then, what's wrong, Anthea? Aren't you sure quite yet of your own feelings for Merry?'

'Oh, no. I do love him.' No one could have doubted the admission, least of all Gwen. 'It…it's just that I'm terrified that if I marry, my life might turn out to be just as unhappy as my mother's once was.'

Gwen was stunned by the disclosure and hardly knew what to say. She certainly didn't wish to appear vulgarly inquisitive by asking a great many highly personal questions. Yet at the same time she felt that Anthea needed to confide in someone in order to attempt to overcome her fears.

'I know that it isn't uncommon for many females of your mother's class to have their future husbands chosen for them at a very young age by their parents. Was this true in your mother's case? Was she coerced into a union with your father?'

Anthea wasn't slow to set Gwen straight on the matter. 'Far from it! It was she who was determined to have him. My father, by all accounts, was the epitome of every young girl's dream of a future husband—tall, exceedingly handsome, and a dashing midshipman, with excellent prospects. My mother fell hopelessly in love at their very first meeting. From what I have discovered from various sources over the years, Mama's family were not so impressed with Gerald Kershaw. But as very advantageous alliances had been made for their three other daughters, my grandparents relented, and allowed Mama her way.'

Thankfully Anthea had regained her poise completely by this time, and appeared in no danger of losing it again. 'Please don't misunderstand. I do not think the family, as a whole, deemed my father totally unsuitable to marry the youngest daughter of an earl. He came from an old and respected family himself, and could boast many distinguished and high-ranking relatives. He wasn't precisely a pauper either, and of course Mama's dowry was not insubstantial. So they would be able to live in comfort, if not precisely luxury. Furthermore, he appeared to be doing well in his chosen profession, though whether his eventual rise to captain at such a young age was through ability or patronage is, I believe, open to debate.'

'Evidently, he turned out to be not quite the dashing hero of your mother's dreams, though,' Gwen suggested when Anthea fell silent, staring broodingly down at some imaginary spot on the carpet.

'By the mere fact that she touches upon her marriage so very rarely is testament to its failure,' Anthea, said at length. 'I suspect, although she has never admitted as much, at least not in my hearing, that she realised she had made a grave mistake quite early in the union. Ralph was born within the first year. I followed some four years later. Our father was rarely at home, sometimes absent for very many months at a time. So, naturally, I do not remember him at all well. But what I do recall is a different, almost chilly atmosphere in the house whenever his tall, shadowy figure was present. Mama seemed different too when he was there. My old nursemaid revealed once that she frequently heard Mama sobbing bitterly during the nights whenever Papa was home… One can only guess the reason why.'

'Indeed, yes,' Gwen acknowledged softly. 'And his cruelty, as I recall, extended to your brother also.' She cast an anxious glance at the woman beside her. 'But you did not suffer at his hands, surely?'

'Oh, no,' Anthea wasn't slow to confirm. 'I mercifully was spared his brutality. It might have been different had he not been killed in battle when I had turned five.'

Now she could perfectly understand those deep-rooted doubts and fears of Anthea's, and echoed her feelings aloud. 'But you don't suspect, surely, that Merry Markham's character bears any resemblance to your late father's?'

'Oh, no. I'm positive Merry's not a whit like him in any respect.'

'Well, thank heaven for that!' Gwen exclaimed, striving for a lighter note. 'I was beginning to think my judgement was becoming sadly flawed, and I ought to re-examine my own circumstances.'

Anthea frankly laughed, and it was a relief to hear. 'You and Joss are so well suited. I don't believe you'd ever consider doing that.'

'Don't you?' Gwen was all seriousness again. 'Then it might surprise you to know I was doing precisely that just prior to your arrival.'

Ignoring her visitor's look of combined surprise and scepticism, Gwen took up her former stance before the window. 'I have no intention of attempting to influence your decision where Merry Markham is concerned, Anthea. But all I shall say is this—I love Joss, and I'm positive he loves me.

Whether that is sufficient in itself to ensure we enjoy, basically, a happy marriage, I don't know. I do know that I'm embarking on this union with my eyes wide open, though. I know my future husband isn't perfect; he knows I am not. I can envisage occasions when we'll not be in complete accord, which might lead to periods of discontentment. But if the alternative is a life without Joss at my side, then I'm more than willing to take the risk.'

Although she continued to stare avidly down at one particular area of the carpet, Anthea appeared noticeably less distressed. 'It would be foolish to suppose that any marriage could be perfect all the time, because people are not perfect. I promised to give Merry my answer when he returns from London. You don't know exactly when they expect to be back, do you, Gwen?'

'I'm afraid not. Joss thought more than likely Friday, but it could be not until early next week.'

Although Gwen received a brief note from Joss apprising her of his return, it was none other than Mr Markham who was the first to pay a call early the following week. Happily abandoning the monthly chore of checking the household accounts, Gwen went along to the sunny front parlour to discover a gentleman who bore all the appearance of someone very well pleased with life, though his first words tended to dispute this.

'I'm sorry to be the bearer of sad tidings, Gwen,' he told her, after coming forward to clasp both her hands warmly. 'Joss doubts he'll be able to see you at all today. Mrs Brice, his house-keeper, suffered a seizure some time during the night. Dr Bartlet doesn't hold out much hope. But Joss is determined to stay close by in case she does come round. You know what he's like with his servants, Gwen. And he's known Mrs Brice since he was a boy.'

'Yes, yes, I quite understand,' Gwen responded softly. 'I would go to Bridge House if I thought I could be of some help. Should she recover, Mrs Brice wouldn't wish to find me sitting beside her bed. She would much rather see a familiar face—one of the maids, perhaps.'

'That's true enough,' Merry agreed. 'And Joss wouldn't expect it of you, anyway, Gwen. He's ever practical, even at times like these. Told me that I could be of absolutely no use to him what-soever, and to clear off to keep my appointment with Anthea in the village.' There was undeniably a suppressed excitement about her visitor now. 'And I'm very glad I did. You see, not all my news is bad…Anthea has done me the honour of agreeing to become my wife.'

'Oh, I cannot tell you how pleased I am for you both!' Gwen placed a sisterly peck on his cheek, before pouring out two glasses of wine. 'This is certainly cause for celebration,' she added, raising her glass in a silent toast. 'Does Joss know yet?'

'No. I thought in the circumstances that I'd leave it until tonight. But I was absolutely longing to tell someone, that's also why I'm here. So you must forgive me calling on you in riding gear. Anthea and I have not long parted company, and I haven't been back to Bridge House to change yet.'

'I don't object to the smell of the stables,' she assured him, before something occurred to her. 'Do I infer correctly that you haven't been over at the Hall?'

He nodded. 'Anthea suggested we met somewhere in private.'

'Oh, I see.' Something in her expression must have betrayed her slight feelings of unease, for Merry frankly laughed.

'It's all right, Gwen. Anthea approached her mother, whilst I was in London, in order to prepare the way, as it were. I'm dining at the Hall this evening, but it's merely a formality. Apparently the Earl is delighted. All those occasions I played chess with him in recent weeks must have done the trick. So I expect it was he who put in a good word for me, for Lady Florence isn't wholly against the match, though I don't doubt for a moment she would have much preferred Pont as a son-in-law.

'Which brings me on to something else I wished to discuss with you,' he continued, after at last seating himself in the chair opposite her own. 'I wondered what plans you had for this place after your marriage?'

It was clear that the question had taken her completely unawares. 'Do you know, Merry, I hadn't honestly given the matter a single thought.'

'Then, will you do so now?' He took a moment to sample the wine that his closest friend appreciated above any other. 'As you might possibly know, I do own my own house in London—not large, but at least situated in a fashionable area. For some time now, I've been considering finding a place in the country as well. Anthea likes it here in the West Country, and so do I. And this place of yours is just the sort of property I would want—adequately sized, but not so large as to cost a fortune to maintain. If you are willing to sell, Anthea would be more than happy to settle here. Not only does she like the house and its peaceful location, it would enable her to visit her mother as often as she wished. Which, I must confess, I should prefer. I wouldn't relish the prospect of having Lady Florence residing under my roof for any length of time,' he was honest enough to add.

'Well, I shall certainly promise to give the matter some thought,' Gwen said, clearly not wanting to commit herself at this juncture.

Her visitor wasn't slow to understand. 'Yes, I appreciate you'll need some time to think it over. I know I've sprung it upon you. But at least will you offer me first refusal, if you do decide to sell?'

'You may be sure of it, Merry.'

Gwen saw Joss the following day, when he called to disclose the sad news that his housekeeper had passed away without once regaining consciousness. Understandably, he didn't remain very long, for he had much to do organising the funeral, which was to take place in two days' time.

Gwen herself chose not to attend, but was more than happy to allow Mrs Travis and Annie to pay their last respects to a woman who had been born and bred in the community, and had been respected by all who knew her.

'Church were fair full, ma'am. Even Mr Northbridge attended the funeral,' Annie related on her return. 'Old Mrs Brice were well liked, so she was. No one had an ill word to say about the poor hardworking soul.'

Pausing in the task of sorting through some dresses, Gwen glanced over at her maid. 'Mr Northbridge suspected the service would be well attended. That's the main reason why I chose not to go. I hardly knew Mrs Brice, and I thought it would be selfishly unfair of me to deprive someone who knew her well of being able to sit in church.'

'I'll say this for Mr Northbridge, ma'am—he saw to it she were given a decent send-off. Bid all those wishful to sample ale and a bite to eat to come to Bridge House after the service.'

'Then, why on earth didn't you go, Annie?' A rather disturbing possibility sprang into Gwen's mind. 'You don't imagine surely that I would have objected?'

'On, no, ma'am, nothing like that,' Annie wasn't slow to assure her. 'But me and Mrs Travis didn't want to take advantage, like.' She shrugged. 'Besides, I didn't want to go there, just in case I started getting ideas above my station.'

Gwen, now, was merely puzzled. 'What on earth do you mean by that, Annie?'

'Well, ma'am, stands to reason Mr Northbridge's going to want a new housekeeper. Happen he'll choose one of his other female servants for the position, though.'

'Yes, he might.' Gwen agreed. 'He has three, I believe, if you don't include the cook—two chambermaids and a scullery maid. I think you can discount the scullery maid, as she's little more than a child. And the other two aren't that much older, either, come to that. How old are you, Annie?'

'Fast coming up to five-and-twenty, ma'am, I reckon. Ma always swears I were born the year of the bad summer storm, when the great oak up at the Hall were struck by lightning and burst into flames. Could be seen for miles around, so I've been told. They kept a note of it at the Hall. That's why I know for certain I were born on the 15th August 1792.'

Gwen couldn't help smiling at this. Then she became serious again. She didn't wish to build up the maid's hopes of acquiring a better position, at least not until she'd discussed the matter with Joss first.

'I'm afraid Mr Northbridge might well consider you far too young. But, thanks to your last mistress, you can read and write quite well.

That should stand you in good stead, besides being a hard worker. I tell you what I'll do. I'll raise the subject when Mr Northbridge dines here tomorrow evening, and put in a good word for you, providing you help sort out these things.'

It appeared for several moments that Annie, unable to believe her good fortune, had lost all power of speech. Then she said, frowning, 'What exactly are you doing, ma'am?'

'I'm heartily sick and tired of wearing these clothes, Annie. My period of mourning ends in a week's time, and I'm replacing much of my wardrobe.'

Looking appalled, the maid held up one of the day dresses. 'But 'tis a sinful waste, Mrs Warrender, ma'am! There's plenty of wear left in these.'

'In that case the poor will appreciate them all the more,' Gwen returned, her resolve not weakening one iota. 'I've promised Mrs Travis she may have the black bombazine and the grey one over there, so we'll keep those to one side. If you want to help yourself to the two woollen shawls, do so. The rest can be packed up and sent to the vicarage for distribution among the needy.'

Annie looked longingly at the gown in her hands. 'I wish I were as trim as you, ma'am. I'd snap 'em up in a trice.' She frowned suddenly.

'Our Betsy's about your size, I fancy. Can she 'ave a look at 'em afore they go to the vicarage?'

'Yes, of course. If you can get a message to her, tell her to come tomorrow.'

'Oh, she'll not be able to do that, ma'am, on account of the summer ball being but a week from now.' Annie wasn't slow to note her mistress's puzzled look. 'Don't you remember me telling you, ma'am? Our Betsy's a chambermaid up at the Hall. There'll be no time off for any of the servants now until next month, and the guests start to leave.'

'In that case, Annie, we'll pack these clothes in a trunk and pop them in one of the spare rooms, until your sister is given an afternoon off.'

Having the most beautiful sapphire-and-diamond ring slipped with loving care on one's finger does tend to dominate ones mind, Gwen discovered the following evening. Consequently it wasn't until after she and Joss had enjoyed the intimate little dinner for two, and had returned to the comfort of the front parlour, that her thoughts returned to recent events, both happy and sad, and the promise she had made to Annie the previous day.

'Have you someone in mind to replace Mrs Brice?'

Only for an instant did Joss's gaze stray from

the chessboard, set on the table between them, to cast his worthy opponent a quizzical look. 'Hardly my province any longer, my sweet. Domestic arrangements are your concern.'

'Oh, heavens!' Gwen hadn't for a moment considered this. 'Yes, I suppose they are. Or very soon will be, at any rate.'

'Well, you've only just over five weeks to effect any changes you think might prove beneficial before you move in to Bridge House permanently,' he reminded her, swooping down on a hapless pawn.

'I have no intention of upsetting your existing servants by making drastic changes, Joss,' Gwen assured him. 'Besides which, your house is so well run there's no need for me to do so. Of course, poor Mrs Brice should have taken most of the credit for that, and her demise might change things somewhat.'

Gwen paused for a moment to ponder her next move. 'Do you consider either of your house-maids suitable?'

'Too young, in my opinion. But as I've said already, it's your department, and I'm content to leave such decision-making to you.'

'I'm very pleased to hear it, Joss. But I'd still value your opinion.'

As always, he wasn't slow to understand. 'Evidently you have someone in mind?'

'Yes, Annie Small, the maid I employ here.' Gwen was determined to be totally honest. 'She's young, some would say too young. And I'm inclined to that viewpoint myself. And it's true that she's never held such a responsible position. But to her credit, she's hardworking and completely trustworthy. Added to which she has had the benefit of some education. Her first mistress taught her to read and write. So I'm inclined to offer her the opportunity, if you've no objections.'

'From what you've told me, I think it's worth giving her the chance to prove herself. But what of your present housekeeper? Have you not considered her?'

Totally abandoning the game for the time being, Gwen leaned back in her chair. 'Yes, and that brings me quite nicely to something else that has been on my mind of late. Has Merry told you he wishes to purchase this house?'

Joss nodded. 'Again, though, Gwen, it's your decision. If you wish to keep it, let it, and not sell it, it is entirely up to you. I've no intention of attempting to influence you in any way.'

'But you would like to have Merry living close

by, wouldn't you?' she persisted, striving for a little guidance once again.

'You won't persuade me to influence you that way, my girl!' Joss told her bluntly. 'There are other desirable properties in the area that he might consider.' He smiled at the exasperated look she flashed him. 'All right.' He finally relented. 'If the house doesn't mean that much to you, then sell it. Merry and Anthea will soon make it theirs, and a happy family home, I'm sure.'

'Do you think they're likely to keep Mrs Travis on as cook-housekeeper?'

'Every chance, I should imagine. Having dined here, they both know what a damned fine cook she is. I'll broach the subject with him when I get back, to make certain, though.' Joss paused for a moment to reduce the level in his glass. 'Apart from Annie and your personal maid, is there anyone else you wish to bring with you to Bridge House?'

At Gwen's shake of the head, Joss said, 'I shall offer Ben Small a position. I can see him running my stables in a year or two. I'll not have a stranger in charge of my horses, and I've known young Ben all his life. He might wish to remain here, of course, and, if so, I'm sure Merry will employ him. It'll be Ben's choice.'

'That just leaves the younger brother, Joe. And Manders, of course,' she reminded him carefully.

All at once there was a steely glint in Joss's eyes. 'I don't doubt that Joe's position here will be safe enough, as he's showing every sign of taking after his older siblings. But if you think I'm offering that idle loafer Manders employment, you can think again. And I'll tell you something else for nothing, my girl,' he went on, having warmed to the subject. 'Merry's one of the most easygoing people you could ever wish to meet. But he's no soft touch. If Manders pulls his weight, as he's surprisingly been doing in recent weeks, taking care of the livestock, no doubt Merry will keep him on. But that's his decision, not mine.'

Gwen knew she would be wasting her breath attempting to influence him. Furthermore, it would have been wrong of her to try. She didn't doubt for a moment that he would allow her her way in a great many things. In certain matters, however, he would remain stubbornly resolute.

But that, in part, was why she loved him so.

Chapter Ten

'If I were of a decidedly cynical disposition,' Gwen said, as she and Joss strolled arm in arm into the ballroom at Cranborne Hall, 'I would be exceedingly tempted to suggest that that perfectly delivered welcome of Lady Florence's just now had been in the gravest danger of verging on the icily polite.'

He frankly laughed, inducing more heads to turn in their direction than had already done so, and instigating many more whispered exchanges too. 'If it's any consolation, my darling girl, my own wasn't a deal warmer, remember? So let's be charitable on this occasion and suggest that the evident reserve possibly stemmed from a surfeit of nerves. Her only daughter's betrothal is also to be announced this night, after all, so she must have a deal on her mind. And let us take comfort from the fact that his lordship's words of welcome couldn't have been more genial.'

She readily agreed with his last statement, and suggested it was more than likely that Anthea's engagement to Mr Markham had been looked upon with far more favour by the uncle than the mother. 'Which would be such a pity,' she continued, after successfully picking out the happy couple among the throng. 'How blissfully contented they look! Especially Anthea. She looks positively radiant tonight.'

'As do you, my darling,' Joss returned, his expression easily betraying the well of pride within him to any discerning soul. 'I can say with some experience in the matter that your appearance leaves absolutely nothing to be desired.' His smile grew a trifle lopsided. 'A circumstance that our esteemed hostess wouldn't have failed to note.'

Gwen thought the adornments at her throat and ears most likely to have captured their hostess's attention, rather than any other part of her attire. Might Lady Florence have viewed the glinting gems as a taunting reminder of what her own daughter would undoubtedly have attained had not a newcomer arrived in their midst earlier in the year? Gwen sincerely hoped this was not so, for no thought of attempting to crow over her more financially advantageous union had once entered her head.

When Joss had presented her with the blue velvet box earlier, announcing that it was his chief engagement gift, Gwen had been too overcome by the sight of the beautiful sapphire-and-diamond set to say very much at all, or to consider what feelings the donning of such gems might arouse in any other person's breast. Then her main thought had been that no other adornments could have better enhanced the dress she had chosen to wear that evening.

The silk-and-lace gown, clearly the creation of a supreme dressmaker, was a most unusual colour. A shade or two lighter than navy, it was none the less a much darker hue than any other blue garment on display that evening. Gwen had chosen the colour with particular care to indicate the clear end to her period of mourning, while maintaining the show of respect for a much-cherished late husband.

'She certainly wouldn't have overlooked the adornment you fastened about my throat,' Gwen remarked wryly, at last echoing her thoughts.

'Or any other aspect of your appearance,' Joss countered, studying the small spray of artificial flowers nestling in the perfectly arranged coiffeur. 'More than once of late, I've been foolishly considering trying to persuade you to employ a fully trained abigail at least for the period we remain in town during the autumn. But I see I was doing your precious Gillie an injustice. She's highly competent.'

'Oh, she is,' Gwen hurriedly agreed, 'when I allow her the time to practise her skills. She learned some very useful tips from one of the most accomplished lady's maids you could wish to find, whilst we resided in Italy. The Contessa is never less than impeccably groomed at all times, as you'll discover for yourself when we remain as her and her husband's guests for a few weeks during our honeymoon.'

'I look forward to it,' Joss assured her. 'Just as I shall enjoy a few private moments with Merry now. If you will excuse me, my darling, I shall leave you in Anthea's excellent care.'

Apart from a brief exchange of pleasantries, Gwen didn't attempt to detain his friend, and Joss was able to steer Merry away to a secluded little niche, behind a conveniently sited potted palm, where in his usual no-nonsense fashion he came straight to the point of his engineering a few moments' privacy.

'Discovered anything worthy of note yet, old friend?'

Although Mr Markham had agreed to Joss's request, it wasn't without a deal of soul-searching first. He was brutally aware now, after Joss had confided in him, that he could well be marrying into a family, any one of whom might turn out to be a rapist and murderer. He fervently believed no stone should remain unturned in an effort to bring the culprit to book. All the same, using his privileged position as a frequent, and now very welcome, visitor to the house in order to spy on those guests now putting up at the Hall certainly left a bitter taste in his mouth; and it was only his high regard for his friend's bride-to-be that had influenced his decision to disregard his principles.

'No, not really, except...'

'Yes, go on,' Joss urged, when Merry seemed disinclined to continue.

'Well, it may be nothing. But I seem to recall your saying something about not suspecting the gamekeeper, because when one or two of the tragedies occurred Furslow was attending some prize-fight or other. Very conveniently out of the way, as you might say. And last night at dinner someone mentioned a few bouts of fisticuffs taking place next weekend, and getting Furslow to go along and place bets on for him. It's taking place some distance away, near Bristol, I believe. So the game-keeper's likely to be away for a day or two.'

Joss digested this with great interest. 'Can't you remember who it was, exactly, who brought the topic up, Merry?'

'No, I couldn't swear to it,' he answered. 'You know what it's like when gentlemen linger over the port. And more than just one bottle was passed round the table last night. But I believe I'm right in thinking it was none other than the abominable heir. The Earl himself, and several others, professed a desire to lay bets on the outcome of the main event, even though they expressed no real wish to view the contest for themselves.'

'Interesting,' Joss murmured, his eyes narrowing speculatively.

He himself hadn't received an invitation to dine. Which was quite understandable in the circumstances, as there were so many guests staying at the Hall this year to celebrate Anthea's engagement. Thankfully, though, Lady Florence had been determined to include her future son-in-law in the celebratory feast.

'And who precisely sat round the table at dinner

on the eve of the summer ball?' He listened with intense interest as he learned each and every name. Some he discounted immediately for varying reasons; others he committed to memory, while all the time appreciating the divulger's reluctance to play the tale-bearer.

'I fully understand that to have complied with my request was an offence to your integrity,' Joss assured him. 'And believe me when I tell you I didn't make use of your privileged situation lightly.'

'I know,' Merry responded without a moment's hesitation. 'I know you want justice for Gwen's sake. And I'm willing to continue to discover what I can for that reason.'

'It would be true to say that my bride-to-be still grieves over the loss of her friend. Maybe she always will. But I didn't ask you to discover what you could merely for her sake.' Raising his eyes, Joss scanned the room. 'I couldn't reconcile it with my conscience if I sat back and did nothing, merely because the one I seek is probably none other than a member of my own class.'

'But how can you be so sure, Joss?'

'Without tangible proof I cannot be one hundred per cent certain, of course. But I'm as sure as I can be a cold-blooded killer is mingling with the guests here tonight—someone badly flawed, but not lacking intelligence. He might appear on the surface quite normal, or he may perhaps hide his lethal imperfections behind a feigned display of harmless eccentricity.'

His searching gaze rested on Felix Lucas, but only briefly. 'It's highly likely that, if not prevented, he'll kill again. Realistically, though, it's perhaps the only way we'll ever succeed in catching the fiend. We must cling to the hope that sooner or later he unwittingly leaves some clue as to his identity at the scene of one of his crimes.'

Mr Markham's expression of disquiet had increased dramatically whilst Joss had been airing his views. 'But couldn't we at least attempt to trap him by setting men to patrol the woods, for instance, at least for the next week or so?'

'It's too vast an area, Merry. You'd need an army of men to do the job properly, certainly many more than his lordship and I could spare at any one time. And I can't see the Earl agreeing to organise help from the militia, just on the off chance the murderer might strike.' Joss shrugged, straining the material of his impeccably tailored jacket. 'Besides, how long would it be before word got about that there were an unusual number of people lurking in the woods…days, maybe only hours? Don't make the mistake of underrating this killer, Merry. As I've mentioned before, he's no fool. He's avoided detection thus far by, I suspect, a combination of brains, cunning, and perhaps a certain amount of luck too. He won't seek his next victim if he suspects for a moment something's amiss. If he learns there are men patrolling the woods, he'll either bide his time, or seek to satisfy himself else-where. And I, for one, believe we'll stand more chance of catching the devil if his hunting ground remains in the locale.'

Across the room, Gwen and Anthea had been having a far more pleasant conversation. They had managed to secure two vacant chairs, and as they hadn't seen anything of each other for almost two weeks, they had plenty to discuss, not least of which had been Gwen's decision to sell Merry the house, together with most of its contents.

'I cannot tell you how much I'm looking forward to residing there,' Anthea disclosed. 'I think it's a delightful property, and you've refur-bished it so very tastefully. Why, we can virtually move in without doing a thing, once we're married!'

'It's as much to my benefit as yours to leave most of the furnishings,' Gwen responded, determined to remain practical about the whole business and not become maudlin over the property which had been her husband's home for so many years. 'Merry will probably have told you that I'll be taking one or two items of furniture with me to Bridge House, those pieces that retain some sentimental value, together with the ornaments. But everything else I'm happy to leave behind…with the possible exception of Mrs Travis, that is.'

She was suddenly serious. 'Merry assured me he was quite happy to keep her on, and I cannot deny it was a relief. She's been at the house for so long that she considers it her home, and wouldn't be happy to leave. But are you wholly agreeable to the arrangement? I should hate to think she's being foisted upon you, if you truly would prefer to find your own housekeeper. I can always offer her a place at Bridge House.'

'Don't you dare, or I shall never speak to you again!' Anthea threatened, though not very convincingly as she was smiling broadly. 'I've been to the house often enough to be sure Mrs Travis maintains high standards. What more could anyone want from a housekeeper? Furthermore, she's a first-rate cook. Merry's no pauper, but he cannot afford to squander money on a French chef. No, Mrs Travis will suit us both admirably.'

Thus assured, Gwen didn't dwell on her friend's future domestic arrangements. All the same Anthea's latter remarks had recalled to mind something else that had been troubling her slightly of late.

'I believe I'm right in thinking that the Earl looks favourably on your forthcoming marriage, Anthea. But what about the other members of your family? Are they as pleased?'

Anthea was no fool, as she proved by saying, 'What you mean, my dear friend, is my mama happy about the match.'

Looking slightly shamefaced, Gwen was forced to admit the truth of it. 'Yes, I cannot deny I had wondered how she received the news.'

'I think the best way to describe it is that she's resigned to it. Once she realised there was no possibility of Joss offering for me, and that I was absolutely delighted he was marrying you, she was content for me to marry Merry—not a poor man, by any means—rather than remain a spinster all my days. And our intention to live close by has certainly pleased her.'

'And what of your brother...? He hasn't raised any objections, I trust?'

Anthea shrugged. 'There's no real bond of affection between us, never has been. Truth to tell, if he is genuinely pleased about the betrothal, and it's impossible to tell what Ralph is thinking and feeling most of the time, I suspect it's because he'll now not be burdened with caring for a spinster sister all his life. But my choice of husband would be a matter of complete indifference to him.'

She laughed suddenly, a light tinkling sound of genuine amusement. 'Why! Merry has been more of a brother to me in recent years than ever Ralph was,' she surprised Gwen by admitting. 'Believe it or not, it was precisely how I looked upon Merry at the beginning of our acquaintance. He was always so kind, so understanding, always ready to guide me on to the dance floor, if I'd been sitting by the wall too long.' Her cheeks were suddenly suffused by a becoming maidenly blush. 'Now, of course, I view him quite differently, and look forward to our union in the autumn.'

'A big London affair, from what Joss was telling me the other day,' Gwen remarked, as she began to scan the throng for a tall figure in military uniform. 'Cynical demon that he is, Joss suspected it was a concession made to your mother.'

Once again Anthea's tinkling laughter rose in the air. 'Well, he isn't far wrong. Merry and I would have much preferred a quiet affair, as you have planned. But we're not wholly against marrying in the capital. It makes it so much easier to invite all our friends and relations. Besides which, Uncle Charles insists on footing the bill. It's as much his wish as Mama's.'

Although having listened to everything said, Gwen had also continued to scan the room, and had finally located that striking dark blue dress uniform that she well remembered. 'Who's that talking with your brother?'

'None other than the heir to this pile, Viscount Carstairs.' Anthea's smile was decidedly twisted. 'Handsome devil, isn't he? Don't be fooled, though, by his wealth of charm and good looks. Believe me, it goes no deeper than the surface.'

Blond locks carefully arranged in the ever popular windswept style, the chiselled features of an Adonis and a perfectly proportioned, though not over-large, frame were certainly physical attributes worthy of more than just a casual glance, Gwen decided, before regarding the female beside her with keen interest. 'But you don't care for your cousin Lawrence, do you, Anthea?'

'Oh, I wouldn't go as far as to say that, exactly.

Sometimes I like him very well,' she admitted. 'But I'm not fooled by his displays of geniality. He uses people for his own ends. Whilst he finds their behaviour novel, he'll continue to pay particular attention, instantly raising their standing in society from the mere commonplace to the more noteworthy. But when he becomes bored with someone's company, he can be quite ruthlessly cutting, cruelly excluding them from his intimate circle without suffering the least pang of conscience over any consequences of his actions. Evidently the friends he brought with him last year have already fallen from favour, for his three hangers-on this time are quite different.'

Interesting, Gwen thought, studying each member of the small clique surrounding the handsome Lord Carstairs so intently that she was hardly aware that Anthea had risen from her chair in order to partner a young gentlemen in a set of country dances that was forming. Nor was she aware that the seat had quickly been taken a moment later by a distinguished naval gentleman whom she had met on just one previous occasion.

None the less, Sir Robert Rawlinson had left her with such a favourable impression on that certain evening she had dined at Bridge House that she was delighted to have him bear her company for a few minutes, when finally she became aware of his presence.

'I'm sorry if I startled you, my dear,' he apologised, after catching Gwen's look of evident surprise. 'I'm afraid aching joints tend to make one forgo basic good manners. I hope you don't object to my rudely sitting beside you. Only it grants me the opportunity to congratulate you personally on your betrothal.' He smiled benignly, instantly reminding Gwen of her late husband. 'I've already told Northbridge he's a damned lucky dog. Young Jocelyn's very like his late father. Sound, very sound! I think you've made an excellent choice, m'dear, if I may say so.'

'I rather think I have too, Sir Robert,' she said when he gently raised her hand to study the sapphire-and-diamond engagement ring with evident approval. It was then she noticed that he too was sporting a most unusual signet ring on his right hand.

'Your own ring is rather fine, too, sir. What is that design on it?'

'An anchor, my dear, a foul anchor. See the rope coiled round it? And that beside it is supposed to be a pelican, would you believe? Looks more like an old crow to me! Had it for years. It still retains some sentimental value, though I don't wear it so very often nowadays, on account of having difficulty getting it over the knuckle, even on the little finger. Good job I never married, eh? I don't suppose a wife would take kindly to my removing a wedding band when it grew too tight. There's no joy in growing old, believe me.'

Sir Robert was silent for a moment, watching the striking blue eyes studying the details of his ring just as keenly as they had been regarding someone across the room when he had first sat down beside her.

'Might I be permitted to know who or what was the object of your interest a few minutes ago? You appeared totally absorbed in something, or someone.'

Gwen saw no reason not to enlighten him. In fact, she thought it might well prove beneficial to attempt to attain someone else's opinion of the Earl's elder son and heir.

'Oh, that young wastrel!' The disparaging tone said it all. 'Impudent young pup! Needs a good thrashing! And I've never been an advocate of the overuse of a whip. Quite the opposite, in fact! Still...' he shrugged 'Cranborne's to blame for the lad's turning out as he has. Spoilt him to death, so he did. Should have curbed his excesses years ago—gaming, women and a great many other vices much worse, I dare swear. I can't imagine the likes of him making old bones. If his excesses don't catch up with him eventually, he'll meet a sticky end, you mark my words. He's made scores of enemies, from what I've heard. And he hasn't turned thirty as yet!'

Certainly no admirer, then, Gwen mused, before she was surprisingly offered the opportunity to judge for herself, when none other than the object of the discussion came sauntering over to request her hand in the next set of country dances.

Although it did momentarily cross her mind to decline, and to remain in the far more agreeable company of the distinguished ex-Admiral, Gwen decided on this occasion to disregard her inclinations. Furthermore, she had no intention of causing offence to the present holder of the title, whose treatment of her had never been less than courteous, by rebuffing his son. So the instant Sir Robert had graciously performed the introductions, she allowed clearly the most handsome man in the room to lead her away.

It took her a few moments only to appreciate that his grace on the dance floor was equal to the high quality of his other physical attributes. He was without doubt a most skilful exponent of the art, possibly the best she had ever partnered.

'I must own to an inquisitiveness that borders on the vulgarly curious where you are concerned, Lady Warrender,' he surprisingly announced, as they once again came together in the set.

As he hadn't attempted much conversation thus far, except for one or two rather trite remarks, Gwen was somewhat startled by the frank admission, and didn't attempt to hide the fact. 'Why so, my lord? Without attempting to indulge in insincere modesty, I'm nothing out of the common way, I assure you.'

'On the contrary, ma'am, I'm sure you must be,' he countered. 'And, without wishing to offend, I strongly suspect it was something rather more than a pleasing countenance that first attracted such a die-hard old cynic like Northbridge. Although you do not need me to tell you that you have been favoured in that department also.'

'I know my limitations, sir,' Gwen returned, never having been one to succumb to flattery. 'But if there is a quality in me that attracts Joss, then I suspect it's my partiality for plain speaking and honesty.'

'Really?' One shapely masculine brow was

raised in a perfect arch. 'Admirable qualities indeed, and uncommon nowadays.'

'Oh, I do not think them so rare, sir. It depends, I suspect, on what company one chooses to keep.'

'Ooooh! A sharp tongue and ready wit! You'll do well in London society with those accomplishments, ma'am.'

'Oh, I cannot imagine I would stand out among the throng, sir,' Gwen countered. 'Besides which, I do not consider the present vogue for cruel barbs, maliciously delivered, a substitute for wit.' She shook her head. 'No, you cannot tempt me, sir. Like Joss, I suspect I'd find the majority of society quite shallow, and not to my taste.'

Lord Carstairs's eyes narrowed ever so slightly at this, but he made no attempt to pursue the topic. He merely changed the subject by touching briefly, but with no real show of interest, upon Anthea's forthcoming marriage, before relinquishing his place to his noticeably taller cousin.

Ralph Kershaw, if not quite up to Lord Carstairs's high standard, proved at least competent on the dance floor, and very adept at keeping his shiny sword from becoming entangled in her skirts. At any rate, Gwen certainly wasn't disappointed with the change of partner, for it offered the opportunity to judge for herself the brother's views on Anthea's betrothal. What did disappoint, however, was that his apathy was almost on a par with his illustrious cousin's.

'Don't misunderstand, ma'am,' he added, evidently having not mistaken the look of reproach Gwen did absolutely nothing to disguise. 'I've nothing against Markham. He's not a particular friend, but I know nothing to his discredit. It's simply that I've never attempted to interfere in the lives of the members of my immediate family.' He shrugged. 'Why should I? They do well enough without assistance from me.'

Gwen wasn't at all convinced. She strongly suspected what was nearer the truth was that he'd never concerned himself about his immediate family.

'You're very like your cousin.' It was out before she realised what she was saying. Yet strangely enough he seemed more amused than anything else.

'I hope you're referring to Lawrence and not Felix,' he returned, slanting her a mocking look. 'Yes, we are alike in many ways.' He almost appeared smugly satisfied about it, too. 'Not so much in looks, though there is a faint family resemblance. But certainly in outlook. We're both selfish devils, motivated by pure self-interest for the most part.'

Gwen couldn't even find it within herself to

commend him at least for his honesty. Yet her look of distaste clearly had no effect upon him, at least not visibly, for his expression remained quite inscrutable, before he belatedly congratulated her upon her own forthcoming marriage.

'Anthea, I believe, is genuinely happy for you.' All at once he was more intense, his eyes probing. 'She has come to look upon you as a friend, so I understand. In one way at least you seem to have had a beneficial effect upon her. She is certainly more assertive where our beloved mother is concerned, at any rate.'

There was no vestige of warmth in the smile that unexpectedly curled his lips, and it certainly came nowhere near to lessening the hard, resolute look in his eyes. 'And Mama would do well to look upon her daughter's union with more enthusiasm. Whilst Uncle Charles remains the head of the household, her position here is assured. But there is no guarantee her presence under this roof would be so welcome once the heir takes up the reins. And I know for a fact she wouldn't care to reside under my roof again. So that just leaves her future son-in-law's benevolence, if she doesn't choose to reside alone, or impose herself upon one of her sisters.'

Gwen was as pleased to be rid of Major

Kershaw's company as she was her previous partner's, and almost sighed with relief when she caught sight of a certain tall gentleman, dressed impeccably yet soberly in conventional black evening attire, making a beeline across the room towards her.

'What a callous, self-centred lot we're being forced to mingle with this evening, Joss!' Gwen declared, as soon as Major Kershaw had moved out of earshot. 'I hope you're not going to expect me to play the gracious hostess to them too often after we're married.'

'Shouldn't imagine so, my darling. I don't know half of 'em for a start. And haven't the least desire to, come to that,' Joss freely admitted whilst searching her face for the smallest sign of distress, and blessedly finding none. 'But they're not all so bad, surely? I saw you talking with Sir Robert not so long ago, and looking very well pleased.'

Gwen readily acknowledged the truth of it. 'Yes, I like him a lot. And many others here, too, of course. I like his lordship and his younger son. Felix might be maddeningly vague on occasions, but at least he's got red blood running through his veins, not like that brother of his.'

Joss squeezed her arm. 'Don't worry, my

darling. We shall be very selective in those we invite to our home, after we're married. And talking of which, the Earl is about to announce the engagements publicly. So you'd best mentally prepare yourself to be congratulated by the cream of the county.

Thus adjured, Gwen did precisely that, knowing full well that among those present there were likely to be many of Viscount Carstairs's ilk. But no matter how close she steered towards dark, unfriendly waters, she was convinced the man beside her would always provide a safe haven.

Chapter Eleven

Although she had willingly complied with Joss's preference for a very short engagement, Gwen began to think that maybe it hadn't been the wisest decision she had ever made in her life. The banns were called in the local church for the first time on the Sunday following the official announcement at the Cranborne ball, and from then on she didn't seem to have a moment to herself.

Several return visits to an excellent seamstress in the local market town occupied much of her time, as did the packing away of those items she intended to take with her to Bridge House. Before she knew it a week had passed, and she seemed no nearer to leaving her present abode in good order for Mr Markham to take up residence immediately after her departure. None the less, rushed off her feet though she was, she still found time to make the acquaintance of Annie Small's younger sister when the poor girl, at last relieved of her hectic duties up at the Hall, was granted an afternoon off.

At first glance the sisters seemed so dissimilar in appearance as to make one doubt a relationship at all. Where Annie was generously proportioned, Betsy lived up to her surname. Small and slender, with fair locks, and a complexion that many society ladies would willingly have sold their pearls to possess, she was without doubt extremely pretty. Only on closer inspection could one detect a similarity here and there—in the shape of their mouths, perhaps, and in the colour of their eyes.

'As you've at last managed to accept your sister's invitation to call here, Betsy, I assume things are now much quieter up at the Hall.'

'Yes, thank you, ma'am. Most all the guests have left now.' The young maid didn't add, 'Thank goodness', but one could sense it hovering there on the tip of her tongue, all the same. 'Lord Carstairs is still there. He usually stays for a few weeks… Expect his friends will stay to keep him company too.'

No one could have mistaken the steadily increasing disgruntled tone, least of all the young maid's more worldly elder sister who demanded to know if her sibling was being pestered again.

'Because if so, Betsy, you must tell the house-keeper at once. She'll see to it you're given different duties until the Hall returns to normal.'

'Don't you fret none,' Betsy returned, all at once looking far more cheerful. 'No need for me to tell anyone anything. Master Felix just 'appened along the gallery at the time, and saw Lord Carstairs's friend chasing me out of the bedchamber.'

She shook her head, appearing genuinely perplexed. 'He's a strange one, is Master Felix. Some say he's queer in the top storey. But I don't reckon that's so. Mind you, he can get as mad as fire at times. Gave Lord Carstairs's friend a proper dressing down, so he did. Told him he had the morals of a tomcat. And much worse besides! Reckon he must have said something to his lordship, or maybe Lady Florence, 'cause nothing's 'appened since.'

'And a good thing too!' Gwen announced, after digesting everything the young maid had revealed. She then changed the subject, drawing both sisters' attention back to the trunkful of her unwanted garments. 'If any of these are of use to you, Betsy, you're at liberty to help yourself.'

The young maid held a plain grey dress at arm's length, and gazed at it in wonder, as though it had been the most splendid ball gown imaginable. 'Oh, ma'am, 'tis lovely, so it is! And it won't need a mite of altering, at least not much, just in length, mayhap. And a matching pelisse, too! I shall feel like a princess when I goes to church on Sunday!'

'It could be made a deal more stylish if trimmed with ribbon,' Gwen suggested, without considering that chambermaids weren't paid sufficient wages to squander what little they did earn on unnecessary luxuries.

Then she noticed Annie cast her young sister a sympathetic smile, and rectified her blunder in a trice by adding, 'I believe there are several lengths of pink ribbon in my workbox, Annie. If there's anything there that's long enough, let your sister help herself. I'll leave you together now to sort out anything else that might be suitable.'

When she reached the door, Gwen bethought herself of something else. 'How are you getting back to the Hall, Betsy? I'm going to Bridge House shortly to take some things over, but if you wish to await my return, I'll get Ben to take you back in the carriage.'

'That's kind of you, ma'am, but there's no need

to trouble,' the young maid at last replied, though still looking slightly taken aback by the kind offer. 'The carrier that brought me 'ere said as how he'd be back along this way, if I were to wait at the crossroads by the church at five.'

'Oh, in that case you'll have time to stay for some refreshments before you leave. But make sure you're at the crossroads in plenty of time.'

'I'll see she is, ma'am,' Annie put in. 'Don't you fret none on that score.'

It was quite late in the evening when Gwen became aware that something was wrong, and instantly felt a shiver run through her.

She was sitting alone, an increasingly unusual occurrence, for Joss tried to spend at least part of every evening with her nowadays. That evening, however, he'd been invited to dine with a business acquaintance of his residing some miles away, and didn't expect to return until quite late.

Consequently the house was unusually quiet, and Gwen had little difficulty in hearing the tiny cry, like a stifled portent of doom, emanating somewhere from the back of the house. A moment or two later Martha Gillingham came into the room, the bearer of grim tidings.

Gwen instantly went along to the kitchen to

discover not only her groom Ben trying his best to comfort his, now, quietly sobbing sister, but a young man who bore a keen resemblance to the two siblings seated at the table.

'This be my young brother Jem…Jeremiah, ma'am, 'im that works in the stables up at the Hall,' Ben was the first to explain, instantly rising to his feet at sight of his mistress. 'Seemingly our Betsy ain't back, 'cause no one up at the big 'ouse 'as set eyes on 'er since she walked up the drive early this afternoon.'

'She was to have returned with the carrier,' Gwen reminded them all. 'Did she leave here in good time?'

'That she did, ma'am,' Mrs Travis confirmed. 'Annie walked with her as far as the gate, and watched her heading off down the road.'

'I should 'ave gone and waited with 'er, so I should,' Annie sobbed, still distraught, but thankfully regaining some of her poise.

Gwen, striving to remain calm, considered for a moment before saying, 'The carrier, I assume, resides in town?'

'That he do, mistress,' Ben confirmed. 'Trapp be 'is name, John Trapp. I knows 'im well.'

'In that case, you'd best not delay in saddling up one of the carriage horses and accompanying your brother on a visit to Master Trapp to discover if indeed he did take your sister up beside him on his return journey.' Gwen turned to the younger brother. 'Should you discover she did return with him, get word to his lordship without delay, if you can. It might still be light enough for him to instigate a search of the grounds.' Again her attention focused on her own groom. 'If you discover she didn't return with the carrier, I'd like you to come back here, Ben, and I'll have a letter ready for you to take over to Bridge House.'

It wasn't until late the following afternoon that Gwen had her worst fears confirmed. Joss, grim faced, came striding into the parlour, not needing to utter one single word.

'Oh, no!' Gwen buried her face in her hands, but only for a moment. 'Like the others, I suppose… That poor, poor girl…so young, so dainty.'

Momentarily forgetting himself, Joss uttered a string of colourful oaths as he went across to fortify himself from the contents of the brandy decanter.

'Who found her?' Gwen asked, hoping it hadn't been one of Betsy's brothers, all of whom had been involved in the search since first light.

Her silent prayer was swiftly answered. 'It was Felix, accompanied by one of the Cranborne footmen, who eventually found her. Felix possibly knows those woods as well as anyone. And he's remarkably sharp-eyed too.' Joss shook his head, the memories of the past hours all too vivid. 'Poor lad looked absolutely ghastly. Which is no very great surprise, considering what he'd discovered. It took several swallows from the contents of my flask to revive him enough for his cousin to see him safely back to the Hall,' he went on. 'He was the only one from that crowd at the Hall, apart from Kershaw, that is, and the servants, who offered to join the search.'

No one could have mistaken the disgust in his voice, least of all Gwen, who had grown to gauge his moods with increasing accuracy. 'Be reasonable, Joss. You couldn't expect the Earl to do so,' she pointed out. 'He's hardly a young man, and not in the best of health either, come to that, as he hasn't fully recovered yet from his most recent bout of gout.'

'But his elder son's got no excuse. Nor that bunch of sycophants he has clinging to his every word!'

Gwen couldn't argue with this, and didn't try. Instead she attempted to steer his thoughts in a slightly different direction. 'I assume you searched the area thoroughly. Any clues found?'

Her ploy was singularly unsuccessful. If anything, he appeared grimmer than before. 'No, confound it! God, Gwen, we're dealing with a clever devil here, and no mistake!' He paused to refill his glass yet again from the contents of the brandy decanter. 'There were footprints of course, dozens of 'em. But which belonged to the killer was anybody's guess! By the time Stubbs and I arrived on the scene there was a crowd round the body. Thankfully, Felix possessed the forethought and decency to cover her with his cloak before anyone else turned up. The clothes you'd given her were scattered about. But apart from those, there was nothing else. Stubbs, Merry and I remained after the others had departed and searched the area thoroughly.'

Sighing deeply, Joss fixed his gaze on the wall opposite. 'I cannot help feeling partly responsible for what has occurred.'

Gwen studied his grim expression intently. 'Why so?'

'Because if I had arranged that meeting with the Earl, after my return from London, this latest fatality might have been avoided.'

'Oh, come now, Joss,' Gwen parried. 'If you're

going to take that view, you'll be suggesting next that the carrier, John Trapp should share the blame too, simply because he chose to enjoy the hospitality of some friends of his living in the next village, and stayed far longer than he had intended. He openly admitted that he forgot all about Betsy, and didn't arrive at the cross roads until gone six. It was little wonder the poor girl set off on foot.'

As his look of self-reproach did not lessen, Gwen added, 'Besides, you didn't expect to return from London to discover your housekeeper gravely ill. Your mind was on other things, remember?'

'True. But I still should have sought that interview with his lordship,' Joss countered, clearly still plagued by a guilty conscience. 'I allowed a surfeit of scruples to influence me. I considered it would be exceedingly ill bred to confront the Earl at a time when he was about to host his famous summer ball, and suggest it was highly probable that he was housing a murderer under his roof. I thought to wait for a more appropriate time to broach such an unsavoury matter, with the result that another young woman now awaits burial.'

Realising it would be futile to argue further while he remained in his present guilt-ridden state, Gwen went over to the window and stared out. It had been a thoroughly depressing day in more ways than one. For early August the weather had been very disappointing—humid and overcast since dawn broke, with an ever-present threat of a storm. She hoped it would rain. At least it might clear the air. Would that it were so easy to obtain a clear image of the demon they sought!

'Do you consider the tragic events of the past two days support the theory that the killer is closely associated in some way with Cranborne Hall, or detract from it?'

Joss regarded her in frowning silence for several moments. As he had long since considered her one of the most sensible women of his acquaintance, he could only assume she had been so affected by this most recent tragedy that she wasn't thinking clearly. 'Naturally, it rather confirms it, wouldn't you say?'

'Yes, and no,' she further confounded him by admitting. 'Let's take a moment or two to go over a few facts we do know. Firstly, most of the guests had left the Hall days before poor Betsy Small was murdered. Furthermore, those three friends of Lord Carstairs, at present still at the Hall, have never stayed there before, as far as I'm aware.'

'No, they haven't,' Joss readily confirmed.

'So you would agree, would you not, that we

may safely discount any one of them? To my reckoning, then,' she went on at his nod of assent, 'that just leaves us with three possible suspects— the heir and his brother, and Major Kershaw. I have discounted the Earl himself on grounds of age, though I'm willing to bow down to your superior knowledge. The Earl has only just turned sixty, after all, and perhaps still desires the company of the female sex from time to time.'

Joss ran a finger along the inside of his cravat, as though it had suddenly grown uncomfortably tight. 'I think we may discount the Earl,' he agreed, 'if not entirely on grounds of age, then because these murders have only occurred in recent years, and he's resided at the Hall all his life. So why start now? Besides which, it's highly unlikely he'd go about killing young women, when he could afford a string of mistresses if he so wished.'

'Yes, but that's just the point I'm trying to make,' Gwen returned in a trice. 'It's common knowledge that Viscount Carstairs has had a string of mistresses since leaving Oxford, and before then, I do not doubt. And you told me yourself Major Kershaw has kept at least one mistress in recent years, and no doubt can continue to afford to do so, if he so desires.'

Returning to her chair, Gwen sighed deeply. 'So that just leaves Felix. He doesn't seem at all interested in women, as far as I'm aware. Is that because he's discreet, and doesn't make a habit of flaunting his *amours* in public, as his brother doesn't scruple to do? Is it because he has no real liking for women, or is he merely uninterested? Or has he, perhaps, some dark, secretive reason for wishing to appear slightly indifferent to members of the opposite sex?'

She looked up at him steadily, as though hoping he would provide the answer. Joss, however, was unable to oblige. 'I honestly couldn't say, Gwen, and do not intend to speculate, except in one thing… If the killer turns out to be one of those three you have just mentioned, then I strongly suspect that you, like myself, hope it isn't Felix.'

Gwen nodded. 'But I can't help wondering, Joss. And what's more infuriating, I cannot seem to make up my mind about him. There are occasions when I believe he cannot possibly be involved. Then, at others, I'm unsure again. I'm certain of one thing, though—he isn't quite what he seems. Betsy herself told me that he came to her rescue when one of Lord Carstairs's friends— she didn't specify which one—was pestering her. A knight in shining armour is hardly how one would picture Felix. But his ire was raised that day, though whether through a sense of chivalry, or merely a selfish desire to keep the girl for himself, is anybody's guess.' She shook her head, both troubled and perplexed. 'But surely he's far too intelligent to lead people directly to the body, if he'd perpetrated the deed himself?'

Leaning back in her chair, Gwen released her breath in a long sigh. 'The only thing we can be certain of is that whoever is responsible isn't normal. Oh, but I cannot deliberate any more,' she declared at last, too tired and too distressed by recent events to think clearly. 'We'll discuss this again, Joss, when I'm more myself.'

Three days later, the very day after the funeral, Gwen was no clearer in her mind, when she received an unexpected visit from none other than Felix himself, accompanied by his cousin Anthea.

'I'm sorry to impose upon you like this,' her friend declared, as she swept into the parlour, shortly before noon. 'I'm sure with organising your move to Bridge House you could well do without unexpected visitors. But Felix and I would have gone insane if we'd remained at the Hall a moment longer.'

'On the contrary, it's lovely to see you both,'

Gwen assured them. 'I'm sick and tired of my own company. I'm tending to brood far too much over recent events.'

'Oh, by Jove, yes! Terrible it was! Can still see her lying there beneath that beech tree. Expect I always will,' Felix admitted, after sampling the wine Gwen had handed to him. 'Pretty little thing she was, too. One of the best chambermaids we've ever had up at the Hall. Always liked her to tidy my room. Never moved my things about—bless her!—unlike the others.'

After listening to this declaration, Gwen was, if anything, more confused than ever. Once again she found herself unable to believe Felix could be responsible. He had sounded so very sincere.

'I understand from Mrs Travis that you both attended the funeral,' she said, turning her attention once again to Anthea.

'Yes, Felix and I represented the family. There was quite a gathering. She was laid to rest beside her father in the servants' graveyard.'

'Little wonder you wished to get away. I can imagine the atmosphere up at the house must be pretty grim at the present time,' Gwen remarked, in an attempt to prevent a lull developing in the conversation.

'Ha!' Felix exclaimed disparagingly. 'At least

some of us know how to comport ourselves. Father, of course, is most upset. Not only was one of his own people involved, but the dreadful deed was committed on Cranborne land this time. A little too close to home for comfort, as you might say.

'He seemed even more concerned after he'd received a visit from Northbridge the other day,' he went on to disclose, thereby revealing to Gwen that Joss had at last talked over his suspicions with his illustrious neighbour. 'Ensconced in the library for most of the morning, they were. The Lord alone knows what was discussed, but Father's been going about hardly saying a word to anyone, least of all Lawrence, who carries on as though nothing untoward has occurred. Laughing and jesting with those mindless cronies of his… They make me sick!'

'Don't fret yourself so, dear,' his cousin soothed. 'I heard it from Mama's own lips that he doesn't intend to stay for very much longer this time, in view of what's occurred. A further week at most.'

'And good riddance is what I say!' Felix clearly wasn't one iota appeased. 'I tell you what, Anthea, as soon as he comes into the title, I'm off! Couldn't stand to reside under the same roof as him for long.'

'You're fortunate enough that you won't be

forced to do so,' Anthea reminded him. 'You've money enough of your own, so don't worry on that score any more. Instead, turn your mind to why you accompanied me today, or have you forgotten?'

'Oh, by Jove, yes!' Finishing off his wine, Felix rose at once to his feet. 'If I might leave my cousin in your care for a while, Gwen? I'll just pop along the road to see Miss Harmond. Promised her at the ball I'd take her in to the woods one afternoon to search for a certain rare orchid. But that's out of the question, now, with that madman still on the prowl. So I thought I might invite her and her mother over for tea one afternoon, instead, and she can explore our gardens. Very keen on plants she is, sensible girl! So, I'll be off now.'

Gwen was so stunned it took a deliberate effort to stop herself from gaping after him as Felix left the room. 'Miss Harmond…? Not Caroline Harmond, the vicar's eldest girl, surely?'

Anthea, wickedly smiling, nodded. 'Isn't it wonderful? And it's all due to you, Gwen. As we always worship in the church on the edge of the estate, Felix had never seen her before. They met for the first time here, at your delightful dinner party, remember? That's why he was so cross about that goose of yours. It startled Miss Harmond whilst he was escorting her round the garden. He wouldn't have cared a jot about the incident otherwise. It was he who insisted she receive an invitation to the ball.'

Anthea laughed again at Gwen's look of utter amazement. 'Didn't you notice how much attention he paid her? He even danced with her twice. And Felix never stands up as a rule, though heaven knows why not. In my opinion he's equal to his brother on the dance floor.'

Gwen shook her head, still somewhat bewildered. 'And here I was thinking he was totally indifferent to our sex.'

'To be truthful, I don't think he notices we're there much of the time. All the same, I don't believe he dislikes females. At least he adored his mother.'

'Did he? That's the first I've heard about it,' Gwen admitted.

'Oh, yes, he did,' Anthea reiterated. 'It was she, in fact, who nurtured his interest in wildlife. They often ventured out together, seeking rare species of wildflowers. He loved her so very much, and still misses her dreadfully.'

All at once Anthea appeared a little subdued. 'I wish Ralph held our mother in such high regard. I have sometimes caught him staring at her with such contempt in his eyes that I think he almost hates her. Then he confounds me by displaying such consideration towards her that I become convinced I've allowed my imagination to run away with me again. It really is most odd!'

Directly after luncheon Gwen received yet another unexpected visit, only this time it was from none other than a member of her own household to whom she had willingly granted leave of absence.

'Annie, what in the world are you doing back here so soon? I told you you might remain with your mother until you felt able to resume your duties.'

'I know you did, ma'am, and it were right kind of you too. But I'm as one with our Ben. He's wanted no time off, 'cepting to go to the funeral, o' course. And I fancy he's got the right of it, ma'am—brooding ain't going to bring our Betsy back. Staying at home with Ma and the young 'uns ain't doing me a mite o' good neither. Work's the best thing. So, if you're agreeable, I'd like to take up my duties again tomorrow. But I were wondering if you'd allow our Ben some time off this afternoon. Just an hour or two, so he can walk with me to the woods. Might seem strange to you, ma'am, but I'd like to see for myself where it 'appened, and maybe place some flowers there.'

'I don't think it strange at all, Annie. And of course you both may have time off. And if you don't object, I'd like to accompany you, and we'll take the carriage. I didn't attend the funeral because, as you know, I considered it a time for friends and family. I hardly knew your sister. But I should like to pay my respects by accompanying you today.'

They left the house an hour later, taking with them flowers, freshly cut from the garden, and Manders, who came along in order to take care of the horses whilst Ben showed them the way to that very poignant spot.

He had no difficulty whatsoever in locating the large beech tree under which the bruised and battered body of his much-loved sister had been discovered after an intensive search. He had tied the length of pink ribbon she had taken with her on that fateful afternoon to the lowest branch, where it now fluttered gently in the light breeze.

Ben didn't remain with them. He moved several yards away, his back turned, as though he couldn't bring himself to look upon that place where his pretty sister had met her end. And

Gwen, at least, could perfectly understand why. Except for that length of pink ribbon marking the spot, there was nothing, absolutely nothing at all to indicate that such a tragedy had occurred at their feet a few days before. It was all so tranquil, so lovely, with just the faintest of breezes rustling the leaves, and bright rays of light piercing the lush, green canopy high above their heads.

With a suppressed sob, Annie placed her flowers upon the ground, before turning abruptly and rejoining her brother. Gwen remained, allowing the siblings a few minutes alone together with their thoughts and their grief. Then, very slowly, she knelt to place the bunch of flowers she held next to her maid's.

At precisely that moment the sun once again broke through the clouds, its shafts of light darting across the dark, peaty woodland earth. It was then she saw it, glimmering briefly—something shiny tucked beneath the edge of one of the exposed, gnarled roots of the tree.

Reaching out, she grasped the tiny, gleaming object, and placed it in the palm of her hand. There was no need for her to study it intently, for she recognised it at once… And remembered all too vividly precisely where she had seen it before.

Chapter Twelve

'I simply can't believe it…won't believe it! It cannot be true. He must have lost it…mislaid it. Perhaps even Betsy herself found it whilst cleaning the ballroom, after the spectacular event had taken place, slipped it into her pocket for safekeeping, fully intending to hand it over to the housekeeper, and had merely forgotten all about it. Yes, that must have been it!'

'What's that you're saying?' Martha paused in the act of hanging the recently laundered day dress back in the wardrobe to look across at her mistress, who had seemed in a strangely subdued mood since her return from Marsden Wood the previous afternoon. 'You shouldn't have gone with Annie and Ben, Miss Gwennie. It were bound to upset you. And here you are now talking to yourself, like a half-wit.' She tutted.

'What with attempting to put together some sort of trousseau, not to mention trying to put the house into good order before Mr Markham moves in, I think it's all been too much for you.'

Completely disregarding the maid's assertion, Gwen continued to stare down intently at the small, shiny object nestling in the palm of her left hand, though she kept her disturbing thoughts to herself this time.

In fact, she had confided in no one about her discovery, not even Joss, who had dined with her at the house the previous evening. Just why she had continued to keep her own counsel, she couldn't have explained. She only knew that until she was absolutely sure, she didn't intend to point an accusing finger at anybody.

'I'm so sorry, Gillie,' she apologised, suddenly realising her maid had spoken again. 'What did you say?'

'I said, do you want that I should lay out your new riding habit? I seem to recall Mr Northbridge saying, before he left last night, about taking you out this morning.'

'Yes, he did,' Gwen confirmed. 'Unfortunately, I shan't be able to keep the appointment. It quite slipped my mind that I had promised to call in to see the dressmaker some time this week for a final fitting.'

Rising from the dressing table, Gwen joined her maid over by the wardrobe and took out a pelisse and a particularly dashing bonnet trimmed with blue ribbon.

Martha frowned. 'But I thought you said you'd go tomorrow.'

Gwen was obliged to acknowledge the truth of this. 'So I did. But I need to see someone quite urgently, and as he resides on the outskirts of the town, I may as well call in at the dressmaker's whilst I'm there, and save myself the bother of doing so tomorrow.'

'Do you wish me to accompany you?'

'No, Gillie. I want you here to ensure that Manders saddles up the pony and rides over to Bridge House, directly after I leave, with my letter of apology, otherwise he's likely to take his own sweet time about it and Mr Northbridge will arrive here expecting to find me at home. Besides which, you know Ben always takes such excellent care of me, and never allows me out of his sight for very long without making enquiries.'

As this was true enough, and Ben had quickly become devoted to his mistress, Martha didn't attempt to argue the point, especially as she had already decided that in all probability the other errand was merely a visit to Dr Bartlet in order to obtain a draught to settle what must surely be premarital nerves.

The instant the maid had departed, Gwen remained in her bedchamber only for the time it took to collect a metal object that she kept safely concealed at the back of the wardrobe, and to write two quite separate letters to Joss, one of which she slipped together with the metal object into her reticule. The other she handed to her maid before going out to the carriage that was already awaiting her at the door.

Throughout the journey to the town, her mind remained in turmoil, a mass of conflicting thoughts. Not even the superb results of the local dressmaker's highly skilled labours could distract her from her real purpose that morning. Consequently, the instant she had satisfied the dressmaker's fastidious eye with a final fitting, she wasted not a precious moment in returning to the carriage in order to achieve her main objective.

In no time at all Ben was drawing up outside a fine brick house. Very like her own in size, and set in a well-maintained garden, the property was undoubtedly one belonging to a gentleman of means and good taste.

The instant she alighted from the carriage her nostrils were assailed by the sweet, unmistakable scent of roses. They grew in profusion everywhere: round the door, along the house walls, gracing what seemed every bed and every corner of the garden.

Gwen frowned as she took a moment to gaze about her, recalling the admission made by the owner of the property that evening when he had sat beside her at table on the first occasion she had ever dined at Bridge House: 'My very favourite flower, my dear,' he had confessed. 'One of the very few things I really missed during my frequent absences from these shores.'

How clearly those words came back to her now. She shook her head. It just didn't make any sense at all. How could someone who loved what must surely be the most romantic of flowers be responsible for such terrible, cruel acts of violence against her sex? He simply couldn't be responsible! There had to be some other explanation… There simply must!

'Are you all right, ma'am?' Ben gazed down in some concern. His kindly mistress seemed disinclined, almost fearful to make the visit now she had arrived at her destination. 'Do you want that I should call for someone to take charge of the 'orses, so that I can, mayhap, escort you inside?'

'No, thank you, Ben. I shall go in alone.' Moving closer to the carriage, Gwen gazed up earnestly. If the worst should happen, Ben must remain safe to relay her gravest fears. 'If I should fail to return within the half-hour, and you are unable to locate my whereabouts, for whatever reason, then I want you to take this to Mr Northbridge without delay.'

She offered no further explanation. She merely handed up the second letter bearing Joss's name, written in neat, sloping characters, and then walked resolutely up to the front door.

Her summons was answered almost at once. Unfortunately the individual who appeared before her, blocking her entry into the house, did little to boost her confidence. Although dressed in smart black livery, he bore little resemblance to any servant she had ever seen before. Small, yet stocky, he had hands the size of shovels, a broken nose and one badly misshapen ear that was very much larger than the other, all of which led her instantly to suppose that his activities at one time might not have been quite as respectable or genteel as they were now.

'Is your master at home? If so, perhaps you would tell him Lady Warrender has called and would appreciate just a few minutes of his time?'

Disconcerting in appearance he might have been, and yet he evidently recognised the name, or had swiftly decided she was a virtuous young woman, visiting for a legitimate reason, for he moved instantly to one side to allow Gwen to enter the small, neat hall.

'If you'd take a seat, ma'am, I'll let the master know you're 'ere,' and so saying he disappeared into a room on the right, returning a few moments later with none other than Sir Robert Rawlinson at his heels.

'Why, Lady Warrender, what a delightful surprise!' Something in her expression, as she rose to her feet and gave him her hand, must have alerted him to her troubled state, for he added almost immediately, 'My dear child! There's nothing wrong, is there? You've not been forced to cancel the wedding for any reason, I trust?'

'Oh, no, no, sir, nothing like that,' she swiftly assured him.

'Well, thank heaven for that! I cannot tell you how much I'm looking forward to it, or how very honoured I feel to be one of the few hereabouts to receive an invitation.'

His delight was all too evident, and almost more than Gwen could bear. She was consumed by an acute feeling of guilt, not to mention disgust at herself, for continuing to harbour the suspicion, slight though it was, that an hon-ourable gentleman might possibly be responsible for a series of such heinous crimes. Yet she had to be sure, and her resolve to discover the truth withstood the ever-increasing pressure of self-reproach as he guided her into a comfortable parlour.

'May I offer you some refreshment? Can I tempt you to join me in a glass of Madeira, perhaps?'

'No, thank you, sir, I want nothing,' Gwen answered, all the while staring at his right hand. 'I came here on what you will perhaps consider a very strange errand—to ask about that very unusual ring you wore on the night of the Cranborne Summer Ball. But I see you're not wearing it today. Not mislaid it, I trust?'

His expression remained one of sublime un-concern. 'No, I shouldn't imagine so. As I believe I mentioned to you, I don't wear it much on account of swollen joints. Old age, m'dear, terrible thing. Find it the most fearful trouble to remove these days.' He turned to his odd manser-vant, who had remained dutifully hovering a few feet away, awaiting further instructions. 'Run along upstairs, Stebbings, and bring down the trinket box off the dressing table, would you? There's a good chap.'

Sir Robert then moved across to a side table, and had only just made his selection from the contents of various decanters, when his strange major-domo, who evidently was regarded as more than a mere servant, returned and promptly handed him a small wooden box.

The briefest of searches among the contents was swiftly rewarded. 'Ah, yes, here it is!' Clasping it between finger and thumb, he held it aloft almost triumphantly. 'Thought I'd placed it back in the box, after I'd returned from the ball the other night. Haven't worn it si—'

Sir Robert broke off abruptly as he noticed his delightful guest unexpectedly slump down into one of the chairs and rest her forehead in her hand. 'Why, my dear child! You're as white as a sheet. Are you not feeling quite the thing?'

'I assure you, sir, I feel better than I have for quite some few hours. It's just the relief, I expect.'

Evidently he didn't quite believe her, for, after dismissing his servant, he insisted that she join him in a glass of Madeira. 'I recall your showing some interest in that ring on the night of the ball,' he said, after he had the satisfaction of seeing her sip the wine and seeing, too, a semblance of colour almost immediately afterwards returning to her cheeks. 'I thought perhaps you'd some notion of attempting to have it copied as a present for that future husband of yours. But I suspect now your reason for coming here is rather more serious.'

Gwen didn't attempt to deny it. She merely drew out the ring she had found the previous afternoon and, reaching forward, placed it into Sir Robert's outstretched hand. 'Foolishly I had imagined your ring was unique. Clearly, sir, it is not.'

Without responding, he studied the ring intently for several moments, paying particular attention to what had been inscribed inside. Then he lowered his quizzing glass and looked directly back across at her, his gaze level, and betraying no evidence of bewilderment whatsoever.

'The inscription is identical to that in my own—*With undying gratitude, E.E.* Therefore I must assume it came from the same source as my own—namely, one of the eight rings commissioned by a Mr Edward Emerson.'

'Eight rings, sir?' Gwen echoed.

'Yes, one given to each serving officer on board *The Pelican*.' Taking a moment to sample his wine, Sir Robert leaned against the back of his chair, his eyes taking on a faraway look, as though seeing something from the distant past. 'We had been on duty in the West Indies for almost three years, attempting to stamp out piracy, and were heading homeward, looking forward to some well-deserved leave, when we pulled Edward Emerson out of the water. A wealthy British merchant, he was a frequent visitor to the islands. Only on this occasion he wasn't so lucky. His ship was taken by a particularly vicious gang of cut-throats. He and the crew were either cut down or tossed overboard. In fact, when we found him, clinging to a piece of driftwood, he was more dead than alive. Needless to say the surgeon on board succeeded in keeping him alive. In recognition Emerson gave a ring to each and every serving officer on board, both commissioned and warrant.'

'Can you recall the names of your fellow officers on that particular mission, sir?' Gwen asked, after digesting everything she had learned.

He remained silent for a full minute, merely staring down into the contents of his glass, then he raised grey eyes brimful of sadness. 'Yes, my dear, I recall quite clearly. Not all the recipients were as touched by the merchant's gesture, as I was. One or two of the rings were sold many years ago, others were never worn. Only one name, I suspect, will be of interest to you, however. But before I divulge it, might I be permitted to know precisely when and where this particular ring was found?'

Gwen's eyes never for a second wavered from the ex-Admiral's face, as she revealed, 'I found it myself, sir, yesterday afternoon in Marsden Wood, at the very spot where a young maidservant's body had been discovered only days before.'

'Oh, dear God!' Sir Robert's despairing groan was clearly audible. 'I feared as much…I'd heard of the latest murder, of course. News of that sort spreads so swiftly… Poor, poor Florence, as if she hasn't suffered enough over the years.'

'Ralph Kershaw, of course,' Gwen murmured, suddenly remembering confidences and a string of incidents that only seemed to corroborate his guilt in her own mind. 'His father was on board that ship?'

'Yes. Like myself, he was a midshipman at the time,' Sir Robert revealed. 'Some say his success over the years was achieved through competence; others put it down to sponsorship—knowing the right people. No one can deny, though, that he had courage. He was a brave captain, if an unnecessarily brutal and unforgiving one. It was common knowledge throughout the Navy that more floggings took place on his vessel than on any other ship of the line. It was said that he never so much as batted an eyelid if a man died under the lash. My man Stebbings can testify to the brutality that took place. He was a conscript on board Kershaw's ship at the Battle of the Nile. Unlike his captain, he survived. It was I who pulled him from the water. And he's been with me ever since, more than once repaying me for the good turn I did him. He's but one of many who still bears the marks on his back of Kershaw's cruelty.'

'And, unless I'm much mistaken, his viciousness was not confined to his life on board ship,' Gwen remarked softly, having now recalled other details revealed by several different people over the past months. As she suspected that the man sitting gravely opposite knew as much, if not a deal more than she did herself, about the Kershaw family, she chose not to elaborate, and merely remarked, 'Presumably Captain Kershaw left his ring to his son. Now I can clearly recall Ralph sporting a signet ring on the evening I held a dinner party at my home. If my memory serves me correctly, unlike you, he wears it on the third finger of his left hand.'

Sir Robert nodded. 'Yes, I have seen it there

myself on several occasions in recent years. I have witnessed too that same pitiless look in his eyes that his father's frequently betrayed... Perhaps I should have guessed...at least suspected. Perhaps at the back of my mind there always lurked the suspicion that he had inherited his ruthless sire's pitiless nature. But for his mother's sake I suppose I tried to convince myself it was quite otherwise.'

He was silent again for several moments, evidently locked in his own private world. For her part, Gwen was happy to leave him there, for she herself had much to consider. Then, as if able to read her thoughts, he said unexpectedly, 'So what are you intending to do now? Finding that ring will not prove his guilt. You must surely appreciate that? He might merely say the ring was lost or stolen, and he thought it not important enough to mention.'

Gwen had already considered this very real possibility. 'Yes, I know, sir. But somehow he must be made to give himself away. It will need some careful thought. I must consult with others without delay.'

This drew his full attention. 'Do I infer correctly from that that no one knows of your present whereabouts?'

'No,' Gwen answered with complete honesty. 'With the exception of my coachman, that is.'

'Good God, child!' Sir Robert's expression was one of staunch disapproval, not untouched by dismay. 'You took an awful risk. Supposing I had been responsible?'

As she had remained for the most part unmoved by Mr Jocelyn Northbridge's forcefully voiced strictures in recent months, Gwen wasn't likely to be much affected by the kindly ex-Admiral's mildly worded disapprobation, and was not. She merely rose to her feet, complete mistress of her emotions.

'It was a risk, perhaps,' she acknowledged, smiling as he too rose. 'But a very small and calculated one. The daughter of a clergyman, I was raised to try to see good in everyone. But I'm not a fool, sir. Nor am I such a bad judge of character either.'

Reaching for his hand, she retained it in her own. 'Let me assure you, I came here because I wanted to justify my belief that you couldn't possibly be responsible for those poor women's deaths, not to prove your guilt. I'll concede I didn't consider for a moment the possibility that more than one of those rings existed,' she went on to admit. 'Sadly, though, I don't think we need look further afield than Cranborne Hall for the guilty party. And, by your own admission, neither do you. There was just something about Ralph Kershaw I never liked from the first. And the more I think about it, the more convinced I become that he is responsible.'

The clasp of his fingers grew stronger as he now held on to her hand. 'Promise me, child, that you won't confront him alone…you won't go to Cranborne Hall?'

'I can safely promise you that,' she returned, without even having to consider the matter. 'I'm for Bridge House.' She smiled that soft, captivating smile that had so quickly broken through Joss's cynicism and captured his heart. ' And will you promise me something…? Will you promise to say and do nothing until you hear from either Joss or me?'

Gwen wasted no time in reaching the house that was soon to become her home. She was momentarily taken aback to be admitted into the hall by none other than Annie Small. Her thoughts had been so consumed by her monumental find of the previous afternoon that she had quite forgotten that it had been agreed between them on the return journey from the wood that Annie should take up her duties at Bridge House the following morning.

The newly appointed housekeeper smiled broadly, the first she'd managed since learning of her sister's death. 'Well, ain't that just like you, ma'am, to look in to see how I go on. I must confess I'm finding it all a bit strange, and expect I will for some time yet. But the staff here seem friendly enough, and I'm enjoying the extra duties.'

'That's good,' Gwen responded, experiencing a twinge of conscience, but insufficient to tempt her to lie in order to spare someone's feelings. 'Truth is, though, Annie, I didn't come here with the intention of discovering how you were getting along. I've the utmost faith in you and am sure you'll do very well, once you've found your feet. And no one expects you to do that in a trice. No, I'm here for one reason only and that is to see your master. And the matter is urgent.'

Such was Annie's understanding of the easy relationship that had existed between her mistress and the master of Bridge House from the first that she didn't even attempt to announce Gwen, and merely informed her where her fiancé was to be found, and that he was not alone.

Joss was slightly surprised when she swept into his parlour. This was not because she had arrived unannounced, of course. It was merely that, after receiving her brief missive cancelling their ride, he had thought she must be feeling slightly under the weather, and had made up his mind to call on her later in the day, when he had hoped to find her feeling more the thing.

Rising instantly from his chair, he captured both her hands. He then took a moment to scan the sweet face he had swiftly grown to adore, and was satisfied with what he saw. 'Evidently you've recovered from your slight megrim.'

'I've suffered no indisposition, Joss,' she assured him, as she seated herself in a chair. 'I've merely been deeply concerned about a certain matter.' Without enlightening him further, she turned to his companion, who had also risen. 'I didn't expect to find you here, Merry. I thought you'd be escorting Anthea out on her ride.'

'I do usually, as you know, weather permitting. This morning, though, she wished to accompany her mother to town.'

'Really? I didn't see them there.'

Joss wasn't slow to digest this snippet. 'Oh, so that's where you've been! So you, too, prefer marketing to spending time in the company of your fiancé?'

Gwen wasn't fooled by the look of mock-hurt. Nor did she allow herself to be distracted from the seriousness of her visit. 'My reason for visiting the town was a deal more significant than a mere desire to visit my dressmaker.'

The soberness of her tone was lost on neither gentleman, least of all Mr Markham, who once again rose to his feet. 'Well, if you'll both excuse me? I've a letter or two I must write.'

'Please do not feel obliged to leave on my account, Merry,' Gwen adjured him, thereby instantly arresting his progress across to the door. 'In fact, I should much prefer it if you remain. What I have to disclose will, I'm afraid to say, ultimately concern you.'

Clearly intrigued, he didn't hesitate to return to his chair by the hearth. Before Gwen could satisfy the evident curiosity of both gentleman, however, an interruption occurred in the form of the housekeeper, who didn't delay in apprising her new master of the fact that there was someone by name of Stubbs wishing to see him.

'And I'm obliged to point out, sir,' Annie added, looking faintly troubled, 'he don't seem quite the thing to me. At any rate he ain't no gentleman, that I do know. And I wouldn't have allowed him into the house, 'cepting as 'ee did say as how you were expecting a visit from him.'

Perfectly understanding his housekeeper's reluctance to admit someone dressed so roughly into a gentleman's abode, especially by way of the front entrance, Joss couldn't prevent a ghost of a smile, even though he was more than just moderately concerned over his future wife's strangely sombre mood. 'You did quite right to admit him,' he assured her. 'Perhaps you'd be good enough to show him into the library and furnish him with a glass of brandy. Tell him I'll be with him presently.'

'I think Mr Stubbs should hear what I have to say too,' Gwen countered, before Annie had a chance to carry out the instructions. So Joss, more intrigued than ever now, nodded his head in agreement, before rising to his feet and pouring his visitor a glass of brandy himself.

'Good to see you,' he greeted the ex-Runner, when Stubbs entered the room a few moments later. 'No doubt you're here to confirm that Furslow was indeed attending that prizefight near Bristol on the day of the latest tragedy.'

'Aye, sir,' he concurred, gratefully accepting the generous measure of his particular favourite tipple. 'The gamekeeper stayed overnight at a wayside inn and didn't get back until Sunday afternoon. There are plenty who'll confirm it too.'

'So, we're back where we started,' Mr Markham put in, sounding decidedly disgruntled. 'We're no closer to discovering who has committed these terrible crimes.'

'On the contrary,' Gwen countered softly. Rising to her feet, she moved across to the window, the cynosure of all eyes. 'I'm very much afraid I now do know the precise identity of the killer.'

Anyone observing the recipients of the startling revelation would have been hard put to it to say which of them appeared most stunned. It was Joss who eventually broke the ensuing silence.

'Are you sure about this, Gwen?'

'Yes, I'm sure. I'm also sure the evidence I've uncovered thus far will be insufficient to convince a jury of his guilt.'

Gwen turned away from the pleasing aspect beyond the window to study the sombre expressions of the three other occupants of the room, all of whom had listened intently to everything she had said. 'Somehow he must be made to confess his guilt before witnesses. And that, I'm certain, will not be so easy to achieve.'

Once again it was Joss who broke the ensuing few moments' silence by demanding to know where she had been that morning. 'Who have you been to see?'

'After discovering a certain object in Marsden Wood yesterday afternoon, I felt obliged to call upon Sir Robert Rawlinson to ascertain if my find belonged to him.'

'You went to the wood?' Joss's tone was anything but mild, but Gwen wasn't unduly ruffled by it, and returned to her chair.

'Yes, I accompanied Annie. We placed flowers on the spot where her sister met her untimely end.'

Joss wasn't one iota appeased to learn that she hadn't ventured there alone, and it clearly showed in the taut line of his jaw and tightly compressed lips. Nevertheless, before he could give voice to his displeasure, Mr Stubbs asked what precisely had been found. 'Mr Northbridge and myself remained long after everyone else had left and searched the area for clues,' he added, after Gwen had delved into the reticule and handed him the ring.

She shrugged. 'No doubt during the attack it came off his finger and was possibly trampled under foot. I noticed scratch marks about, as though an animal had been foraging. Maybe that is how it was eventually unearthed.'

Stubbs handed the ring to Joss, who studied it for a moment, paying particular attention to the two symbols on the square face of the ring and the inscription inside. 'And you'd seen Sir Robert sporting just such a ring?'

There was an unmistakable hint of disbelief in

his voice that Gwen didn't quite understand. 'Why, of course, otherwise I wouldn't have had reason to call upon him, now would I?' No response was forthcoming, so she added, 'Haven't you ever seen him wearing it before?'

Once again his mouth became a taut, straight line. 'I do not pay too much attention to gentlemen's adornments.'

'Understandable,' she conceded. 'And I know he doesn't wear it too often, on account of his swollen finger joints. He just happened to do so on the evening of the ball and I noticed it.'

'And having done so, you then willy-nilly pay a visit on a man who might well be a murderer?' Joss clapped a hand to his forehead, as he stared ceilingwards. 'God give me strength!'

'Don't be ridiculous, Joss!' Gwen snapped back, annoyed herself now by the belittling tone. 'I didn't go to see Sir Robert because I believed him guilty of those crimes. I went because I wished to confirm his innocence beyond doubt in my own mind.'

Striving to regain control of her temper, Gwen once again rose to her feet and went across to join Joss before the empty hearth. 'Even though I was almost convinced that Sir Robert couldn't possibly be guilty of such horrible deeds, I'm ashamed to admit that a niggling doubt did remain, and so, naturally, I was obliged to take necessary precautions?'

'What precautions?' Joss demanded to know, not one ha'p'orth appeased by the explanation.

'This.' Delving into her reticule, Gwen revealed to all what she had extracted from her wardrobe before leaving her bedchamber earlier that morning.

'Good gad!' Joss exclaimed, momentarily taken aback. 'Is the dratted thing loaded?'

'Well, of course it is!' Gwen retorted. 'What possible good would it have been otherwise?'

'In that case, don't level the confounded thing in my direction, girl!' Joss returned, an unmistakable thread of amusement in his voice now.

Stepping forward, he easily wrested it from her grasp, and then examined it carefully. Small and well balanced, the pocket pistol was the ideal weapon for a woman's smaller hand.

'And I'm assuming you can use it with a reasonable degree of accuracy?'

'I'll have you know I'm highly proficient in the use of firearms,' Gwen returned with simple pride. 'Percival was a crack shot, as you may well remember. He took the time to teach me whilst we were in America.'

'Did he, by gad!' Joss gave an unexpected bark of laughter, which instantly dispersed the tense atmosphere in the room. 'Good old Sir Percy! We'll hold a contest after we're married, my girl. Then we'll see just how good you really are.'

It was then that Merriot Markham appreciated fully, for perhaps the very first time, just why Gwen had so captivated his friend. There was no denying that she was always well groomed and very pleasing on the eye in both face and figure. All the same, Joss's name had been linked with some quite exceptional beauties during the past ten years or so. Yet not one of them, as far as Merry was aware, had ever stood up to his friend the way Gwen did. He looked upon her as an equal. He was proud of her too. It was there in his eyes for anyone to see.

The little interlude had provided some light relief for all. None the less, Merry, asking to see the ring, eventually recalled everyone to the seriousness of the discussion. Joss absently handed it over, but as he was still studying the pocket pistol, he didn't detect his friend's sharp intake of breath. Gwen, on the other hand, most definitely did, and stared intently at the holder of the incriminating evidence.

'You recognise it too, don't you, Merry?'

'Are you sure it isn't Sir Robert's?' he said by way of an answer.

'Positive. His was in a small, wooden trinket box. He showed it to me.'

Gwen once again resumed her seat, the cynosure of all eyes once more as she retold the story Sir Robert had related about the eight rings. 'Apparently not all the recipients appreciated the gesture as much as he himself did. By all accounts some were sold, and others were passed on to other family members. The one Merry now holds, I firmly believe, was once the property of a midshipman on board *The Pelican* by the name of Gerald Kershaw.'

One could have heard a pin drop in the silence that followed before Mr Markham unexpectedly said, 'I suppose I should have been suspicious, but foolishly I wasn't. Ralph has been exercising Lord Cranborne's prize hunter ever since he arrived at the Hall, you see? The animal has earned the reputation of being unruly, something of a biter. I know for a fact all the grooms are wary of him. So when Kershaw came down to dinner on Saturday evening with his left hand heavily bandaged, I never gave it another thought. Now, though, I cannot help wondering whether his injury was inflicted by a gelding or…a little filly.'

'Betsy Small was undeniably a dainty thing,' Gwen reminded them all. 'But I suspect, like other members of the family, she didn't want for spirit. It wouldn't surprise me in the least if she attempted to put up a fight.'

Joss ceased his sombre contemplation of the empty hearth to reveal, 'And I happen to know for a fact, after my recent visit to the Earl, that Kershaw was one of those staying at the Hall at the times of the other murders and disappearances. But that, too, won't prove his guilt.'

'No, of course, it won't,' Gwen once again acknowledged. 'He must be goaded into a confession. And I suspect only a member of the sex he so obviously holds in such low esteem will succeed in getting him to do that.'

Chapter Thirteen

Joss had been as one with Gwen when she had made the suggestion that some attempt must be made to induce Kershaw into making a confession. Surprisingly enough, he hadn't even attempted to disagree when it had been proposed that a woman would be more likely to succeed. It was only when she had put herself forward as the inducement that her half-formulated scheme had met with staunch opposition.

For a full hour and more Joss had stood firm against every argument put forward by both Gwen and Merriot Markham, ably supported by Mr Stubbs. Then, quite without warning, Joss had walked across to his parlour window, and had stared out in the general direction of Marsden Wood for what had seemed an eternity, before he had finally agreed to the scheme. Even so, he had gone on to make two unexpected stipulations: firstly, that only those present in the room would be involved; and secondly, no matter the outcome, he and he alone would decide what, if any, action would be taken thereafter.

Gwen glanced across at the tall man riding alongside her. Even now she wasn't perfectly sure why he had pledged them all to such secrecy. She only knew that, no matter what had prompted his eventual agreement, he was still, almost twenty-four hours later, wholeheartedly against her involvement. He had not strung more than half a dozen sentences together since he had called at the house a short time earlier in order to escort her to the Hall, and his expression had remained a mask of grim disapproval.

'Oh, will you snap out of this mood of doom and despondency!' Gwen urged him. 'What can possibly go wrong? You went over and over it yesterday in the most minute detail with us all. You even had me outside proving that I could handle firearms, for heaven's sake! Merry knows what to do, Stubbs knows what to do, and if you should attempt to go over it one more time you shall induce a fit of the vapours in me the like of which you've never witnessed before.'

The empty threat did produce a flicker of a

smile, but it was fleeting in the extreme. 'Even the most well-laid plans can go wrong,' he reminded her. 'Luck has seen fit to favour us thus far. Merry paved the way for your part in the scheme yesterday evening whilst dining at the Hall. If all has gone well, he and Anthea should have set off on their ride by now. You turn up at the Hall expecting to find Anthea there. All being well, Lady Florence will still be abed, or at her *toilette*, and therefore unavailable to bear you company in order to await Merry's "supposed" return. We must just hope that Kershaw himself will then offer his services, as he should be taking his customary exercise in less than an hour's time.'

Joss took a moment to glance up at the sky. 'Even the weather has chosen to be kind to us. But a lot can still go sadly awry.'

'Yes, a lot can,' Gwen agreed sombrely. 'But we still have to try...I have to try.' Releasing her breath in a sigh, she cast a brief glance skywards herself. 'Heaven only knows it isn't revenge I want, Joss. Nothing can bring Jane back...any of them, for that matter. But I do want justice for all those women. I simply cannot ignore what I feel in my heart to be true, and do nothing.'

'I know that. Just as you know yourself that that ring is not conclusive proof of guilt. When confronted, he's likely to say it was stolen, possibly by Betsy Small herself. And there isn't a way on earth you'll be able to prove otherwise.'

'Maybe not,' she was obliged to concede. 'But as I've already told you, I don't underestimate him. If I should fail to goad him into an admission of guilt, then I still don't imagine for a moment he'd be foolish enough to violate anyone else hereabouts, knowing full well that he has been under suspicion. But whether or not he ever commits another murder, anywhere, is a different matter entirely. Nevertheless, I shan't ever go back on the promise I made to you yesterday. No matter the outcome, I'll not involve myself further in the matter after today.'

'We're almost there,' was her escort's only comment.

But Gwen wasn't fooled. She knew he was having to exert every ounce of self-control he possessed not to abandon the scheme there and then, and take her back by force if necessary.

'I shall be all right, Joss. If all else fails, I have my trusty pistol.' She tapped the pocket of her skirt. 'You know I can use it. And you may be sure I will, if I feel the need. And if Lady Luck continues to favour us, I shall see you at the rendezvous in just over an hour's time.'

'I sincerely hope you won't catch a glimpse of us at all, otherwise the whole confounded escapade is doomed to failure almost before we start!' And with that curt response he turned his mount, leaving her at the imposing south gateway to Cranborne Hall.

Gwen watched until he had disappeared from view round the bend in the road. If he had not altered his original plans, he would soon cut across the fields to Marsden Wood's southern-most edge, where hopefully he would discover Stubbs already awaiting his arrival. From there they would venture into the wood together on foot, leaving their horses securely tethered for Merriot Markham to find in due course. If all went well, and she achieved her objective, a shot would be fired to instruct Merry to bring the horses to the spot where poor Betsy Small had been found.

As she turned her mare between the solid stone pillars, Gwen was under no illusion that she might so easily fail, no matter how positive she had tried to appear in front of Joss. It was true that she wasn't unduly concerned for her own safety. Not only was she armed, but once she had arrived at that certain spot in the wood, she would be guarded at all times by Joss and Stubbs, well concealed in the undergrowth. Only if the need arose would they reveal themselves in order to protect her; if not, they would remain hidden for as long as possible, listening to whatever conversation did take place between Kershaw and herself.

The Hall suddenly appearing before her succeeded in claiming her attention. Nestling amid gently rolling countryside, and surrounded by a substantial deer park, the mansion was situated in the ideal setting, picturesque and tranquil. It was hard to believe that within the stone walls of such architectural splendour sheltered a being capable of the most despicable acts. Yet it was true. In her own mind she was convinced of it. Now it was up to her to prove his guilt beyond doubt by inducing him to admit to his crimes within the hearing of two independent witnesses.

Finding no one about at the front of the mansion to take charge of her horse, she didn't hesitate to ride directly round to the stables; there to discover none other than the very person she was determined to bring to justice about to mount a fine chestnut hunter.

This was just the sort of unforeseen occurrence that Joss had feared. Major Ralph Kershaw, a man of habit as a rule, had from his arrival at the Hall, three weeks before, exercised his lordship's prize hunter at the hour of eleven, or very soon thereafter. Yet here he was today—of all days!— ready to set forth a good half an hour before his customary time. Curse him!

Now what on earth was she supposed to do? Gwen was in two minds. Ought she to try her best to detain him, thereby allowing ample time for Joss and Stubbs to take up their positions, and maybe risk rousing her quarry's suspicions at the start? Or leave it to Providence to provide the means by which to delay the Major's immediate departure?

'Why, Major Kershaw! Good day to you, sir.' Quickly deciding that an exchange of pleasantries would be considered quite natural in the circumstances, she decided to stick to her original plan as far as she could, and trust to divine intervention. 'I hope your sister is well, and ready to accompany me out?'

He appeared surprised, but thankfully not in the least suspicious, because he must have known that Gwen and his sister had ridden out together on several occasions before, even though they had never arranged to meet at the Hall. 'I'm afraid not, Lady Warrender. She went out almost directly after breaking her fast, with Markham, I believe.'

He turned to the groom for corroboration, and received a vigorous nod in response. 'That she did, sir. Left, mayhap, almost an hour ago, and took young Jem along as usual.'

'Oh, dear.' Gwen did her best to appear disappointed, but not too disheartened. 'It must have quite slipped her mind that we'd arranged to ride out together today.' Then she shrugged whilst waving a hand in a dismissive gesture, hoping to convey the impression she had accepted the misunderstanding with a good grace. 'Oh, well, never mind. One must make allowances for people in love, I suppose. Perhaps Lady Florence will be kind enough to bear me company for half an hour or so, or until they return.'

Although his response was not quite what she might have wished, it didn't completely dash all hopes. 'I hate to be the bearer of more bad tidings, ma'am. But my mother is keeping to her bed this morning, on account of succumbing to one of her headaches.'

There was an unmistakable edge of intolerance in his deep voice. Clearly he, like Joss, had little patience for females who made much of trifling ailments. Thank heavens the similarities between the two men ended there!

'Oh, how vexatious,' Gwen declared, 'not only

for your mother but for me also. I didn't trouble to bring a groom with me, as you've probably observed. Joss himself escorted me as far as the gateway, as he has an appointment in town. Unfortunately he'll not be back this way until after noon, so I was hoping I might take advantage of your mother's kind hospitality by remaining here in order to persuade Mr Markham to come to my rescue and escort me home when he returns with your sister.'

'There's no need to concern yourself, ma'am. If you choose not to await Markham, one of the grooms here can escort you.'

Gwen had half-expected just such a suggestion, and had her response already hovering on the tip of her tongue. 'As your mother isn't receiving, I shan't await Mr Markham. And there's no need for one of the grooms to neglect his duties on my account. I shall be fine on my own.'

His inclinations might have been the furthest removed from those of a gentleman. Yet when he chose he was able to give a peerless performance of a man of honour, as he displayed there and then by saying, 'I couldn't in good conscience permit you to return on your own, ma'am. If you are disinclined to accept one of his lordship's people, perhaps you would allow me to act as escort?'

Not wishing to appear too eager, she remained silent for a few moments, before finally graciously accepting. 'I sincerely trust you'll not find it too onerous a task, though, Major,' she added, as they left the stable yard together. 'That hunter of yours looks eager to be off, but I know my limitations. At best I'm a competent horsewoman, and therefore never attempt more than a decorous trot.'

But would attempting to maintain a sedate pace give Joss enough time to reach the destination? Gwen thought not, and was just wondering how on earth she was going to delay her departure a little longer, again without arousing suspicion, when Providence did come to her rescue by providing the means to an end. The mount beneath her companion was indeed restive. Champing at the bit, he was frisking about like a restless colt.

'Why not take the edge off your mount's stamina by putting him through his paces, Major, before we set off? He looks a fine animal, and I should enjoy seeing him in action. Besides which, it's a lovely morning. I'm in no immediate hurry to return home, and I've been told by your sister you're a fine horseman.'

In point of fact it had been his mother, not Anthea, who had sung his praises. He wasn't to know that, of course. He just appeared moderately pleased by the compliment, before he acceded to the request and set off across the park at a gallop.

Grudgingly, she was silently obliged to own that Lady Florence had not been dotingly maternal and overgenerous in her praise. Her son had an excellent seat and, as far as Gwen could judge, was equal to Joss in the saddle.

She continued to watch with keen interest, marvelling at the way the rider's undeniable ability made crossing wide ditches and clearing hedges and gates with inches to spare look effortless, as though horse and rider were as one. Eventually, though, she was obliged to bring the peerless display to an end by hailing vigorously. The last thing she wanted was for Anthea to return and innocently betray the fact that no arrangement to go riding had ever been made between them.

'Sir, I have rarely seen your equal in the saddle,' Gwen was able to tell him with total sincerity. 'You make me feel quite ashamed, because I shall be put into the shade by such superior horsemanship during the homeward journey. But return some time I must.'

He made no demur, and thankfully they reached the little-used west gateway without

coming face to face with his sister and her favourite groom, or anyone else for that matter. Nor did
he so much as raise a brow when Gwen turned
her mount off the highway to make use of the
bridlepath that skirted the entire wood on its
northernmost side.

The area of woodland they had entered did in
fact belong to the estate. The Earl, however, had
never attempted to question the public's right of
way, providing users kept strictly to the path and
did not attempt to venture further on to his land.
The gamekeeper Furslow was usually to be found
patrolling this section of the wood. On the
lookout for those trespassers who left the bridlepath in order to shorten their walk, no matter
which direction they were heading, or those with
notions of attempting a spot of poaching, the
gamekeeper had been responsible for bringing
several people before the magistrates over the
years, and, in consequence, wasn't so very
popular with local inhabitants.

'It's hard to believe that a picturesque place
like this one has earned itself such a sinister reputation in recent years, is it not?' Gwen
remarked as casually as she could, when the
Major, who, like Joss, could never have been
accused of being garrulous by nature, continued

to ride alongside in silence. 'I would never dream of venturing here alone.'

'Very wise, ma'am,' he responded laconically.

'Of course, most of those poor women who have sadly perished here had no choice, I'm sure,' Gwen continued, not in the least disheartened by his callous lack of interest. 'I'm reliably informed that, despite the gamekeeper's almost constant vigilance, the woods are frequently used as a shortcut. Little wonder when it can lessen the journey for those visiting the local town on foot quite considerably.'

There was no response at all this time, but Gwen refused to admit defeat so early in her campaign for justice. 'You may not be aware of it, Major, but the last victim had, in fact, paid a visit to my home on the day she died. Yet another unfortunate soul to whom I have had some connection.'

Again she won no response.

'And, in part, I blame myself for that young maid's death.'

At last he betrayed a grain of interest. 'Why so?'

'I knew the girl had arranged to return to the Hall with a local carrier. But I should have made it clear that she was to return to my house if the carrier failed to turn up. I didn't, and so, when Betsy Small thought she'd missed her ride, she set off on foot.'

Once again he took refuge in silence. Gwen, however, remained doggedly determined. 'Anthea mentioned that you yourself had joined in the search for the young maid.'

At least she received a nod this time.

'But I understand it was poor Felix who eventually found her.'

'Yes. I was searching in quite another area of woodland with one of the grooms.'

He was so coolly dispassionate, Gwen was forced to turn her head away, lest her expression betray her utter disgust. 'That's a pity,' she managed at length.

'Why so, ma'am?'

Gwen drew her mount to a halt, obliging him to do likewise. 'Call it morbid curiosity, if you will, but I should have liked to see where it happened. Some folk believe the places where people die, at least those who have met a violent and untimely end, retain the spirit of the deceased.'

His expression was openly scathing. 'You don't believe such nonsense, surely?'

'Perhaps not,' Gwen conceded. 'But I should

have liked, none the less, to look upon the place where she was found, if only to pay my respects. Felix mentioned she was discovered on his father's land, so it must have been somewhere not too distant. It was mentioned too that you returned with him to the Hall, as he wasn't feeling quite the thing. So I assume, Major, you yourself must remember roughly where it happened. But then,' she added, 'I must not take advantage of your kindness simply because you're here. You must be wishing me quite otherwhere so that you can continue putting that fine hunter through its paces.'

'Not at all, ma'am,' he responded promptly enough. 'As you say, I do vaguely recall where she was found, though whether I could now take you to the exact spot is quite another matter. You must appreciate it was several days ago.'

Gwen didn't doubt the truth of this. She didn't suppose for a moment that he took too much notice of his precise surroundings when he was committing his terrible crimes.

'Of course. And I do appreciate you putting yourself to such trouble on my account.'

Without offering him the opportunity to change his mind, Gwen slipped lightly from the saddle and, entering the wood, began to lead her mount along one of the wider tracks, one possibly used by estate workers collecting firewood for the Hall. She wasn't perfectly certain they were heading in quite the right direction. When she had made that visit with her servants, they had entered at a different location. All the same, she had the feeling they couldn't be too far off course.

Amazingly enough, Gwen continued to feel remarkably composed considering she was walking alongside someone who had undoubtedly been responsible for the deaths of three women, and possibly several more. Nevertheless she remained acutely aware of his every movement, ever alert to the slightest nuance in his voice that might suggest a subtle change in his mood. He was for the present, she felt sure, not in the least suspicious of her motives in wishing to enter his killing grounds, and until that moment came for her to accuse him outright, she must endeavour to keep him in his present unwary state by continuing to behave as naturally as she could.

'You will be silently cursing me long before we part company, sir,' she said lightly, after they had walked some distance in stony silence. 'I notice that hunter of yours either doesn't care for his surroundings, or has acquired his second wind. I must say he is a skittish creature. Hardly a suitable mount for someone of his lordship's advanced years. The Earl's so sensible as a rule.'

'It might surprise you to learn, ma'am, that my uncle, when not suffering the gout, still shows to advantage in the saddle,' he countered, surprising her somewhat by this show of loyalty, for she had not supposed he had that much regard for any member of his family. 'Having said that, I do not consider this particular animal was the wisest purchase he has ever made. The hunter can be headstrong and in need of a firm hand on most occasions.'

Instinctively, Gwen glanced at his left hand, encased now in a tan leather glove and, after a moment's indecision, decided to take the risk. 'Ah, yes! I seem to recall Mr Markham mentioning the animal had earned himself the reputation of being a biter. The grooms up at the Hall are all wary of him, so I understand. And am I right in thinking, also, that you yourself have been a recent victim of this ill-natured vice?'

'Very true, ma'am. Entirely my own fault, though,' he revealed, after a moment's hesitation. 'I should have taken more care.' There was a suspicion of a sneer about his mouth that instantly sent a shiver scudding down the length of her spine. 'I shall certainly endeavour always to do so in future.'

Once again Gwen was forced to look away to conceal her disdain. Had she needed more proof that what she was attempting to do was right and just, she had been given it now. If he wasn't stopped, it wouldn't be too long before he would seek yet another victim, she felt sure.

Gwen felt her trusty little pistol brushing against her thigh as she walked, and took heart. If the worst came to the worst, she knew she wouldn't suffer any lasting pangs of conscience if she was obliged to put a period to such a loathsome creature's existence.

'I cannot be perfectly sure, ma'am, but I believe the maid was found somewhere about here,' he said stopping quite without warning, and waving vaguely off to his right.

Gwen, however, was equally certain it was not the place. In her considered opinion they were still too close to that bridlepath. They needed to venture deeper, much deeper. Besides which, there were no statuesque beech trees in sight in this particular location, not one, and certainly no fluttering pink ribbons to mark the spot.

Evidently he considered her silence quite natural, a mark of respect, maybe. Which was perhaps just as well as Gwen was concentrating her thoughts on attempting to calculate precisely where they were. She had a vague recollection of crossing a wide track when Ben had brought them into the wood two days before. Whether it was the one she now stood upon, she couldn't have said with any degree of certainty. Yet she remained hopeful, and determined to keep searching for that all-important length of pink ribbon.

'I thank you for your escort, sir. I think we'd best move on now.' Having deliberately kept her voice low, she hoped she hadn't sounded too eager to be gone from the spot. 'Do you suppose if we carry along this track it will eventually bring us back on to the bridlepath and the lane beyond? If so, it will save us the walk back.'

'It may possibly do so, ma'am,' he said, sounding as though he genuinely wasn't sure. Gwen, however, wasn't prepared to give him the benefit of the doubt this time. She strongly suspected he knew precisely where they were.

'But I see no reason why we cannot ride,' he added, cupping his hands in order to assist her back into the saddle.

Gwen did not demur at the suggestion they continue on horseback. More importantly, she managed not to recoil when he assisted her to remount the mare, and could only wonder at her lack of reaction. Yet, in another way, she could perfectly understand—could understand, too, why his victims had, perhaps, experienced no alarm when first coming upon him. It seemed to her that there were two completely different entities existing inside that well-muscled frame: one, punctilious, gentlemanly and controlled; the other, ungovernable, brutal and pitiless. Something drew this darker side of his nature to the fore on occasions. And it was up to her to find that all-important trigger. But not yet a while.

Without attempting to hold him in further conversation, she made a play of taking a casual interest in her surroundings, while all the time keeping a sharp eye open for that length of pink ribbon. For a short period of time they rode deeper into the heart of the wood. Then, when finally the track began to bend in the opposite direction, taking them back towards the bridlepath on the northern side, and the narrow lane beyond, Gwen at last glimpsed that poignant marker she had been so determined to find.

'Great heavens, Major! What do you suppose that can be over there?'

'Where, ma'am?' He was alert in a trice. 'I cannot see what has claimed your attention.'

'Over there!' She pointed between the trees,

before once again slipping from the saddle. 'Why, that must surely be the spot! I distinctly recall my groom mentioning he'd tied a length of ribbon to mark the place where his sister had died.'

Without waiting for him to follow, Gwen secured her mount's reins to a conveniently low-hanging branch, and then made her way that short distance through the undergrowth. She could only pray that Joss and Mr Stubbs were somewhere close, already in position, for she could see absolutely no sign of them.

'Yes, yes! This is the place,' she called back over her shoulder to the erect figure on horseback, who had made no attempt whatsoever to follow. 'Do come and see, Major,' she coaxed. 'See if I'm not right.'

She dared not say more, lest she put him on his guard at this, the most crucial stage. Fortunately there was no need for further prompting. She heard the sound of a twig breaking some few feet behind her a moment or two later, his approach having been as stealthy as that of a predatory beast.

Strangely enough, though, she still didn't feel in the least threatened by his close proximity, as she continued to glance about with feigned interest. 'And look! Someone has placed flowers here.'

With her back still towards him, Gwen lowered herself gracefully on her haunches. Then, very carefully, she extracted that vital piece of evidence from the safety of her jacket pocket, and whilst reaching out her fingers to grasp one bunch of wilted blooms, she tossed the ring deftly beneath one exposed gnarled root, almost within an inch of where it had been originally found.

'How sad,' she murmured, momentarily staring down at the drooping flowers in her hand, before glancing over her shoulder to find him staring off to his left, as though he couldn't bring himself to look at the spot.

His tone was clipped, too, as he said, 'Quite! But I think, ma'am, it's time we were gone.'

Gwen had no desire to delay proceedings either. So, after replacing the flowers, she made as though she were about to rise. 'But wait! What is this?'

The Major had already moved several yards away, eager to be gone, it seemed, but turned back at her exclamation of surprise. Out of the corner of her eye, Gwen could see him watching intently, as she made a great play of using her handkerchief to clean the soil from her fingers, thereby neatly concealing the object she deliberately held from his view.

'What have you found?'

There was a definite trace of urgency in his voice that Gwen found most encouraging. 'Why, it's a ring, sir! A gentleman's signet ring. And, do you know, I believe I've seen it before. Yes, I'm positive I have!'

He had come to stand within a yard or two of her again. 'May I see it?'

Holding up the ring so that he couldn't fail to recognise it, while at the same time keeping it safely out of his reach, she blatantly ignored the request. 'This might turn out to be evidence, Major. After all, it was found here, at the scene of a crime.'

'I shouldn't imagine so, ma'am,' he returned, waving his injured left hand in a dismissive gesture. 'Unless I'm much mistaken, it's none other than my own, the one I mislaid some days ago.'

Feigning surprise, rather than betraying suspicion at this stage, Gwen echoed, 'Yours, Major? But I understood yours wasn't lost. You'd merely ceased to wear it on account of your swollen hand and fingers.'

He was silent, but only for a moment. 'I cannot recall informing you of that, ma'am.'

'You didn't,' she admitted at once, only to lie in the next breath by adding, 'It was Mr Markham who told me so.'

His expression was decidedly sceptical now. 'And why should Mr Markham choose to discuss my late father's ring with you?'

'Nothing sinister, Major, merely seeking advice,' Gwen returned, maintaining her composure and, more importantly, without suffering the least pang of conscience for the tissue of lies about poor Merry she was about to utter in order to further her cause.

'He wished to know whether I would object if Joss chose to sport a signet ring rather than the more usual wedding band. I told him I shouldn't mind in the least. He hoped Anthea would hold a similar view because he preferred the heavier and more masculine style of the signet ring. He then went on to say he was particularly taken with the one you sported, and mentioned too that you'd ceased to wear it for the time being on account of your injury.'

She gave him a moment or two to digest what she'd told him, uncaring whether he believed her or not. 'What I do not perfectly understand is why it should have been found here, unless you yourself had dropped it.'

'A mystery, wouldn't you say, ma'am, since the last time I saw it, several days ago, it was in my bedchamber back at the Hall?'

Although he had sounded completely unperturbed, Gwen strongly suspected he wasn't as untroubled as he was striving to appear. 'As you say, a mystery, indeed, sir. And one the authorities will undoubtedly insist needs clearing up. Naturally, it might be difficult, not to say embarrassing, for your uncle to conduct enquiries into your movements on Saturday last. But I'm sure one of his colleagues on the Bench will undertake the task.'

She paused for a moment to study his impassive expression. 'That you were out exercising his lordship's hunter, and alone, when the girl was attacked might prove a little awkward for you, especially as your ring was found at the scene of the crime.'

All at once eyes were glinting down at her between half-shuttered lids. 'I could almost imagine, ma'am, that you are convinced of my guilt already.'

For answer Gwen tossed the ring into the air, and caught it again deftly in the palm of her hand, complete mistress of her emotions still. The time had come to confront him. And confront him she would!

'I'm aware the ring alone will not convince the authorities. But perhaps when I remind them that you were staying at the Hall when my dearest friend

Jane Robbins was murdered and, indeed, at all those times when the other women went missing, it might be considered necessary to look into your activities in recent years a little more closely.'

During the previous evening she had been granted ample time to mull over precisely what she would say, when the moment came. The accusations, assumptions and possible courses of action open to the authorities had all been mentally rehearsed, and were now ready to trip off her tongue in quick succession.

'They might choose, for instance, to discover if any women have been reported missing, or were found in similar circumstances in and around the Portsmouth area during those times you were in residence at your home,' she continued smoothly, without so much as the slightest falter. 'After all, you took the necessary steps at a very early age to ensure that you had complete privacy and freedom of movement by making it impossible for your mother and sister to remain under your roof, did you not?

'The magistrate in charge might also find it interesting to discover whether similar murders or disappearances of young women occurred in those places where you have been sent to—er—maintain law and order in recent years.' Gwen was unable to keep the derision from creeping into her voice as she said this. 'But before any of these enquiries are put into place, I personally will recommend that a doctor examines that injured hand of yours very carefully in order to ascertain whether the bite was made by a horse…or a human.

'Yes, I'm convinced of your guilt, Major Kershaw,' she admitted at last. 'And have been ever since I discovered this ring belongs to you.'

There was now an unpleasant curl to his mouth. 'I infer from that that you found the ring before today.'

Gwen was very well aware she had induced him to admit nothing as yet, and that how she proceeded from here on was vital. All the same, her suggestion that it might be worth investigating his postings in recent years had certainly induced him to stiffen, and his expression to darken noticeably.

'Indeed I did,' she confirmed, deciding to stick to the truth as far as possible. Pitiless he might be, but fool he was not. Furthermore, she had never made a convincing liar. 'I found it two days ago when I placed those flowers here.'

The sneer disappeared momentarily as he pursed his lips. 'I cannot help wondering, then, why I have not been approached by the authorities already.'

'Simply because I have yet to inform them, sir,' Gwen returned without hesitation. Which was not so far removed from the truth. 'Firstly, I was obliged to discover the identity of the owner of the ring. You must know, as well as I do, that Sir Robert Rawlinson owns just such a style of ring. Paying a morning call on that worthy gentleman was all that was required to assure me of the true owner's identity.'

Gwen was able to mimic his sneer perfectly. 'I remembered, you see, the night of my dinner party when your ring scratched my arm—remembered, too, that my goose was hacked to death that night…remembered also that you wore your sword. By a few discreet enquiries here and there, it was no difficult matter to discover that you were in the locale on every occasion a female was either found murdered or reported missing. And last night I recalled that there had been no disappearances occurring during that three-year period when you were with your regiment across the Channel.'

She regarded him in silence, before she shook her head in wonder, genuinely perplexed. 'Perhaps I can understand why someone might react instinctively and lash out in defence if under attack by a goose or any other creature. But what

I fail to comprehend is why a man, such as yourself, who cannot lack female admirers, should feel the need to force himself on innocent women and then murder them.'

His shout of laughter simply oozed derision. 'Innocent women? Scheming, selfish harpies, the lot of 'em!'

'Your hatred of my sex comes as no surprise to me, Major,' Gwen admitted, after a few moments' intense thought, during which a germ of an idea had begun to develop. 'I know for a fact you have little or no affection for your sister. But how you can actively dislike your mother, the woman who gave birth and protected you as a child, I quite fail to—'

'Protected me!' Kershaw cut in, his voice razor sharp. 'Where was my mother during the first nine years of my life? Where was she when I was forced out in all weathers from the age of five, rowing a boat until my hands bled so much I couldn't grip the oars. Where was she when my father took a belt to me, or anything else he could lay his hands on, for the slightest misdemeanour, and I became so afraid I couldn't even speak without stammering whenever he was near?'

'Your mother suffered too, Major,' Gwen reminded him gently, hoping to rouse at least a modicum of sympathy in him. His reaction, however, was not quite what she might have expected. If anything, his expression hardened, and his eyes seemed almost glacial, though not through any threat of tears.

'Oh, I know she did, ma'am,' he said silkily. 'And it was some recompense to know I was not the only one to suffer my father's brutality, believe me. Many was the time I stole out of my bedchamber at night when he was home on leave, and entered my father's dressing-room in order to peer through the crack in the door and watch, and listen to my mother's whimpering cries. My father's coupling could never be described as gentle. Her pleading fell on deaf ears. But she never put up any resistance.'

If anything, his expression became even more disturbing. 'Now, I like women to resist. That friend of yours put up almost as good a fight as that pretty maid t'other day.' The sneer had returned in full measure. 'And I don't doubt you will do exactly the same.'

'Aren't you forgetting one very important thing—that I was seen leaving the Hall in your company?' Gwen reminded him, whilst trying to suppress a *frisson* of fear at the possibility that Joss might not be close at hand.

'No, I wasn't forgetting that. It's unfortunate, but not disastrous. I shall merely be put to the trouble of making sure your body is not found, at least not for some considerable time. Then I shall merely say that, at your insistence, I left you at the edge of the wood. Your mount will undoubtedly be found quite quickly, confirming my story.'

'My, my, you really do have little regard for my sex,' Gwen purred, striving to retain her nerve, 'if you supposed for a moment that I was foolish enough to accompany you anywhere completely unprotected.'

His response to this was to peer intently at the various clumps of dense undergrowth surrounding them. By the time his attention had returned to her, Gwen had already extracted the small pistol from her skirt pocket and had it levelled at his heart in a remarkably steady hand.

'And if you suppose for a moment that I couldn't or wouldn't use this, I would strongly urge you to think again, Major,' she advised. 'And now I believe it is time for us to leave.'

Surprisingly he did turn, just as though he meant to obey, and Gwen made to follow. Unfortunately her heel caught one of those exposed roots of the beech tree, the very one under which she had originally found the ring. Her foot twisted beneath her, sending a sharp pain darting through her ankle, and resulting in her losing her balance completely. She was powerless to prevent herself from falling backwards. Her head cracked against the beech tree, and a moment later her back was sliding down the smooth trunk, just as she herself was sliding into unconsciousness.

Chapter Fourteen

Joss's forbidding expression didn't lessen even so much as marginally when he arrived to discover Henry Stubbs already awaiting him at the pre-arranged rendezvous.

'Change of plan,' he announced, dismounting with sublime ease, thereby once again displaying that surprising agility for a man of his size. 'We're now to await Markham's arrival before proceeding into the wood. He'll then take the horses back to Bridge House and return with the carriage.'

'I'm sure you've got your reasons for doing so, sir. But mayn't I know what they are?'

'You may,' Joss answered without hesitation. 'It's simply that I've little taste for melodrama. If, and I say if, Lady Warrender is successful in her endeavours, I have no wish to cause a sensation by being seen by all and sundry escorting a close relative of the Earl of Cranborne, bound and gagged, and at gunpoint, to stand before one of his lordship's fellow magistrates. The less public interest we arouse, the better I shall like it. A carriage will afford privacy, you see.'

'Point taken, sir,' Stubbs acknowledged, before he caught sight of a familiar figure on horseback. 'And here's Mr Markham now!'

'The little ploy evidently worked,' Joss remarked, at last managing a semblance of a smile as his friend drew his mount to a halt beside him.

'Better than I could have hoped. I merely repeated what you suggested last night, and said I'd completely forgotten a prior engagement with the solicitor in town to clear up a few minor details with regard to purchasing Gwen's house. Naturally Anthea wished to accompany me. But when I said it would be devilish dull business in a stuffy office, and that she'd be much happier enjoying a ride in the fresh air, she didn't argue. In fact, I persuaded her to return by a more circuitous route. So all being well, Gwen will have safely departed long before Anthea arrives back at the Hall.'

Joss, his mind swiftly returning to their grim

purpose, consulted his fob-watch. 'I make it wanting only a minute to the half-hour, gentlemen, so we'd best not tarry. Return to Bridge House now, Merry. As I also remarked last night, my head groom isn't likely to question your wishing to tool the carriage yourself, if you merely say you've a fancy to try your hand at tooling my team. He knows I trust you with my horses. Then, as we agreed, enter the wood by means of the track the loggers use on the southern side. Go far enough so that you cannot be seen from the road, but not so far as to risk Kershaw either seeing or hearing the horses, and await my signal.'

As farewells were brief, Joss was soon leading the way into the wood. He had been blessed with a most remarkable sense of direction. Once having visited a town, village, or place of interest, no matter the size, he never had much difficulty in locating its whereabouts a second time. And so it proved to be with the exact location of the latest crime.

His approach was of necessity slow and careful. He wished to alarm as few woodland creatures as possible in case Gwen and Kershaw should not be far away. He could see no sign of them as yet, and could hear nothing either. All the same, he was determined to remain cautious at all times. The last thing in the world he wanted was to alert

Kershaw to potential danger. His possible reactions were too disturbing to contemplate.

'You know, sir, this be a damned eerie place, and no mistake!' Stubbs remarked in an undertone, as he settled himself, belly down, alongside Joss on the woodland floor. 'Thought so the first time I clapped eyes on the spot, with that poor mite of a thing still lying there.'

'Get a grip, man!' Joss adjured, after he had watched his companion rub a hand back and forth across the nape of his neck as if to flatten the hairs there. 'I would have thought you'd have been used to it by now. You must have viewed dozens of crime scenes in your profession, and corpses too, come to that.'

'Too many,' the ex-Runner admitted. 'But you never get used to it, not really, 'specially not the ones where women and children are concerned, them that can't defend themselves.'

'If what Markham now suspects is true, then that young maid attempted to do just that. A close look at Kershaw's left hand might prove most interesting, if the injury hasn't already healed,' Joss suggested, a moment before his acute hearing detected the unmistakable sound of hoofbeats.

Seemingly Stubbs had heard it too, for both men peered between the dense foliage surrounding them to see two horses, together with riders, appear round a bend in the track.

Seeing the woman he loved totally unharmed, and looking so remarkably composed, too, in the circumstances, induced Joss to release his breath in a protracted sigh of relief. That and the slight rustling of clothing as both men, almost simultaneously, withdrew pistols from their pockets and prepared themselves to watch and listen were the last sounds either of them were destined to make for some little time.

During the following fifteen minutes or so, Joss believed he experienced as many diverse sentiments as it was possible for a human being to feel.

Intense relief quickly gave way to a surge of expectation, as he listened to Gwen coaxing her companion to the spot only a matter of a few yards from where he and Stubbs remained safely hidden. Then he went through a short period of acute pessimism, when he was convinced it would all be for nothing and no confession would ever be forthcoming. The despondency was thankfully vanquished by a surge of renewed hope, when his bride-to-be—clever little minx!—suggested that a thorough investigation into the Major's movements in recent years might prove interesting.

Even though he was several feet away, Joss couldn't fail to detect the paling of the Major's skin. The darker expression of unalloyed hatred that quickly followed, and which accompanied the final admission of guilt, did not go unnoticed either, and ignited a further surge of apprehension, especially when the person responsible for ending so many lives unexpectedly turned and stared at the shrubbery, almost at the exact spot where he and his companion were hiding.

The most disturbing experience of all came when he watched Gwen, quite without warning, fall heavily against the tree. Although he quite failed to understand what had happened, Kershaw's immediate response spurred Joss himself into action. He was standing over the Major in a trice, his gun pressed against the soldier's temple, as Kershaw knelt and reached out gloved hands, ready to encircle the slender neck.

'Attempt to touch her, and you're a dead man,' Joss warned, a moment or two before he brought the pistol down hard on the side of the Major's head.

'My God, sir!' Stubbs exclaimed, as he came to stand beside Joss. 'Did you ever see such a face? It weren't human.'

'I saw,' Joss confirmed. 'That's why I wasn't

prepared to take any chances. He's little more than stunned. He'll come round soon, too soon in my opinion, so you'd best bind his hands behind his back now.'

While the ex-Runner sensibly followed the advice, Joss turned his attention to his main concern, and quickly had his suspicions confirmed when he located the sizeable lump already forming on the back of Gwen's head.

Wasting not a precious second, he picked up her small pistol and discharged it into the air, instantly shattering the silence. Then he scooped Gwen up into his arms and carried her over to where the horses were tethered. With a little assistance from Stubbs, he succeeded in getting himself and Gwen safely positioned on the hunter's back. He well knew the animal's reputation. All the same he swiftly justified his future bride's faith in his abilities by maintaining a firm control over the restive gelding, while cradling her with infinite gentleness in one arm.

'I'll be of little help until I have Lady Warrender safely in my carriage,' Joss admitted with brutal frankness. 'Can you guard the prisoner until I return? I'll be as quick as I can.'

'Don't you fret none, sir. As soon as he comes round, I'll lead your lady's mare, and we'll follow on foot. And if he be daft enough to try to make a run for it, I'll not be afraid to use this,' he assured Joss, brandishing his pistol.

The journey back to Bridge House was the worst Joss could recall making in his life. Not only did his concern over Gwen's well-being increase with every passing minute, as she betrayed no sign whatsoever of regaining consciousness, he was well aware that Mr Markham was under intense stress too.

There seemed no depths to which Ralph Kershaw would not stoop. Evidently not satisfied with his past iniquities, he was quite willing to add emotional blackmail to his list of misdeeds by suggesting strongly that his sister would find it hard to forgive anyone remotely connected with the scheme to have him put to death.

'I do believe, Merry, it was a grave error of judgement on my part to suggest Stubbs tool the carriage on the return journey in order to give you a rest. I believed, you see, that I knew the depths to which this profligate would stoop. I was in error.'

'Don't concern yourself on my account,' Merriot responded. 'If I appear perturbed, it's merely that I find it offensive having to remain in such close proximity to slurry. Besides, anyone well acquainted with Anthea would know that she would never be such a hypocrite as to mourn the loss of someone who has treated her with such indifference throughout her life.'

What Kershaw might have chosen to respond to this was destined never to be known. For the carriage had at last turned between two tall wrought-iron gates, and Joss was suggesting the untying of their prisoner even before the carriage had come to a stop in the stable yard at Bridge House.

'Untie him? ' Merriot looked decidedly sceptical. 'Are you sure that's wise? I wouldn't put it past him to make a run for it.'

'Then shoot the blighter!' Joss returned, with complete unconcern. 'But I don't think he'll make the attempt,' he went on, taking a moment to look Ralph Kershaw over from head to foot. 'He's everything despicable, but not an absolute imbecile. At the present time four people only are certain of his guilt. If, however, he chooses to announce it to the world at large, he'll behave rashly. And that, my dear, Merry, is not in his nature.

'I'll leave you to apprise Stubbs,' he added a moment later, as the ex-Runner himself threw wide the door for Joss to alight. 'Await me in the library.'

Not even delaying to see if his instructions were

being carried out, Joss went striding across the stable yard and into the house by way of the side entrance. Consequently few people witnessed his arrival. None the less, by the time he had carried Gwen upstairs to his own bedchamber, his entire household seemed aware that all was not as it should be, for no sooner had he placed his precious burden down on the four-poster bed than his new housekeeper came bustling into the master bedchamber.

Sensible as always, Annie Small didn't try her new master's patience by asking a stream of needless questions, once she had been informed that her young mistress had met with an accident whilst out riding, and now had a sizeable lump on the back of her head.

It was the removal of her boots that finally roused Gwen to consciousness and alerted her two concerned attendants to the swollen state of her right ankle.

After detecting the low moan, Joss felt untold relief to see those strikingly lovely eyes open a matter of moments later, and to detect the unmistakable flicker of instant recognition in the wonderful blue depths.

'Did we succeed, Joss?' she asked, her voice barely above a whisper, though clearly audible.

'Better than we could have hoped, my darling,' he answered. 'But no more talking now. I'm going to leave you in Annie's capable hands for a short while. The doctor will be here presently to look you over, and I shall return soon afterwards.'

Deeply concerned though he remained, Joss, ever the pragmatist, knew his presence was more urgently required downstairs. Consequently, after receiving his housekeeper's assurance that she could manage perfectly well on her own, he went straight down to his library to find the one responsible for his present unsettled state still being ably guarded.

After assuring Merriot that Gwen had at last regained consciousness, and would suffer, he felt sure, no lasting damage, he suggested that Stubbs position himself outside, lest their prisoner should foolishly attempt to escape by way of the window, and that Merriot himself might like to await him in the front parlour.

'I shall be quite all right, Merry,' Joss assured him, when his friend suggested he too remain. He then drew out his own pistol from his pocket once more to corroborate the statement. 'It's just that I wish to have a word or two with Kershaw in private before informing the authorities.'

'I cannot imagine what you can have to say to me,' the Major remarked the instant they were alone together. 'We have enjoyed, at best, little more than a cordial acquaintance over the years.'

'True enough. And that is because I am particularly careful in my choice of friends,' Joss returned, after going across to the decanters and pouring out two glasses of a particularly old and excellent brandy. 'But I didn't wish to speak to you in private in order to exchange insults.'

'Then why did you?' Kershaw returned, sounding remarkably composed in the circumstances, though he did glance briefly at the pistol clasped in one strong and steady hand, before accepting the glass held out to him in the other.

'In order to offer you something you ill deserve, but which your family most certainly does—namely, a chance to stop the name Kershaw degenerating into a byword for iniquity.'

The manic glint had long since left the steely-grey eyes. Yet the unpleasant curl to those lips remained, a constant reminder, should it be needed, that behind the seemingly rational façade lurked a dangerous being capable of the most despicable acts.

'The only way that that can be achieved is if no charges are ever brought against me.'

'Quite so!' Joss concurred. 'And that is precisely why I have taken it upon myself to offer
you a choice. When I leave this room I shall not
delay in making arrangements for you to be
handed over to the authorities. You will undoubtedly be placed in the local lockup for at least one
night, and possibly longer, before you appear
before a magistrate.

'Make no bones about it, Kershaw,' Joss continued, his voice level, containing no vestige of
emotion, 'news of your arrest will rapidly spread
throughout the county. Don't misguidedly
suppose you won't be held in custody until your
trial, simply because you're the nephew of a peer
of the realm. Should it become necessary, I shan't
hesitate to make it clear that it would be the
height of folly to allow such a deranged being as
yourself out on bail. If you don't end your days
dangling from a rope, then it will be in Bedlam,
or some other equally diabolical institution. Long
before then, you will have lost everything, your
reputation in tatters. And if you should, by some
mischance, manage to escape before the trial,
you would be for ever on the run, for ever peering
over your shoulder, for ever wondering if
someone, somewhere, has recognised you.'

If Joss's tone had been impassive, Kershaw's

expression had remained equally so. Perhaps only his voice betrayed the faintest timbre of disquiet as he asked, 'And the alternative you offer?'

'In the top right-hand drawer of my desk is the brother to this, primed and ready to fire.' Joss raised his pistol slightly. 'If you've any sense at all, you will take it out and put a period to your own existence, and by so doing very likely take your guilty secrets with you to the grave.'

After tossing the contents of his glass down his throat, Joss placed the empty vessel on the corner of his desk, and then moved over to the door. 'As I mentioned earlier, at the present time four people only are convinced of your guilt. If I can attain their agreement, and I have every reason to suppose I shall, I'll make it known that you died as a result of an accident. That you were fortunately at hand when Lady Warrender took a tumble from her horse, and assisted me in bringing her back here after the accident. Whilst waiting to discover how badly she was hurt, you occupied yourself by cleaning my pistols, which resulted in a tragic accident.'

Never once taking his eyes off the other occupant of the room, Joss reached into the pocket of his jacket for his desk key, and placed it on the table by the wall. 'The choice is yours, Kershaw. But so that you do not misunderstand me…if you should be foolish enough to attempt to leave this room before the authorities arrive, I shan't hesitate to use my own pistol.'

Closing the door quietly behind him, Joss moved slowly across the hall. He had almost reached the door leading to the parlour when he heard the high-pitched manic laugh. A moment later the house echoed with a deafening report.

Chapter Fifteen

'Naturally, I heard the shot,' Gwen admitted, the following morning, when Joss came to apprise her in person of Kershaw's demise. 'But I was in such discomfort with my ankle, I paid it little mind. Then, as you know, Dr Bartlet arrived and, after a brief examination, filled me so full of laudanum that I remember absolutely nothing until I woke this morning to find my own dear Gillie sitting in the chair by the bed.'

She cast a brief glance at one particular corner of the room, where her personal maid was doing her best to appear inconspicuous. She knew Joss would never reveal what had truly taken place in his library while there was someone around to overhear.

'Leave that now, Gillie dear, and be good enough to take my breakfast tray down to the kitchen,' she called, rampant curiosity having rapidly quashed any thought of adhering to the proprieties. 'I should appreciate some lemonade later. But first I should like to speak to Mr Northbridge in private.'

After the slightest hesitation Martha did as bidden, and Gwen once again turned her attention to the tall figure standing beside the bed. 'Sit down do, and tell me what really happened, because if you think I'll ever believe Kershaw accidentally shot himself, you must—'

'Of course I know you don't believe it,' Joss acknowledged, availing himself of the invitation to sit, but not in the chair. As his lady surprisingly voiced no objection, he swung his legs, boots and all, on to the bed, and leaned back against the mound of pillows, gathering her in his arms as he did so. 'But that is what I trust you will continue to tell the world at large.'

'What really happened, Joss?' Gwen demanded to know, at this juncture unwilling to commit herself.

'He took his own life rather than face a hangman's noose.'

'But how did he get hold of the pistol? He hadn't one on him, surely?'

'I placed it in the top drawer of my desk the evening before,' Joss at last admitted. 'I did so in the hope that he would choose that way out, and save the family much anguish. What I wished to avoid from the beginning was Anthea and her mother having to live with the consequences of Ralph Kershaw's actions.'

Gwen was silent for a few moments, turning things over in her mind. 'Well, I for one am not in the least sorry it's ended this way. As I told you, I wasn't seeking revenge. Nor did I have any desire to see him hanging from a gibbet. And at least no other woman will die at his hands. But I'm rather surprised he chose to do the honourable thing in the end.'

'That knock to the head must be more serious than I supposed. Don't be such a simpleton, my darling!' Joss lovingly scolded, genuinely amused. 'Honour didn't enter into it. Kershaw availed himself of the opportunity to take his own life because it was preferable to the alternative. I doubt he even gave his mother or Anthea a thought before he placed the barrel to his temple and squeezed the trigger. He was thinking only of himself.'

'Yes, I expect you're right. I suppose it's just that I'd like to think there was some good in him somewhere.' Gwen sighed as she positioned her head more comfortably on the large expanse of chest. 'You heard, I suppose, everything he said about his childhood, his father and mother. It was his mother who unwittingly produced that hatred of women in him.'

Joss was distinctly unmoved. 'I've crossed the path of dozens of women I could quite cheerfully have strangled during my lifetime, my sisters included. But I've refrained from throttling any of 'em thus far.' He shrugged. 'No one will ever know what truly made Kershaw behave as he did. But I saw for myself, if only briefly, that insanity surface. I know what those poor women saw before they died.'

Joss then obliged her by filling in the gaps so that she knew precisely what had occurred after she had clumsily knocked herself unconscious. Gwen listened intently, and then at last gave her word never to reveal that Major Ralph Kershaw had been the Marsden Wood Killer.

'As far as I'm concerned, he can take his guilty secret to the grave. But what of the others—Merry and Stubbs? Have they agreed to say nothing?'

Joss nodded. 'As you might imagine, Merry is more than willing to spread the accidental shooting story abroad in order to protect his future wife and mother-in-law. And as for Stubbs…' Joss shrugged '…he's no axe to grind.

His reputation has been built on trust and discretion. He's been well paid, and is already on his way back to London, satisfied that the job has been done. He's more to lose than gain by revealing what he knows. Besides which, he's given his word, and I believe him.'

'And what of the family…? They were apprised of Ralph's death yesterday, I assume?'

'Yes, Merry and I rode over, directly after the doctor's visit. Dr Bartlet examined Kershaw, but it was merely a formality. Naturally Anthea was sincerely shocked and her mother was deeply upset. The Earl, however…' Joss shook his head. 'Of course he suspects, more than just suspects, because he knows his nephew was among those few that were at the Hall on those significant occasions. He also belatedly remembered that his nephew had returned to the Hall with his clothes covered in mud on that day in January when Jane Robbins died. Sensibly, though, he will keep whatever suspicions he has to himself for the family's sake. Also, whilst I was there, I managed to slip that ring back into Kershaw's room, so I think we've managed to cover just about everything.'

Gwen, suddenly recalling something to mind, gave a start. 'Except you've forgotten my visit to

Sir Robert. He knows of Kershaw's guilt, or strongly suspects him.'

'Don't concern yourself, my darling. I rode over to see Rawlinson first thing this morning. I didn't attempt to lie to him. As it happens, he'd already heard the news, and guessed the truth. Rest assured, though, he's far too fond of Lady Florence to breathe a word of what he knows.

'He'll not be attending the funeral, however, and neither shall I,' Joss went on to reveal. 'For his sister's sake, the Earl is willing to allow Kershaw to be buried in the grounds with other close family members. But he's insisted on a private affair— immediate family only. He's also surprisingly insisting that Anthea's wedding is not postponed, unless she wishes it to be. In the circumstances, though, he's suggesting one like ours, a private affair, with few guests. Merry's in full agreement, and I think, once she has recovered from the initial shock of losing her brother, Anthea will be too. She's no hypocrite, and will not pretend to mourn a relative who meant little to her.'

'So it's over at last.' Gwen breathed a sigh of relief. 'Women can safely stroll through Marsden Wood once more without fear.'

'Yes, all except you,' Joss countered, appearing wickedly pleased all of a sudden 'You won't be walking anywhere for several days, according to the doctor. And to ensure you obey those instructions to the letter, you're to remain here at Bridge House, where I can keep an eye on you.'

Sensibly preventing any argument, Joss pressed his mouth to hers very briefly, before swinging his feet to the floor, and sauntering over to the door. 'I'm endeavouring, you see, to maintain my high standing among the *ton*. You are perhaps totally unaware of it, but I've already caused a deal of rumour and speculation by announcing my engagement to the little-known widow of an elderly gentleman. If it's reported you were seen hobbling down the aisle on our wedding day, everyone will naturally assume I have taken leave of my senses by marrying an aged harridan. My reputation would suffer as a result. And that, my dear, would never do!'

'Much you'd care!' Gwen scoffed. 'But I do happen to care about mine.' She wagged an accusing finger at him. 'What do you mean by placing me in this bedchamber? And don't you dare to suggest this room isn't yours, because Annie has already told me it is.'

Dark brows were raised in exaggerated surprise. 'Well, I couldn't place you in Merry's, now could I? Anthea wouldn't have approved at all,' he said outrageously. 'Furthermore, apart from the fact that no other room had been ready at the time, it's afforded you the golden opportunity to try out the rooms we'll be sharing after we're married. Damned good notion, I thought.'

She attempted to appear primly disapproving. 'You are outrageous, Jocelyn Northbridge.'

'Very true,' he agreed, wickedly grinning once again as he opened the door. 'Just think of how much enjoyment you'll attain reforming me after the knot is tied.'

Gwen chose not to waste her breath in a pointless response. Apart from the fact that she thought she stood little chance of success, she wasn't very certain she wished to try. Oh, yes, her darling Gillie had been so right! Foolish though it might be, she rather liked the man she had chosen to marry just the way he was.

HISTORICAL

LARGE PRINT

THE LAST RAKE IN LONDON
Nicola Cornick

Under a blaze of chandeliers, in London's most
fashionable club, Jack Kestrel is waiting. He hasn't
come to enjoy the rich at play; he's there to uphold his
family name. But first he has to get past the ice-cool
owner: the beautiful Sally Bowes. And Jack wants
her to warm his bed – at any price!

THE OUTRAGEOUS LADY FELSHAM
Louise Allen

Freed from her unhappy marriage, Belinda, Lady
Felsham, plans to enjoy herself. She suspects that the
breathtakingly handsome Major Ashe Reynard is exactly
what she needs… The outrageous couple embark on an
affair – and Belinda becomes increasingly confused.
She has no desire to marry again, but Ashe is a
man she cannot live without…

AN UNCONVENTIONAL MISS
Dorothy Elbury

Miss Jessica Beresford is headstrong, impetuous and
poorly dowered. Benedict Ashcroft, Earl of Wyvern,
knows he should steer well clear of her, however dazzling
her beauty. His late brother has lost the family fortune,
and Ben's last hope is to marry a well-behaved heiress!
But Jessica's loveliness is matched by her kind heart, and
Ben is soon torn between duty and desire…

MILLS & BOON®
Pure reading pleasure

HIST0908 L

HISTORICAL

LARGE PRINT

UNTOUCHED MISTRESS
Margaret McPhee

Guy Tregellas, Viscount Varington, has a rakish
reputation, and when he discovers a beautiful woman
washed up on the beach he is more than intrigued.
Helena McGregor must escape Scotland to anonymity in
London – for the past five years she has lived a shameful
life, not of her choosing. But she needs the help of her
disturbingly handsome rescuer…

A LESS THAN PERFECT LADY
Elizabeth Beacon

At seventeen, Miranda Braxton shocked the world by
eloping with her brother's tutor. Now, a wiser and
widowed lady, she returns to Carnwood – and finds
herself engaged in a battle of wills with Kit Alstone,
the new Earl of Carnwood. Soon Kit begins to wonder
if a scandalous lord might ask for nothing better than
a less than perfect Countess!

VIKING WARRIOR, UNWILLING WIFE
Michelle Styles

With the war drums echoing in her ears, Sela stood
with trepidation on the shoreline. The dragon ships full
of warriors had come, ready for battle and glory.
But it wasn't the threat of conquest that shook Sela
to the core. It was the way her heart responded to the
proud face of Vikar Hrutson, leader of the invading
force – and her ex-husband!

MILLS & BOON
Pure reading pleasure

HIST1008 LP

HISTORICAL

LARGE PRINT

THE VIRTUOUS COURTESAN

Mary Brendan

Gavin Stone discovers on his brother's death that, to inherit his estate, he must also take on his mistress! Sarah is horrified – she never thought she would be passed on as if she were a chattel – but what choice does she have? And Gavin will expect a practised seducer – when in reality she is as unschooled as a debutante...

THE HOMELESS HEIRESS

Anne Herries

Runaway Georgie is disguised as a boy, living life on the streets after fleeing her scheming aunt and uncle. Cold, hungry and desperate, she is forced to pickpocket – but she thieves from the wrong man: the dashing Captain Richard Hernshaw! And the consummate Captain very soon discovers the grubby boy is actually a pretty young woman...

REBEL LADY, CONVENIENT WIFE

June Francis

Driven from her home by accusations of witchcraft, Lady Anna Fenwick embarks on a dangerous quest. Her reluctant protector is darkly brooding Jack Milburn, a merchant venturer with a shadowed past... Jack exists only to exact revenge on the man who killed his lover and his son – but slowly Anna teaches him to feel again...

MILLS & BOON®
Pure reading pleasure™

HIST1108

HISTORICAL

LARGE PRINT

MISS WINTHORPE'S ELOPEMENT
Christine Merrill

Shy heiress Miss Penelope Winthorpe was only trying to escape her bullying brother. She didn't mean to wed a noble lord over a blacksmith's anvil! And Adam Felkirk, Duke of Bellston, had no intention of taking a wife. But Penelope's plight moved him. Now the notorious rake has a new aim: to shock and seduce his prim and proper bride!

THE RAKE'S UNCONVENTIONAL MISTRESS
Juliet Landon

Miss Letitia Boyce didn't begrudge her sisters the pick of London's available bachelors. She'd chosen her own path, and knew that book-learning and marriage rarely mixed. Lord Seton Rayne, one of the most notorious rakehells in town, had every heiress hurling herself at him. So his sudden kissing of unconventional Letitia took them both by surprise…

RAGS-TO-RICHES BRIDE
Mary Nichols

Impoverished beauty Diana Bywater must keep her circumstances secret – her job with Harecrofts depends on it! Then an unwanted marriage proposal from the younger Harecroft son threatens everything… Captain Richard Harecroft is suspicious of this gently reared girl who has turned his brother's head. But the closer he gets, the more the mystery of Diana deepens…

MILLS & BOON®
Pure reading pleasure™

HIST1208 LP